He was laughi

'My papa outlined
specifically, I do no

Philip chuckled. 'He did no more than ask me to escort two beautiful ladies to a ball. That is not a duty; it is a pleasure.'

Pretty compliments as well as good looks! Was she supposed to be impressed?

'Do not think I am misled by flattery, Mr Devonshire. Young I may be, but I am not such a goose as to be taken in by compliments.'

Born in Singapore, **Mary Nichols** came to England when she was three, and has spent most of her life in different parts of East Anglia. She has been a radiographer, school secretary, information officer and industrial editor, as well as a writer. She has three grown-up children and four grandchildren.

Recent titles by the same author:

THE LAST GAMBLE
TO WIN THE LADY
A DANGEROUS UNDERTAKING
DEVIL-MAY-DARE

THE RUBY PENDANT

Mary Nichols

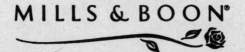

*MILLS & BOON and MILLS & BOON with the Rose Device
are registered trademarks of the publisher.*

*First published in Great Britain 1997
Harlequin Mills & Boon Limited,
Eton House, 18-24 Paradise Road, Richmond, Surrey TW9 1SR*

© Mary Nichols 1997
ISBN 0 263 80444 5

*Set in Times 10 on 12 pt. by
Rowland Phototypesetting Limited
Bury St Edmunds, Suffolk*

04-9711-71208

Printed and bound in Great Britain

Chapter One

1813

There were three people in the garden of Viscount Martindale's country home on the southern outskirts of Peterborough, three people who made unlikely associates. One, a young man, fair-haired and thin as a reed, was dressed in what had once been the resplendent uniform of Napoleon's Old Guard, covered in silver lace and gold braid. Now it was shabby and devoid of any decoration; even the silver buttons had been removed and replaced with leather ones.

His boots were worn down at the heel and his hands, still long-fingered and expressive, were brown and dirty and the nails cracked.

Lieutenant Pierre Veillard, prisoner of war, had given his parole not to attempt to escape and was being employed on his lordship's estate as a gardener. Not that he was gardening at this moment. He was standing at an easel, paint brush in hand, putting the finishing touches to the portrait he was making of the second

5

of the trio, his lordship's daughter, Juliette.

The young lady, sitting beneath an apple tree in full blossom, was clothed in a simple gown of spotted muslin over a matching silk petticoat, with a velvet ribbon round the high waist and threaded through the puff sleeves. Her figure was slim, though well-rounded enough to satisfy the fashion of the day.

Her hair was so fair it was almost silver and framed an oval face with high cheekbones, a firm, well-defined mouth and eyes as blue as the spring sky above their heads, which was, the young man had decided, very extraordinary, considering Lord Martindale was dark as night and his wife was certainly not fair.

He had wanted to paint her the minute he had set eyes on her several weeks before; his artist's eye stirred not only by her beauty but by something indefinable, a faded memory of he knew not what, but it had taken a great deal of toadying to her ladyship before permission had been given and then the execution of his task had not been easy. Miss Martindale found it extremely difficult to sit still.

Juliette wanted to talk, to find out about this handsome Frenchman. She knew his name and that he was, at twenty years old, a year older than herself, and had been captured at the Battle of Salamanca the previous July. She understood she was supposed to look upon him as an enemy, but how could she do that when he was so charming to her and to Mama? It was not his fault he had had to fight. It was all the fault of that fat Corsican, Napoleon Bonaparte, who had set the whole of Europe into conflict.

If only this dreadful war could be over and Napoleon defeated, the aristocracy of France could return to their homes and everything would be as it was before and young men like the lieutenant could take their rightful place in society again.

At nineteen and carefully nurtured, Juliette was too innocent of the world to know the harsher side of war, though she could hardly be unaware of the conflict when the newspapers that arrived at Hartlea were full of it and it was so frequently the topic of conversation between her parents.

The lieutenant was an officer and a gentleman, so her parents believed. She smiled slowly. Would an English gentleman have lured her away from her maid and into the summer house to kiss her so fervently? If Papa or Mama ever found out about that, he would be sent back to the camp at Norman Cross and not allowed out again, parole or no parole.

It was the first kiss she had had from any man apart from her papa and she knew she should not have allowed it. She should have run away or shrieked for help, but she had done nothing of the kind. Always ready for new experiences, new sensations, she had allowed it to go on and nothing dreadful had happened as a result.

The heavens hadn't fallen in; she had not been visited by some dreadful calamity and no one had treated her any differently, though she felt sure her guilt was written on her face.

But then, she asked herself, what was so very wicked about a kiss? Lips on lips that had given her a frisson of excitement at the time, but which was difficult to recall now. That, surely, was not love? There was no one she dare ask, not even Anne Golightly, her maid, and the third member of the trio.

Anne was acting as chaperon, a task she found tedious
in the extreme and though she had brought some mend-
ing to keep her occupied, she frequently dozed off. Her
head was nodding now, her hands idle in her lap.

No one had spoken for several minutes. The early
bees buzzed among the apple blossom, a rook cawed
in an elm and the stable cat stalked along the top of
the garden wall, its attention riveted on something in
the long grass.

'Is it nearly finished?' Juliette spoke at last. 'I do so
hate sitting still.'

'That I know, *mam'selle*.' Lieutenant Veillard smiled
as he cleaned his brush on a piece of rag and stood
back to look at his handiwork. 'There, it is done.'

'Anne, wake up, do!' Juliette turned to her maid. 'Go
and tell Mama it is done. She must be the first to see it.'

The maid, startled into wakefulness, picked up her
sewing and hurried towards the house, a large square
mansion, which had stood there since before
Cromwell's time, impervious to war and riot, flood
and fire.

Juliette jumped up and ran to look at the painting.
She stood transfixed, her mouth a small round 'o' of
surprise. Here was no gentle English girl clad in muslin—here was a French aristocrat in all her costly
splendour.

The face and figure were Juliette's, but the silvery
hair was piled up *à la* Madame Pompadour; the clothes
were sumptuous satin and brocade, padded and hooped,
the bodice cut low to show off a necklace so elaborate
and crowded with gems it must have weighed the wearer
down. There were diamonds, emeralds and rubies along
its whole length, with a silver filigree pendant at the

bottom in the shape of a heart with a huge ruby in its centre.

Her hands, in her lap, clutched a fan and there were rings on all her fingers. The pastoral English setting had become very French, with bougainvillea and plumbago and vines climbing against a mellow brick wall. In the distance was a French château.

'Why did you do it like that? Oh, I do not know what Mama will say.'

Her mother, who had arrived at that moment, said nothing. She simply stared for several minutes, then, with a hand that shook visibly, snatched the painting from the easel and, taking Juliette's arm, marched her back to the house without speaking.

'Mama, I know it is not what you expected, and I confess it surprised me too,' she said, almost running to keep up. 'But do you not think it is well done?'

'Well done?' It was said through gritted teeth, though she had released her grip on her daughter as soon as they were safely indoors. 'Just who does that young man think he is?'

Juliette was perplexed. 'Why, you know who he is, Mama. Papa does, at any rate, or he would not have allowed him to come and work here.'

'Has he been in the house?'

'I do not know. Why do you ask?'

'He hasn't been upstairs, wandered into any of the rooms? My boudoir, for instance?'

'Goodness, Mama, I should not think so. If he has been in at all, it is only into the kitchen when Cook has offered him food and drink. Why would he go anywhere else? You surely do not think he is a thief?'

'I sincerely hope not.'

'Oh, I am sure he is not. What do you imagine he has stolen?'

Her mother did not answer, but hurried up to her boudoir with Juliette at her heels. Juliette remained in the doorway as Lady Martindale stood the picture on a chair, then crossed the room to her escritoire and, extracting a key from the bunch on the chatelaine at her waist, unlocked one of the drawers and took out her jewel case.

Intrigued, Juliette watched as she checked its contents and then replaced it. 'Mama, surely you do not think he would steal your jewels?'

'No, of course not.' Although she sounded relieved, there was still a note of doubt in her mother's voice.

'Then what has your jewel box to do with the portrait? You have nothing like that, have you?' She pointed to the picture, realising the necklace it portrayed was so large that it would not have fitted into the box in any case, and so costly that it would not have been left in a drawer, even a locked one.

'No, I have not,' she said somewhat sharply. 'It would be far too ostentatious for my taste, but all the same I think we have been sadly deceived by that young man.'

'Why?' Juliette was perplexed. Her mother's behaviour was so uncharacteristic of her. She was usually very cool and dignified, almost too repressed sometimes. 'Is it because he has painted me as a French aristo? I suppose that is how his imagination conjured me up. Perhaps I should be flattered.'

'Flattered! It is disgraceful. Humiliating. You will not speak to the lieutenant again. We were fools to trust him, to trust any Frenchman. And as for you. . .' She stopped suddenly. 'Go to your room and stay there.

Until that man has been sent packing, you will stay indoors. Now go.'

Juliette turned and went along the gallery to her room where she sat in the deep window seat, leaning against the cool stone of the embrasure, gazing out on the garden, her thoughts in a turmoil. What had come over her mother? She had not expected her to like the picture—she hadn't been very sure of it herself—but it had been very well painted and the likeness was most definitely there, so why could she not have simply said so and left it at that?

No one had behaved with any impropriety, except for that stolen kiss and her mother knew nothing of that, so *what* was the lieutenant being accused of—theft? Of what? That glittering necklace? She leaned forward to watch as the lieutenant came from the garden with his easel under his arm and disappeared in the direction of the stables. He had a room above one of them where he slept and kept his painting materials.

Her mother had spoken of humiliation; it must have been that and more for the lieutenant to live among the horses and do menial tasks when by all accounts he came from a good family. Perhaps that was why he had portrayed her like that; it reminded him of home.

The sound of hooves and wheels on the gravel of the drive caught her attention and she looked down to see the Viscount's carriage drawing up at the front door. She left her room and stood looking over the gallery rails as he came into the hall and a footman took his hat and travelling cloak. Her mother, who had gone downstairs again, hurried out of the library to meet him, still very agitated.

'Edward, thank heavens you are home. There is something I must show you.'

'Can I not change out of my dusty travelling clothes first?'

'No. Please, Edward.' She took his hand and almost pulled him into the library and closed the door.

A few minutes later, her ladyship emerged and ordered one of the footmen to fetch the lieutenant, then she went back into the library. Juliette held her breath, wondering if they would also send for her, but no one came to her.

Five minutes later, the Frenchman was brought through from the rear of the house. He did not look up and did not see Juliette, standing at the head of the stairs, as he was shown into the library. His escort closed the door on him and disappeared down the hall again.

Overcome by curiosity, Juliette crept downstairs and put her eye to the keyhole. She could see her father standing before the hearth. He was a fine figure of a man in his fifties, still very handsome though his black hair was greying a little at the temples. He looked sombre but not as agitated as her mother had been. The lieutenant was standing a little to one side, the offending portrait propped on a chair between them.

She could not see her mother, who was out of her limited field of vision. Her father was speaking, but the door was a thick one and she could not hear what was said, except an odd word here and there. 'Pendant. . . Where. . .? Who. . .? Innocent child. . .' That was her, she supposed, but she resented being called a child. And the Frenchman had a frightened look. Was Papa threatening him? He seemed to be protesting about something, swearing he could not remember. Remember what?

'Juliette!' The door had been opened suddenly. 'What do you think you are about?'

Juliette straightened up, scarlet-faced, to face her mother. Lady Martindale's usually even features were pinched and her dark eyes betrayed something that might have been anger but which could equally have been fear. She did not look like the handsome, youthful mother whom everyone teasingly likened to a sister. It frightened Juliette a little.

'Nothing, Mama, but why is Lieutenant Veillard being grilled by Papa in such a rag-mannered way? He has done nothing very bad.' She tried to peer past her mother to see what was happening in the room, but her ladyship came out into the hall and shut the door firmly behind her.

'That is for your papa to judge. Now, run along. Find some sewing to do.'

'I don't feel like sewing, I am too agitated.'

'Agitated?' Her ladyship was displaying signs of that herself. 'Why should you be agitated?'

'Because of what has happened. There is something smoky going on and I want to know what it is.'

Her mother took a deep breath and her next words were said in her usual well-modulated voice. 'There is nothing going on, Juliette. Your papa is concerned that the lieutenant should have taken such liberties. He is simply trying to find out why and it is very impertinent of you to call him rag-mannered. Have you no respect?'

'I beg pardon, Mama. I did not mean that, but he does seem somewhat up in the boughs. And you are not yourself at all.'

'That is enough, Juliette. Now, run along do, and no more listening at keyholes or I shall have to tell your papa.'

Reluctantly Juliette returned to her room and fetched out her needlepoint, but she was eaten with curiosity. What were the two men saying to each other? The lieutenant would surely not confess that he had kissed her. Supposing he offered for her? No, he would not do that.

Even if he were so presumptuous, her father would soon put him right. She was a considerable heiress, being her father's only child, and was expected to make a good marriage. An offer from a defeated French officer, who could not even afford to buy a new suit of clothes, would never be entertained.

She sighed. He was such a romantic figure, with his classic good looks and Gallic charm, not stiff at all, like so many young men of her acquaintance who treated her as if she were made of porcelain and would break at a touch.

She had expected the painting to portray her like that, but instead it had given her a robust, rather coquettish appearance, almost like a courtesan. She giggled suddenly. That was what had so infuriated her papa. Oh dear, poor Lieutenant Veillard!

It was at supper that night she learned that the lieutenant had been sent back to the camp and, more importantly, that she was to go to London for the Season. 'It is time you came out,' her mother said. 'We were wrong to postpone it last year.'

'But, Mama, you were not at all well. You said it would wear you out.'

'So I did, but that was last year.'

It was obvious that her parents intended to separate her from the lieutenant as soon as possible. It was a deal of fuss over nothing at all. She liked the young man, had even encouraged him to talk about himself, which was how the kiss had come about, but she had no wish for a closer relationship with him; nor, indeed, with any young man of her acquaintance.

Now she was going to have a Season and would be expected to choose a husband from the eligibles about town before the end of it, fortune hunters, most of them. To her mind the whole process was nothing but a gamble and the odds of coming out of it with any chance of lasting happiness were very long indeed. And marriage would mean leaving her beloved Hartlea. Her protests that she did not want to go were met with stern implacability by her father.

'You will go, Juliet, and you will deal with the offers we allow you to receive with decorum. Your mama will ensure that you are seen in all the right places and with the right people.'

'Did the lieutenant offer for me, Papa?'

Her father stared at her in astonishment. 'You surely have not developed a *tendre* for that young man?'

'No, but I thought that was why. . .' She stopped in confusion.

'Whatever gave you that idea?' He paused and looked at her closely. 'He has not been taking liberties with you, has he? I'll thrash him within an inch of his life, if he has.'

'No, Papa, nothing like that.' She wasn't at all sure what 'taking liberties' meant, but she guessed that kissing had something to do with it and she didn't want the lieutenant to be in more trouble than he already was.

'I'm glad to hear it. It seems to me the sooner you are suitably married the better.'

'I don't understand. What have I done?' she cried in real distress. 'How have I displeased you?'

His voice softened. 'You've done nothing, dear child. I am a little put out by other things. Now finish your supper. Tomorrow you may start packing, though your mama will supervise the purchase of a new wardrobe when we arrive in town. You will need that if you are to take well.'

The thought of shopping cheered Juliette and she soon forgot her father's apparent irritability. He had an important position at the Horse Guards which he never spoke of, but it meant he was often away from home and when he did return was weary beyond imagining, as if the whole conduct of the war rested on his shoulders.

Her mama had often asked him to give it up because it took such a toll of his health, but he always smiled and said he could not, not until Napoleon was defeated, but a few days at Hartlea would soon put him to rights.

He loved his country home above everything, saying it was where he felt most at peace and where he could recoup his strength. Now he was proposing to spend the summer in London, at the beck and call of anyone who thought they had need of him, and all because of Lieutenant Veillard and that portrait. It was a mystery she intended to solve.

In no time at all, the family was established at their London home in Mount Street and the shopping was done, resulting in an array of gowns for mornings, afternoons and evenings, carriage dresses and riding habits, not to mention cloaks, pelisses, bonnets, shawls, shoes, half-boots, petticoats and stockings, which cost her father a small fortune.

Within days of arriving Juliette and her mother were receiving and paying calls and filling up their diaries with engagements—visits to the opera and the ballet, concerts, routs, dances, carriage rides in the park, museum visits. The Viscount seemed to view the move as an opportunity to spend more time at Horse Guards on the conduct of the war and only accompanied them when Lady Martindale insisted that his absence would cause gossip.

'Everyone knows how important he is to the War Department,' Juliette said. 'And if his work helps to bring the war to a speedy conclusion, then I suppose we must decline Lady Carstairs's invitation.'

They were sitting in the morning room, having finished breakfast, and were discussing their engagements for the week. Lady Martindale, in a simple taffeta gown of deep blue, looked much younger than her forty-odd years but there was a frown creasing her brow which had been more evident of late.

Juliette in pale lemon muslin looked fresh and innocent, as became a young lady in her come-out year, but she was far from the silly, empty-headed, just-out-of-the-schoolroom miss that seemed to typify other young ladies in her position. Her father had always encouraged her to seek enlightenment, to question and ponder, to read improving books.

Now, according to her mother, she must suppress her natural intelligence and not put herself forward because it was not becoming; men contemplating marriage did not look favourably on young ladies who voiced opinions of their own.

'Yes, of course, dear, but he is wearing himself out.' Her mother picked up the gilt-edged invitation card that had arrived that morning. 'He needs a little light relief. And I do think he should be there to see the young men who dance with you.'

'You are worried about fortune hunters, is that it? You think I shall fall into the arms of the first rake who asks me to stand up with him. I am not such a fribble, Mama. Sometimes I wish I were as poor as a church mouse and not the daughter of a viscount, then I could marry for love.'

'Don't say such things, Juliette. You do not understand what it is like to be poor and pray God you never do, but to deny your father. . .'

'Deny Papa! Oh, Mama, how could you think I would do that? He is the dearest man and I think it is a shame he has to work so hard. But how are we to go to the ball without him? Won't two ladies on their own cause raised eyebrows?'

'Certainly they would, but we shall not go on our own. Your father has arranged for Mr Devonshire to escort us.'

'Mr Devonshire? Who is he?'

'He is a very close friend of your papa and has been for many years. I know very little more than that.'

With that Juliette had to be content. That Mr Devonshire would be a poor substitute for her beloved father she did not doubt. He was sure to be old and fat and pompous and if he took his escort duties seriously, her enjoyment was bound to be curtailed.

*　　*　　*

She realised how wrong she had been in her conjecture on the evening of the ball when Mr Devonshire arrived in a hired carriage to escort them.

Juliette was wearing a gown of the finest silk gauze in a pale blue-green, which covered a slip of matching satin. Its puffed sleeves were ruched with a darker green silk, which also decorated the high bodice. The skirt hung straight over her hips down to feet shod in satin slippers.

Her hair had been piled up in a classical Greek style, threaded with ribbon on which had been sewn clusters of tiny pearls. More pearls made up her necklace, with a single large drop hanging between the cleft of her breasts. She looked the picture of girlish innocence. Hearing the sounds of their escort being greeted by her mother in the hall, Juliette picked up her reticule and fan and made her way down to join them.

Philip Devonshire looked up when he heard her tread on the stairs and their eyes met and held for a brief moment. He was not old, or pompous, for there was a gleam of amusement in his dark eyes, as if he knew how much he surprised her.

He was about thirty, she guessed. His evening breeches and silk stockings displayed legs that were lean and muscular and his satin coat sat on his broad shoulders as if it had been made on him, so meticulously was it tailored. His white frilled shirt and carefully tied cravat did credit to a valet, or at least a laundress of the highest order.

She reached the bottom of the stairs and he came forward to bow to her. It was when he straightened up that she realised how tall he was; she found herself looking up at clear-cut features, a firm mouth, a dimpled chin and those deeply intelligent eyes that held her mesmerised.

She heard her mother introducing him and heard him say, 'Your obedient, Miss Martindale,' felt him take her gloved hand and put it to his lips, all in a dream. It was like coming face to face with her girlhood fantasies.

But then she came to her senses. If her parents thought it would be easy to divert her, they were in for a surprise because good looks and an easy manner would not win her over. She smiled and withdrew her hand. 'Good evening, Mr Devonshire. It is very good of you to escort us. I do hope you will not be bored.'

He, too, had been surprised. Not by her clothes, or her manner, or particularly by her even features and striking hair, but by something indefinable, a sparkle of mischief in her blue eyes, a spirit of independence, almost defiance, as she met his gaze unwaveringly. And yet there was gentleness too, a kind of warmth that he would hate to see spoiled by disillusionment. How could eyes alone tell him so much?

He pulled himself together and smiled at her. 'How could I be bored with two such charming companions?' he said, offering them an arm each. 'I shall be the envy of the whole gathering.'

The ball, given for Lady Carstairs's daughter, Lucinda, was a glittering affair. No expense had been spared to make it the most talked-of event of the Season. It had to be because Lucinda was no great beauty, being plump and rather short-sighted, although she had an exceptionally fat dowry in her favour.

Juliette was inclined to feel sorry for her, because Lucinda so obviously wanted to please her parents and make a good match that she had subdued her natural intellect and good humour to be a poor copy of those silly young ladies who flitted about the social scene like butterflies, beautiful for a day and useful only for breeding more of the same. Except she wasn't beautiful, but intelligent and sweet-natured.

Standing beside her parents, she greeted Lady Martindale and Juliette with a small curtsy and down-cast eyes, before offering her hand to their escort.

'Miss Carstairs, I hope you will do me the honour of standing up with me,' Mr Devonshire said, as he bowed over her hand. Then he gently removed her card, which dangled on a ribbon from her wrist, and wrote his name with a flourish beside the second country dance. Then, smiling, he returned it to her and accom-panied Juliette and her mother into the ballroom.

For some reason she could not define, Juliette felt put out. Mr Devonshire was her escort and yet he had not asked her for a dance. Surely he was not attracted to Lucinda Carstairs? He must be like all the other young bloods, looking for a fortune.

Who was he, anyway? As far as she had been able to ascertain, he had no title, or even the prospect of one, and his fortune or lack of it had not been the subject of any of the gossip she had heard since coming to London.

And there had been plenty of that among the young ladies she had met at the various social events she had attended, besides conjecture about the marital prospects of each and every one of them, linked to the names of the eligibles of the Season.

They also discussed who had offered for whom; who had won a fortune at the card table; who had been ruined by gambling debts; which married ladies had taken lovers, and stories about the Prince Regent that her mother maintained were too shocking for her ears. In all of that, Mr Philip Devonshire remained an enigma.

The ballroom was brilliantly lit by myriads of chandeliers that made the ladies' jewellery sparkle and the silks and satins of their gowns shimmer as if they had a life of their own.

A full orchestra played on a balcony at one end of the long room and there were exotic plants and hothouse flowers everywhere. The dance area was surrounded by chairs, some occupied by chaperons, others awaiting new arrivals. It was a tremendous crush and the sound of voices and laughter mingled with the music to assail their ears.

Mr Devonshire escorted them to seats and stood behind them as they surveyed the room, waiting for their presence to become known and, in no time at all, Juliette's card was being filled.

She loved to dance and was soon on the floor with Arthur Boreton, the younger son of the Earl of Wentworth. He was followed by fat George Macgregor who kept treading on her toes, and then Lord Hart, who was forty if he was a day, and who was, in turn, followed by young Selwyn Lampeter.

She pretended not to notice what Mr Devonshire was up to, but from the corner of her eye she saw him take up his dance with Lucinda Carstairs and after that to dance with her mama. Lady Martindale had refused all offers up to then and Juliette wondered what had made her mother change her mind; flattery and cajolement, she supposed. The man was very good at that.

The dance finished with a flourish and Juliette dropped into a deep curtsy to her partner before laying her fingers on his arm to be escorted back to her seat. She was flushed and smiling and unaware of the looks of admiration and envy she attracted.

Almost as soon as she had taken her place beside her mother, they were approached by a tall young man in black evening breeches, black velvet coat and a white shirt with points so tall they grazed his cheeks. He bowed over her mama and asked if she would consent to him dancing with his cousin.

Juliette was startled, wondering whom he could mean, but her mother inclined her head and said. 'Good evening, Mr Martindale. I am sure Juliette will be pleased to stand up with you.'

He turned and favoured Juliette with a broad smile as he bowed and held out his hand. Bewildered, she rose and allowed herself to be led into the set.

'Mr Martindale,' she said as the music began and he executed a flourishing leg, 'you said cousin. Are we cousins?'

'That is what I have been led to believe.' He had even white teeth, she noticed, and dark eyes that seemed to flicker about as if he needed to take in everything that was happening all about him. 'Viscount Martindale and my late father were brothers.'

The dance steps parted them but as soon as they reached each other again, Juliette took up the questioning again. 'Why have I never heard of you before now?'

'You must ask his lordship, Miss Martindale. It is not for me to comment.'

'Good gracious, it all sounds very mysterious. Did Papa and your father quarrel?'

'They may have done.'

Again they parted and again returned to each other. 'What about?'

'I do not know. Money, I shouldn't wonder. My father, being a second son, had very little of it.'

'Oh, but Papa has always been most generous. I find it difficult to believe he would deny his own brother.'

'Then perhaps I am wrong.'

'Are you my only cousin, or are there more?'

'No, there is just you and me. And Hartlea.'

'Hartlea?'

'I am the heir. Did you not know?'

'Oh.' She was silent as he took her hands and they moved up between the ranks of their fellow dancers. It was extraordinary that she should learn all this at a ball and not from her parents. Why had they not spoken of family connections before?

'Did you suppose you would inherit?' he asked her. 'I am sorry if I have disappointed you.'

'You have not disappointed me,' she said sharply. 'I had not given it a thought, but if I had, I would have come to the conclusion that there must be a male heir.'

'How very sensible of you!'

She wondered if he were being sarcastic, but his expression was bland and she decided to take his remark at face value. 'Mama did not seem at all put out by your appearance and she consented to me standing up with you, so the quarrel, if there was one, could not have been so very serious. Perhaps it was all in your papa's head.'

'Perhaps.' He smiled. 'We shall never know, for he died several years ago.'

'And where have you been hiding yourself since then?'

'Hiding, Miss Martindale? I have not been hiding. In truth, it is you that has not been out and about in Society, or we should have met.'

She acknowledged the truth of that. 'Papa prefers the country when he is not working,' she said. 'He has an important position at the Horse Guards.'

'Yes, everyone knows the war could not run without Viscount Martindale.'

She looked up at him sharply because she thought there had been a note of acrimony in his voice, but he was smiling pleasantly and she supposed she had imagined it. 'I am sure he would be the first to say he is not the only one,' she said. 'There are others.'

'Among whom I include my humble self,' he said. 'But I am merely a cipher.'

'A very important one, I am sure,' she said. 'We must all play our part.'

'Indeed, yes.'

The dance came to an end and she put her hand lightly on his arm to be escorted back to her seat beside her mother. Of Mr Devonshire there was no sign. She supposed he had found more congenial company in the card room. She told herself she did not care what he did and constantly looking about for him was a futile exercise.

James smiled as he relinquished her to her mama. 'May I claim the first waltz, Miss Martindale?' he asked before leaving. 'I believe it is to be the dance after next.' He took her card from her. 'I see it has not been spoken for.'

'It is not for want of asking,' she said, more pertly than she had intended. 'It is because Mama was not at all sure I should be waltzing.'

He turned to Lady Martindale, smiling easily. 'Aunt Elizabeth, you surely do not object to Miss Martindale dancing with me. I am her cousin, after all, and everyone is waltzing these days. It is only at Almack's they are so stuffy about it.'

Her mother, who had been very sombre of late, as if she had a heavy weight on her shoulders, returned his smile, though it did not light up her eyes. 'I do not see why not. You are family after all.'

He waltzed supremely well and Juliette found herself carried along by the music, though she was uncomfortably aware that Mr Devonshire, who had returned to the room as the dance began, was standing near her empty chair, watching them from beneath lowered brows, as if he disapproved.

Well, it was not for him to approve or disapprove; her mama had given her consent and that was all that mattered. When they returned, it was the supper dance Mr Martindale requested.

'No, I am afraid that is taken,' Mr Devonshire put in before Juliette could answer. 'By me.'

Chagrined, the young man left to seek another partner and Juliette turned to the tall man at her side, eyes flashing. 'Sir, you have not marked my card at all, so why did you say the supper dance was taken?'

He smiled. 'Because I have taken it. Mr Martindale has already danced twice with you and to claim a third would invite comment of a disagreeable nature. Your papa would not forgive me if I did nothing to prevent that.'

'Mr Devonshire is quite right, Juliette,' her mother said. 'We must do things properly.'

'Then I shall sit the supper dance out, Mama. I would

hate to put Mr Devonshire to the trouble of having to dance with me simply to prevent gossip.'

'Juliette!' Lady Martindale exclaimed. 'How can you be so rag-mannered?' She turned to Philip. 'I must apologise for my daughter, Mr Devonshire. She is very young and unused to Society. . .'

'There is not the slightest need for apology,' he said, smiling, as the supper dance was announced and the music began. 'I understand perfectly.' Then turning to Juliette, he swept an elegant bow before her and offered her his hand. 'Will you do me the inestimable honour of joining this country dance with me?'

He was laughing at her and it infuriated her, but short of cutting him dead and creating a scene she could do nothing but take his hand and allow herself to be led onto the floor.

'Do you always take your duties so seriously?' she asked as they stepped between the line of dancers.

'Naturally, I do.'

'And my papa outlined your duties for tonight most specifically, I do not doubt.'

He chuckled. 'He did no more than ask me to escort two beautiful ladies to a ball. That is not a duty, it is a pleasure.'

Pretty compliments as well as good looks! Was she supposed to be impressed? A man needed more than that to become a lifelong partner, though she could not exactly define what it was. A kind of empathy, she supposed, a meeting of minds, mutual love. Oh, yes, love above all things. 'And where did you learn your social accomplishments, Mr Devonshire?' she asked.

They parted at the end of the line and he was not able to answer until the dance brought them together again at the far end. 'Social accomplishments,' he repeated. 'I was not aware of any in particular.'

'Flattery, for one. Do not think I am misled by that, Mr Devonshire. Young I may be, but I am not such a goose as to be taken in by compliments.'

She left him to circle around another dancer, while he did the same and then they came together in the middle, stepping round each other like a pair of fighting cocks. 'In that case, what shall we talk of?'

'I am intrigued to know why Papa asked you to escort us.'

'He trusts me, as I trust him.'

'How long have you known him?'

'His lordship? Since I was ten years old.'

'As long as that?' She was surprised for the second time that evening. In truth, life seemed to be full of surprises just lately. Was that all part of the process of growing up? When you are young, she thought, you accepted people without troubling yourself with questions about how and why they came to be the kind of men and women they were.

There was, for instance, more to her father than the devoted husband and parent, and this man, with his easy elegance and brooding good looks, knew more than she did. She was torn between her need to know and her reluctance to let him see her ignorance. And her natural curiosity won. 'How did you meet?'

Again they parted and again they returned to each other. 'He found me in somewhat straitened circumstances and helped me to find my feet. I owe him my life, my education, my ability to earn a living, for without the education I could have achieved nothing.' His voice took on a husky tone as he spoke, as if it was something he found difficult to speak about, but it was full of sincerity, nothing like the light voice he had used to pay easy compliments.

She tilted her head to look up at him and wished that she had not. He was looking at her with an expression which seemed to say, 'I know all about you, everything there is to know, I can see into your soul. Nothing can be hidden from me.' She gave an involuntary shiver which spread from her body down to her toes and fingers.

'Oh. Then you would do anything he asked of you?'

'Anything within my power. Even attending functions I have no particular interest in and being interrogated by a young lady who seems to forget her manners at times.' His smile belied the severity of his words and she realised he was teasing her. And instead of being annoyed, she laughed.

'I beg pardon for that, indeed I do, but how else am I to learn if I do not ask questions? No one sees fit to enlighten me unless I do.'

He smiled as the dance came to an end and offered her his arm to go into supper. Her mother followed, escorted by Lord Hart. 'What do you wish to be enlightened about?'

'Why I am here at all.'

'You mean why you exist? That is a profound question indeed.'

'No, I meant why I was brought to London. And why I have never met Mr Martindale, or even heard of him before. It all seems so strange. Do you know him?'

'Before tonight I had not met him.' He settled her in a seat at one of the small tables dotted around the dining room and sat down beside her, but she was more interested in the answers to her questions than in eating, delicious though everything looked.

'How old are you?' he asked, offering her a plate of little tartlets filled with fish in a creamy sauce.

She took one and put it on her plate alongside a chicken leg, wondering whether to refuse to answer, but as he was treating her in a very avuncular fashion and her mother, though out of earshot, was looking at her, she decided she might as well humour him. 'I am nineteen.'

'There you are, then. It is surely time you came out. Most young ladies are not only out, but married by your age.'

'Perhaps they are, but Mama has not been well these last two years and we were obliged to postpone my Season. We had planned it for next year when Mama had fully recovered and Papa hoped to be less occupied with the war. His change of mind was so sudden and all because of Lieutenant Veillard and that portrait. . .'

She stopped in confusion, wondering why she had mentioned that. Did she think he knew the answer? Or was it that his manner invited confidences?

He smiled, putting food on his own plate and beckoning a waiter to pour wine for them both. 'Now it is my turn to be intrigued. Tell me, who is Lieutenant Veillard? The name sounds French.'

'It is. He is a prisoner of war, but he is gentleman and a great artist.'

'Oh. I see. An unsuitable liaison. . .?'

'It was nothing of the kind. It is all on account of him painting me like a French aristo. He made me look older, in a great hooped gown and dripping with jewels. It upset Mama.'

'It is hardly surprising. You are the embodiment of
a young and innocent girl and an English one at that.
No wonder Lady Martindale was upset. She could
hardly hang the picture, could she? Or show it to her
friends.'

'No, but she need not have accused poor Lieutenant
Veillard of stealing.'

'Stealing what?'

'I don't know. That is where the mystery comes in.'
She turned to face him, her cheeks flushed and her eyes
bright. She had gone this far, she might as well go on.
'You could not find out for me, could you?'

'Me? Certainly not.' His answer was immediate and
somewhat acerbic. Seeing the pained expression on her
face, he wished he had paused long enough to ask her
why it was so important to her, why she had asked him
and not someone closer to her.

Did she suppose he would be like clay in her hands,
soft and malleable? Or was she clutching at a straw, a
last resort because no one else would take her seriously?
His answer had been the correct one, but he wished
he had not spoken so sharply. 'I am sorry,' he added
more gently.

She sighed. The answer was no less than she
expected. If Mr Devonshire had such a high regard for
her father, he would not do anything behind his mentor's
back. 'I mean to find out,' she said. 'I mean to discover
why Mama is so afraid and why I have suddenly
acquired a cousin I knew nothing of.'

'You have not suddenly acquired him. If any acquir-
ing has been done, it is surely the other way about; he
is undoubtedly two or three years older than you are. I
imagine your arrival put his nose severely out of joint.'

'He is still the heir; my arrival did not change that.'

'No, but you need to be plump in the pocket to run an establishment like Hartlea. What do you suppose he will do for funds when the time comes?' He smiled. 'Not that I expect that to happen for many years. I sincerely hope his lordship has a long life before him.'

'Oh, so do I,' she said. The thought of her father dying was not to be entertained. 'Let us talk about something more cheerful.'

Which is what they did and she discovered that he was not so stuffy as he had at first appeared and his sense of humour matched hers. Before long he had her laughing at some anecdote about the Prince Regent, whom he appeared to know quite well and the rest of the evening passed so pleasantly she forgot her unanswered questions, but they were still there, ready to surface again as soon as the heady evening was over.

As for Philip; he had not enjoyed himself so much for years, though he was only too aware that as a prospective suitor, he had nothing to offer the delectable Miss Martindale. And, wending his way back to his lodgings in the early hours, he laughed at himself for even allowing the thought to cross his mind.

Chapter Two

Country hours of early to bed and early to rise and dinner at three were impossible in London. Too much happened in the evenings and hardly anything before mid-day, so that Juliette constantly found herself going to bed at dawn and rising at noon. Dinner was more often at five or six and supper nearer midnight.

It played havoc with her sleep and her digestion, and she began to wonder if her mother's fragile health would stand the strain for a whole Season. But Lady Martindale would not hear of having a quiet day or two with no engagements.

'We might as well have stayed at Hartlea if we are going to sit at home doing nothing,' she said, the day after the ball. They were in the morning room, having only just come down from their bedchambers, although the day was well-advanced. Her ladyship was examining the invitations that had arrived earlier. 'You will never take if you are not seen out and about.'

'Mama, I do so hate that expression. It makes me sound like a cow at market or a custard you are afraid will curdle. And it is so one-sided. I want to have a say in what happens to me.'

'Juliette, you are not old enough and wise enough to make a suitable choice without some guidance. But your papa will not force you to marry someone you take in dislike, I am sure.'

For the first time Juliette felt brave enough to question her iron-willed mother. 'What about you, Mama? Do you not believe in marrying for love?'

'Love comes later, if you are so fortunate. Your papa was chosen for me by my father, but I would not change him for the world.'

'And have you anyone in mind for me? Mr Martindale, perhaps, or Mr Devonshire.'

'Mr Devonshire!' Her mother's astonishment was genuine. 'Good gracious, that never entered my head. He has no title and no fortune and besides, I do believe he has foreign connections.' She looked closely at Juliette as she spoke. 'You have not formed an attachment there, have you?'

'No, indeed not,' she said, aware that her cheeks were flaming and angry with herself for not being able to prevent it. 'He is too pompous by far. He behaves towards me like an uncle who has been entrusted with my moral welfare. . .'

'Which is exactly the truth of the matter.' Her mother laughed. It was the first time Juliette had heard her laughter since the episode over the portrait. 'At least it was so last night because your papa asked him to escort us and you are vexed because he prevented you dancing a third time with James Martindale.'

'Is Mr Martindale really my cousin? I find it hard to believe that we have never met before. He hinted that

Papa and his father quarrelled. It doesn't sound the least like Papa to hold a grudge for so long.'

'It is not. If any quarrelling was done, it was all on one side, I can assure you.'

'What was it about?'

'I really do not know.'

'Why has nothing been done to mend the rift?' she asked, wondering why she did not altogether believe her mother did not know the reason for it.

'I do not know that either, but now you have the opportunity to set all to rights.'

'Me?' Juliette asked in surprise. 'How can I do that?'

'James is very taken by you, he made no effort to hide it. . .'

'Oh, Mama, you surely do not think he will offer for me? We have only just met.' She was not ready for offers yet. The thought of receiving a proposal filled her with apprehension. What was she supposed to do? How was she to know whom to accept? Her reading of romantic novels had led her to believe she would know when she fell in love because it would be like a bolt from the sky and there would be no doubt in her mind at all.

But no one she had yet met had delivered such a blow, certainly not Pierre Veillard, or Mr Martindale. There was something about him that sent shivers of apprehension down her spine and she had no idea why that should be.

As for Mr Devonshire, he was, according to her mother, not even to be considered and yet he was the one who made her heart beat faster and he was easy to talk to. She had confided in him about Pierre and the

portrait without a second's hesitation. But that wasn't
love, was it?

Her mother did not answer because at that moment
a footman appeared to announce the arrival of Mr
Martindale.

'My respects, my lady,' he said, sweeping confidently
into the room dressed in biscuit coloured pantaloons, a
blue superfine coat with darker facings, a blue and yel-
low striped waistcoat and the most extravagantly tied
cravat Juliette had ever seen. He bowed before her ladyship, who smiled and offered her hand to be kissed,
which he did with aplomb. Then turning to Juliette, he
asked, 'And how are you, Miss Martindale?'

'I am very well, Mr Martindale.'

'I hope you are not too tired after last night because
I was hoping for the favour of being allowed to escort
you for a carriage ride in the park this afternoon. I have
recently acquired a brand-new barouche and a pair of
matched bays.' He turned to Lady Martindale, smiling.
'That is, if your mama will consent to accompany us.'

'I have not been in the best of health and am much
fatigued, Mr Martindale,' her ladyship said. 'And I have
promised myself a comfortable coze at home with an
old friend, but if Juliette wishes to go, then her maid
may accompany her.'

Juliette suppressed a little gasp. This was the first
she had heard of her mother meeting a friend and she
had never heard her tell an untruth before. Was she
trying to throw them together?

In view of the story of the family quarrel, she was
not at all sure she should accept the invitation without
first asking her father. It would put her mother out of
countenance if she should point that out in front of the

young man, so she hesitated, wondering if she ought to make some excuse to decline. She had almost made up her mind to do so, when Mr Devonshire was announced.

Wearing a military-style frockcoat and kerseymere pantaloons, he came into the room, smiling easily, and strode over to the ladies to make his bow before them and ask how they did. On being assured that both were well, he added, 'I had hoped to speak to his lordship. . .'

'I am afraid he is not at home,' Lady Martindale said. 'But please sit down.'

Philip turned to James, apparently noticing him for the first time. 'Good day to you, Martindale.'

'Good day to you.' James grinned at him, though his eyes flickered, as if he could not quite meet the other's steady gaze. 'You see, I beat you to it. I am to escort Miss Martindale in the park this afternoon.'

'I congratulate you on your good fortune,' Philip said. Then, to the ladies, he added, 'Please excuse me, I will withdraw and return another time, if her ladyship and Miss Martindale will do me the honour of receiving me.'

Her ladyship smiled a little stiffly. 'Of course.'

The grin on James Martindale's face as he watched him go, was one of unalloyed triumph and Juliette found herself feeling sorry for Mr Devonshire. Was she supposed to be pleased that two men were so obviously at daggers drawn over her? Or was there more to it than that?

And now it had been taken out of her hands; James had assumed she had consented and there was no opportunity to contradict him because her other partners from the ball arrived in quick succession, bringing flowers and sweetmeats, and after a few desultory remarks about the success of the occasion, James took his leave, saying he would call for her at three o'clock.

Lord Martindale returned to the house from the House of Lords a little after two. He went straight into the library, ordering food and wine to be taken in to him. Juliette waylaid the servant with the tray and took it in herself.

'My,' he said, smiling up at her from his armchair on one side of the hearth, 'what have I done to deserve such attention from the belle of the ball?'

'Who said I was the belle of the ball? Surely not Mama?'

'Why not Mama? She is as proud of you as I am and it is due to her that you looked so well. She said you had been a great success.'

Juliette smiled with pleasure; her mother rarely praised. 'Oh, but I have to own that I was tempted to accept a third dance with the same partner.'

'Oh,' he teased. 'And who had the temerity to ask you three times?'

'Mr James Martindale. He called earlier and asked me to take a carriage ride with him in the park.'

'Did he, by Jove!'

'Papa, should we be receiving him? He told me you and his father had quarrelled.'

'So we did, but it was a long time ago and all forgotten now.' He sounded unnaturally jolly.

'Then you have no objection to my going?'

'None at all, my dear. But do not let him monopolise you. I want you to meet every eligible in town and make your own choice. You must have met and danced with others.'

'Indeed, I did. There was Mr Arthur Boreton and Mr Macgregor, but he is so fat he had no idea where he was putting his feet. And Lord Hart took me on the floor for the Lancers, which must have been very unwise at his age. He hardly had breath left at the end to speak. I began to think he would have a seizure.

'And there was Selwyn Lampeter, but he is hardly out of the schoolroom and I think he was using me to practise his dance steps. And Mr Devonshire, but he danced with me out of duty.'

'How can you say that? I am sure he did not.'

'He implied it was to prevent me making a fool of myself over Mr Martindale, Papa.'

'Were you about to make a fool of yourself?'

'No. I simply had not taken note of the number of times we had danced. I cannot see that it matters anyway.'

'Oh, it does—you ask the tabbies who sit round the floor counting. I am indebted to Mr Devonshire.'

'He came this morning, too, but he left very quickly when he saw Mr Martindale was here. Mr Martindale was crowing over him. Papa, I do not think they like each other. Do you know why?'

'No, except a little rivalry perhaps. You are a very beautiful young lady, you know.'

Juliette sighed. She didn't understand the ways of Society, in spite of her mother's careful instruction. It all seemed so false. 'Mama has said I may accept Mr Martindale's invitation and Anne is to come too.'

'And you were doubtful, is that what all this is about?' He reached across and patted her hand. 'Do not worry, my dear. If you wish to go, you may.' He smiled suddenly. 'And if Mr Devonshire were to ask to escort you on another occasion, I shall give my blessing to that too. If they are to be rivals. . .' He smiled knowingly.

'For me, Papa? I hardly know either of them. It seems to me that Mr Martindale is too flamboyant and confident of his own charm and Mr Devonshire is too sombre. He rarely smiles, unless he is laughing at me, which isn't at all the same thing.'

'Mr Devonshire has not had an easy life, my dear, and perhaps the social graces have passed him by, but he is an excellent fellow.'

'Oh, he is not graceless, Papa, far from it. In fact. . .' She stopped, blushing furiously. 'I do not know quite what to make of him.'

He smiled. 'You are not alone in that. Half London has become curious about him, but do not let that concern you.'

'And Mr Martindale?'

'Until recently, I have had little to do with him, and it is not fair to condemn him for the intolerance and sheer cupidity of his father.'

'What was the quarrel all about, Papa? May I not know?'

'It wasn't exactly a quarrel. I had no heir. You know yourself that it was three miscarriages which ruined your mother's health. My brother was due to inherit. Nothing could change that and, indeed, I had no wish to do so.

'But he took exception to your arrival on the scene when I made it quite clear that he might have the title and the estate, but that the bulk of my wealth would be passed to you, the best dowry I could manage. At that time he was himself a very wealthy man, he had no need of it. But he was also a gambler and his wife was a spendthrift. By the time they died, there was little left.

'I have been supporting James with an allowance for some time now and recently found him a clerical post at the War Department, though he chooses not to acknowledge his indebtedness and has never until now visited us. Pride, I suppose.'

'Is he like his father, Papa?' she asked, wondering if her father knew about the new carriage and pair. The allowance and his salary must indeed be generous if they stretched to such luxuries.

'That I do not know. We will doubtless find out.'

'Mama seems to like him.'

'Yes, I believe she does; who am I to quarrel with her judgement? She chose me, after all.' He smiled and poured himself a glass of wine. 'Now you had best run along or you will keep James waiting.'

She jumped up and bent over to kiss his cheek. 'Thank you, Papa, you are the best of fathers. I shall remember what you said.'

The carriage way in Hyde Park was crowded with vehicles of all kinds, from barouches and town coaches, to phaetons and curricles which paraded at a pace that was little more than a walk, so that their occupants could see and be seen. On the other side of the fence, riders walked or gently cantered, showing off themselves and their mounts.

Juliette, sitting on the padded seat of the open carriage, in a matching skirt and jacket of red and green checked cloth, her pale curls topped by a green bonnet trimmed with a peacock feather that swept across the brim and down on to one cheek, looked very fetching and James was not slow to tell her so.

She pretended to accept his compliments coolly and sat with her gloved hands in her lap, looking about her. She recognised Lady Carstairs and Lucinda in one barouche and James asked the driver to stop so that they might pass the time of day and thank her for an enjoyable evening.

Lucinda blushed scarlet when James spoke to her and seemed to be concentrating on one of the buttons on her pelisse, unable to look him in the eye until her mother dug her in the ribs with her fan.

'Poor thing!' Juliette said, as they bowled away. 'She is so dreadfully shy.'

'And so dreadfully plain, too.'

'Mr Martindale, that is very unkind of you! And it is not true. She has wonderfully expressive eyes and lovely hair.'

He turned to smile at her. 'You can afford to be generous, Miss Martindale, when you have so much to commend your own appearance.' He grinned and leaned forward to whisper in her ear. 'You are lovely, cousin, quite lovely. We make a handsome couple, don't you think?'

'Mr Martindale!' she exclaimed.

'Could you not call me James when we are alone?'

'We are not alone.' She glanced across at Anne, who was pretending not to listen.

'Then I think we should take steps to remedy that. We will stop and take a stroll, shall we?' He called the driver to pull up. As soon as the coach came to a standstill under a group of trees a little off the road, he stepped down and turned to offer her his hand. She hesitated and he added, 'Come, you have nothing to

fear. There are a great many people about and your
maid will watch over us.'

She took his hand and stepped down on to the grass,
but before Anne could follow he shut the door. 'From
here,' he said, smiling at the maid. 'We will not go out
of sight.'

Before Juliette could protest, he had taken her elbow
and was guiding her along a path away from the coach.
'I am very fond of walking, Miss Martindale,' he said.
'Are you?

'At home in the country, yes.' She was very appre-
hensive and wishing she had never left the carriage.
What did he want with her that necessitated leaving
Anne out of earshot? Surely not a proposal? It was far
too soon for that. Her heart was beating uncomfortably
fast. She must control her breathing and converse with
him as naturally and impersonally as possible.

'To be sure, in the country,' he said, apparently
unaware of her doubts. 'Hartlea is quite an extensive
estate, is it not?'

'I suppose it must be. I never thought about it. Have
you not seen it?'

'I have passed by, skirted it, you might say, but I
have not been privileged to see it properly.'

'But it is your inheritance.'

'Yes, but it will not fall into my hands for some time
and by then I hope my fortunes will have changed and
that I will have the means to see to its upkeep.'

'You have expectations?'

He smiled. 'Oh, yes, I have expectations.' He stopped
suddenly. 'Oh, forgive me, we should not be speaking of
so sad a happening. His lordship is your father, after all.'

She did not know why this statement made her shudder, as if someone had poured cold water over her. On the surface he was charming and attentive, but there was something about those flickering eyes that told her to beware.

On the other hand, perhaps she was being fanciful. A match between them might be considered by her parents to be ideal. He would have her dowry to spend on the upkeep of the estate and she would still be able to live in her beloved home. She could not imagine living anywhere else. But where was love?

They turned back towards the carriage and she gave a gasp of surprise to see Mr Devonshire standing beside it, holding a beautiful black horse by its bridle and talking to her maid.

He doffed his riding hat as they approached. 'Miss Martindale, your obedient.'

She wanted to ask him if he had followed them and, if he had, why he had taken so much upon himself, but she found she could not find the words. He was looking directly at her, his dark eyes seeing right into her heart, understanding her discomfiture. She was forced to look away.

'Devonshire, what are you doing here?' James demanded, barely hiding his annoyance.

'I saw the carriage and the young lady sitting in it, looking distressed. I thought it had broken down and rode over to offer assistance. Miss Golightly informed me she was waiting for her mistress and very upset she was, too.'

Anne blushed furiously at the way Mr Devonshire used her name and title, as if he had mistaken her for a lady! 'Oh, Miss Juliette, you said you would not go out of sight, but you did. I did not know what to do.'

'As you see, there is no cause for alarm, Anne, no harm has come to me,' Juliette assured her.

'On the contrary,' Philip said, 'leaving the carriage and going off alone with Mr Martindale in full view of half London's tabbies, will certainly not enhance your reputation, as Mr Martindale well knows.'

'It is none of your affair, sir,' James said. 'Miss Martindale is my cousin.'

'And what is that to the point? Are you bent on ruining the young lady, sir?'

'Ruining her?' James repeated pleasantly. 'Nothing was further from my thoughts. Come, Juliette, into the carriage. I must take you home. Stand aside, Devonshire.'

Juliette, annoyed by James's use of her given name without permission, felt his hand under her elbow and stepped up into the carriage, wondering why it was that Philip Devonshire always seemed to come off worse in his encounters with James. It was not weakness, she was quite sure of that, but there was something holding him back. Was he simply being careful of her, not wishing to quarrel in her presence? Or was there more to it?

As the carriage pulled away in the direction of the Stanhope Gate, she was conscious that Mr Devonshire had mounted and was sitting his horse, gazing after them; she could feel those dark eyes boring into her back.

There was something very mysterious about the man; this was borne out the following afternoon, when she and Lady Martindale called on the Countess of Wentworth. The Countess had invited a few of her friends to take tea with her, simply to gossip, as Juliette soon found out.

Lady Carstairs and Lucinda were also there, and the two younger ladies sat together, taking no part in the conversation, but intrigued by the way the characters of those who had not been invited were pulled to shreds. Juliette thought it was cruel and once or twice was tempted to put in a good word for the absent ones, but a look from her mother quelled her.

'I was surprised to see you escorted by Mr Devonshire the other night, Elizabeth,' Lady Wentworth said, during a pause in the flow of talk. 'He is such a strange man.'

'Strange?' her mother queried vaguely. 'I see nothing exceptional about him. He is a business associate of my husband.'

'He may be the sort of man with whom another man might do business, but that's not to say he is the sort I would countenance as a suitor for my daughter.'

'Why not?' Juliette demanded before her mother could stop her.

'Well, I declare!' her ladyship said, fixing her with a look that was intended to make her quake.

'Please forgive her,' Lady Martindale put in quickly. 'I am sure Juliette did not mean to be impertinent. I am afraid she has been used to saying what she thinks and questioning everything.'

'Such traits will not serve her well,' her ladyship said, somewhat mollified. 'I cannot conceive of a young man who would entertain them in a wife.'

Juliette longed to say that in that case, she would stay unwed, but she dare not. She had embarrassed her mother quite enough for one day. She remained silent, while Lady Martindale tried to retrieve the situation.

'Mr Devonshire was asked by my husband to escort us both as he was unable to do so,' she said, while Juliette wondered why her mama should feel obliged to justify herself to this pompous woman. 'There is no more to it than that. Mr Devonshire has no interest in Juliette and she certainly has no liking for him.' This statement astonished Juliette, who had offered no opinion to her mother on the subject. It was also untrue.

'I am glad to hear it. After all, what is known about him? He has no family that anyone can discover, no title or even the sniff of one and though he appears to be plump in the pocket, that may only be a temporary state of affairs.

'He comes and goes and when he goes, no one has the least idea of where he goes to. And then he reappears as if he had never been away, frequenting White's and being seen everywhere. I have heard it said he made his money in trade. India, I heard.'

'A nabob!' exclaimed Lucinda. 'Perhaps he has an Indian wife.'

'That is a possibility,' the Countess went on. 'I had thought you might know, Elizabeth dear. You would hardly countenance him escorting your daughter if there were any chance of that. And he certainly could not be invited to any other social occasions.'

So that was it, Juliette thought, they were after information. She felt like telling them he had several native wives and his wealth was so immense he could buy up all of London several times over, just to see what they would say, but one look at her mother silenced her.

'I believe he is unmarried,' Lady Martindale said coolly. 'And Lord Martindale tells me he comes from a very good family. You do not suppose my husband would allow me to entertain a mountebank, do you?'

'No, that is just what I said,' Lady Carstairs put in, though somewhat overawed by their hostess. 'I would not have invited him to the ball if I had had any doubts about him. Viscount Martindale has vouchsafed him, I told myself. Do I need more than that?'

Very soon after that, Juliette and Lady Martindale took their leave. Her mother was seething with indignation. 'How dare they quiz me like that,' she said, as their carriage left the door. 'Accusing me to my face of harbouring a snake in my bosom.'

'Oh, Mama,' Juliette said, laughing at her mother's imagery. 'It does not matter what they think, does it? If you are worried, you have only to ask Mr Devonshire for the truth.'

'And what would your father say if I did that? That I did not trust him to know the character of those with whom he associates. It impugns his judgement.'

'Yes, especially as he has told me to look favourably on the gentleman and not let Mr Martindale monopolise me. He would hardly have done that if Mr Devonshire had a wife already, would he?'

'He said that?' Her ladyship was astounded. 'He thinks of that man as a suitable husband for you?'

'He said he would trust him with his life.' Realising she had said too much, she added quickly, 'Not that I would countenance Mr Devonshire if he should offer for me, which I am sure he will not. I do not think I am at all the sort of person he would look for as a wife.'

Her mother did not reply. She said very little for the remainder of the short journey from Piccadilly to Mount

Street and as soon as they arrived went up to her boudoir, pleading a headache.

Juliette spent the remainder of the afternoon reading the latest of Miss Austen's novels, though her thoughts constantly strayed to Mr Devonshire. The popular conception of him and the high esteem in which her father held him were at odds and she wondered who was being deceived, her father or Society in general.

And why did Mr Devonshire and Mr Martindale dislike each other so much? She was not so conceited as to think it had anything to do with her, but if her father had intimated to them both that they were rivals and therefore in competition for her dowry, it might account for it. She wished she had no dowry, then she would not be constantly looking for motives and she could choose for love.

She smiled to herself. James Martindale had certainly seized his opportunities but Mr Devonshire, though never far away had not shown his hand. If she were a flirt, she might play one against the other, but it was not in her nature either to deceive or to tease.

By the time she had dressed ready for a visit to the opera that evening, she had decided to put them both from her mind and enjoy the occasion.

Although it was her first Season, she was a year or two older than was usual and, because white did not suit her very fair colouring, Lady Martindale had decreed that she might wear muted colours. She came downstairs at seven dressed in a gown of pale blue crepe over a white silk slip. It had a high waist and a round neck and was topped by an evening cape of dark blue velvet.

Anne had spent over half an hour on her hair and the result was a young lady who was confident of her looks and not over-awed by the prospect of meeting the Prince Regent, who was expected to occupy his box. It was, so her father had told her, to be a celebration of Lord Wellington's latest success in the Peninsula. He had completely routed Napoleon's brother, Joseph, and driven him out of Spain and back into France. The country was beginning to sense victory.

Her parents were in the library; she could hear them talking as she descended the stairs, but just as she was about to join them, she was halted by their raised voices.

'I was never so humiliated,' her mother was saying. 'Sylvia Wentworth was gloating over it. And then for Juliette to tell me you had encouraged him to offer. . .'

'I said nothing to him.' Her father's voice was pitched a little lower than her mother's but she could tell he, too, was annoyed. 'I spoke to Juliette, not to him. It is my wish that she should think carefully before accepting anyone.'

'Yes, I am perfectly aware that you would like her to have her own way in this as in everything else. I know that she is everything to you, but sooner or later, the truth will out and then what will you do?'

'Nothing.'

'It would be easier if she were safely married.'

'And is her husband to know?' her father asked, so quietly that Juliette could barely hear him.

'Her dowry will keep him silent. And better it were James Martindale, who probably has an idea of the truth anyway and is too poor to care.'

'That is exactly my point. I should like to think that,

above everything, whoever marries Juliette cares for her. And she for him.'

Dear, dear Papa! But whatever were they talking about? What truth? She was so busy questioning herself that she did not hear her mother's reply, until she became aware of the words, 'She is *your* daughter, Edward, you must do what you think is best. But I wish you would consider my position.'

'Oh, I do, my dear, believe me, I do. I would not for the world have you embarrassed, but Mr Devonshire's services are unique and important. And truly the gossip will die down. Hold your head up and pretend not to hear it. . .'

Juliette was astonished to hear her mother say, 'Bah!' in a most scathing tone. 'There is no talking to you.' She retreated a little way up the stairs and stood waiting so that when her mother opened the door and came out, she appeared to be just descending.

Lady Martindale was dressed for the opera, except for her cloak, which lay across a chair in the hall. She looked up when she saw her daughter and visibly pulled herself together. 'There you are, Juliette, we must hurry or we shall be late.'

Lord Martindale appeared behind her, smiling up at Juliette as if nothing had happened and ushered them out to the waiting carriage.

Juliette could not afterwards recount anything of the opera or the host of well-known people who attended it. She vaguely recalled dropping a curtsy to the Prince when she was taken to his box to be presented, but what he said or what she replied, she could not remember.

Her whole being was filled with the conversation she had overheard. None of it made sense. Her mother had been concerned about the truth. What truth? She could not rest nor choose a husband until she knew what it was.

Lady Martindale was indisposed the following morning and it was left to Juliette, chaperoned by Anne, to entertain their callers. There were a great many and she was sure they came as a result of the Countess's remarks about Mr Devonshire, hoping to find out more. It was all she could do to be polite to them.

And then the gentleman himself arrived. He had come, he said, to speak to his lordship, but the Viscount had gone to Horse Guards and was not expected back until the afternoon and she had perforce to invite him to join them.

He was soon chatting amiably with all her mother's friends, making them laugh with his wit, until he had won them all over. By the time he took his leave, everyone was convinced that the Countess of Wentworth would one day be cut by her own tongue and you did not need a title to be a true gentleman. Juliette, catching his eye, knew with certainty that he was doing it for her benefit and was grateful.

'Thank you,' she said, as she accompanied him to the door when he took his leave. 'I truly could not handle them all at once.'

'It seemed to me you were handling them very well, Miss Martindale.' He did not know what it was that attracted him to her. She was very young, possibly too young for a man such as he was, but she had a charisma that was lacking in other young ladies of her age and gentle upbringing. She had character as well as beauty. It was as if she had been touched by tragedy and had become a stronger person because of it.

He recognised something of himself in her, a lone spirit, someone with an inner strength who would not allow life's little ironies to subdue her. Which was all palpable nonsense, of course. And then, to his own considerable surprise, he went against his resolution to remain free from entanglements, and added, 'But if you really wish to thank me, perhaps you would come riding with me one morning. You do ride, do you not?'

'Oh, yes. I ride most mornings when I am at Hartlea. I have a mare in the stables here—not my usual mount, because he is a little spirited for town, but she goes well enough.'

'Then tomorrow morning. At ten, shall we say?'

It was very early, but she decided there was no harm in agreeing, so long as Thomas, one of the grooms, accompanied her. 'I shall look forward to it.' Which was nothing less than the truth.

She decided to forget all the gossip and intrigue, forget why she had been hurried pell-mell to London and was supposed to be choosing a lifelong partner, and enjoy the ride for what it was, a chance to fill her lungs with fresh air, to see the park from a different perspective and exercise her horse at the same time. She chose to ignore the fact that her companion was the subject of gossip. Her father did not think it mattered, and that was good enough for her.

And she was beginning to revise her opinion of him. He was not the boring uncle she had described to her mother; the frisson of excitement she felt whenever he was near could never be attributed to an uncle, or indeed to any relation. It was something that struck at the very core of her, made her feel more alive, aware of him as a man. It was as if they had always known each other and the thought of seeing him and being in his company filled her with happy anticipation.

He called at exactly ten. She was ready and dressed in a dark blue riding habit that set off her shining silvery hair and clear complexion. He was put in mind of the contrast of the moon against the night sky and felt a kind of glow inside him, which he refused to recognise as anything more than pride to have such a beauty at his side. And she rode with an easy grace as they walked their horses along Park Lane and in at the Cumberland Gate, with her groom just behind.

For the first time in his life Philip found himself tongue-tied. Given something specific to do—an order from Lord Martindale, a game to win, a fox to hunt, even a room full of babbling ladies to entertain—he knew exactly what was expected of him and he did it with confidence, but now he was half afraid of saying the wrong thing, of angering her or embarrassing her, of driving her into the arms of someone else, not least her scapegrace cousin.

He had only known her a few weeks, but she had already taken a firm hold on his heart. Not only was she beautiful and delightfully innocent, she was forthright and spirited, thoughtful and intelligent. He had never expected to find all those attributes in one person and having found her, he wanted nothing so much as to hold on to her.

He sat there, jogging along the North Ride, thinking how pleasurable it would be to have her in his arms, to kiss her, and a smile played about his lips.

'Why are you smiling?' she demanded suddenly.

'Have I done something to amuse you?'

'I beg your pardon.'

'You were grinning from ear to ear. I should like to share the jest.'

'I am simply happy,' he said. 'The morning is fine, no hint of rain, and it is good to be alive, to be free, and in such lovely company. What more could anyone ask?'

'Thank you, kind sir,' she said, laughing. 'But why did you mention freedom? Were you perhaps referring to freedom from the constraints of matrimony?'

'No, nothing was further from my thoughts.'

'But you are not married?'

'Oh, you are referring to that ridiculous piece of tattle about an Indian wife?'

'You have heard it?'

'One could hardly fail to hear it; it is all round London.'

'It is not true?'

'Pure fabrication, I assure you.'

'Then why do you not deny it?'

'It amuses me not to.'

'Do you not mind that people are telling lies about you?'

'Not in the least. My friends—my true friends—pay no heed.'

'And Papa is one of them,' she said, determined to find out all she could. 'But it seems strange to me that you have never visited us at Hartlea, when you have known him so long.'

'There has been no opportunity. My work never took me in that direction.'

'Just what is your work?'

He paused, unable to give her a put-down but struggling with an answer that would satisfy her. 'I work for the War Department, as a kind of commissar, locating supplies, recruiting, that sort of thing.'

'But you are not a soldier?'

'No.'

'Neither is Papa,' she said, accepting his explanation equably. 'But that does not mean his work is not important. It must be the same for you.'

He let out his breath in relief. He hated deceiving her and yet he could not tell her the truth. Not now. Not until the war was at an end and there was no longer any need for secrecy. And by then it would be too late, she would be married and out of his reach.

For the first time he cursed his circumstances and wished wholeheartedly that Lord Martindale had not asked him to accompany his wife and daughter to the ball. Then they would never have met and he would not now be suffering such torment.

But if he managed to stop thinking about the possible consequences, the torment was of a pleasurable kind. He ought, of course, to withdraw, to take himself off, but he could not bring himself to do it, to deprive himself of the joy of her company.

'Tell me about Hartlea,' he said, to change the subject. 'You must love it very much.'

'Of course I do. It is my home, I have known no other and it has always been a happy place.'

'Tell me about it.'

'The estate covers a large area, I do not know how many acres, and the house is very substantial. I believe it was given to our ancestors by Cromwell after the Civil War as recompense for the support they gave him. Somehow it avoided being taken back when the

monarchy was restored. It has been handed down from
father to son ever since. . .'

'Only now there is no son.' He spoke quietly, inviting
her to go on, to tell him how she felt and she found it
surprisingly easy to do that.

'Yes. It is entailed and will go to Mr Martindale
when the time comes.' She felt sad for a moment, then
added cheerfully, 'But that will not happen for years and
years yet. It is not something that occupies my mind.'

'No, of course not, but Mr Martindale seems bent on
bringing it to the fore.'

She turned to face him. 'You do not like him,
do you?'

Her bluntness took him by surprise. 'Does it matter
whether I like him or not?'

'No, but I do not like my friends to be at daggers-
drawn.'

'I am flattered to be considered one of your friends,
Miss Martindale.'

She patted the neck of her horse and smiled. 'If you
wish to stay my friend, you will refrain from quarrelling
with Mr Martindale. Papa does not hold a grudge against
him in spite of having good reason and he has told me
that I may entertain his suit, if I so wish.'

'And do you wish?'

His dark eyes were boring into her again, making her
squirm in her saddle. She could not look away, could
not lie to him, could only feel herself melting inside
from the heat in his gaze, so that it took all her concentration to keep her horse steady. 'That is for me to
decide, Mr Devonshire.'

'Of course. But what about others? He cannot be
your only admirer.'

'No, there are dozens of others. I am free to choose.'
It sounded like boasting, but she couldn't help it. It was
her way of defending herself.

'Then choose wisely, Miss Martindale, choose
wisely.'

'I may not choose at all. I will not marry for expediency, or for a title or wealth, or even to stay at Hartlea,
though I love it dearly. If I cannot marry for love, I
will remain unmarried.'

'I cannot see you staying single for long,' he said
softly. 'You would be remarkably easy to fall in
love with.'

She felt the colour flood her face. She had not meant
to speak of her private dream of love and marriage, but
the words had just come out. Had she been testing him,
trying to find out his intentions? How very forward of
her if she were! And his reply had confused her more
than ever. What answer could she give to that?

'Tell me, Mr Devonshire,' she said, deciding she
might as well continue being frank with him; he seemed
not to mind. In truth, he was paying careful attention,
looking into her eyes as if what she had to say was
important to him. 'Has my father encouraged you to
offer for me?'

He was visibly taken aback but then chuckled suddenly. 'He has not spoken to me on the subject.'

'I am glad of that,' she said, tossing back her head
so that the long feather in her tall hat, brushed against
her cheek. It was all he could do to refrain from reaching
out and stroking it away. 'I should not like you to
entertain false hopes.'

'Oh, you have decided against me without giving me
the pleasure of pressing my suit?' He was laughing at

her now, his dark eyes full of mischief. 'You know, if you are so blunt to every young man you meet, you will earn yourself a reputation. There will be more gossip, not less.'

'I don't understand it,' she said, suddenly dropping her bantering tone. 'There is so much going on I do not understand. It is as if some deep dark secret were pressing down on me, something so dreadful it cannot be spoken of. And we left Hartlea so suddenly.'

'I do believe you have been reading too many Gothic novels, Miss Martindale,' he said lightly.

'I am not a fribble, Mr Devonshire. I do not have flights of fancy.' She sighed, wishing now that she had not spoken of her hopes and her fears. Put into words, they sounded so frivolous she was afraid he must think her missish, when she wanted so much to appear cool and gracious. 'But there, you are probably right.' Then suddenly, as if she had put it all behind her, she suggested, 'The horses are fresh, what do you say to a canter?'

Instead of waiting for a reply, she put spur to her horse and drew away from him. She dug her heels in and was soon galloping, her ears filled with the thunder of hooves, her body low and eyes down as the ground rushed past beneath her. This was heaven! She knew she could not outrun him using a side saddle and on this particular mount, but it was fun to try.

Determined not to behave as James Martindale had done and lure her away from her chaperon, in the shape of the young groom who plodded on a sturdy cob behind them, he did not follow. She would stop when she realised he was not behind her and wait for them both to catch up. But she did not pull up and he was at an impasse.

'Sir! Sir!' the groom cried behind him. 'Go after her, sir, for I cannot.'

Cursing under his breath, he set off after her. She was a fine horsewoman, he noted as drew closer, but she was riding side saddle and that was not easy at that speed. And how to stop her safely when he did ride up alongside her, he did not know. He could not seize her reins, it would be asking for trouble. He could hear her laughing and he feared for her at the same time as he appreciated her skill.

'Miss Martindale,' he shouted. 'Juliette, pull up please, I own myself beaten.'

She seemed to be galloping straight for the lake, but suddenly she drew up and brought her horse to a blowing, sweating stop beneath a chestnut tree, whose blossom filled the air with its scent. She jumped easily to the ground and turned to face him.

He threw himself off his horse and found himself standing so close to her, he could see the gentle heaving of her bosom and a laughing mouth that simply asked to be kissed. He took her arms in his hands and pulled her towards him, lowering his head to her upturned face.

Her laughter turned to an expression of astonishment, but there was no fear there, no anger, but that was merely her innocence, he knew; she did not understand what was happening. Just in time he realised his folly and drew away, dropping his hands to his sides and stepping back. 'Are you hurt?'

'Goodness, no.' Afraid to admit, even to herself, that she had wanted him to kiss her and was disappointed that he had not, her voice was unusually hearty. 'Did you think the horse had bolted with me?'

'Had it?' he queried with a smile.

'Certainly not! If I had been on Diablo and riding astride, as I am used to do in the country, you would not have caught up with me.'

'But this is not Hartlea, it is London.' He was still so shaken by desire he could hardly look at her. Of all the stupid things to do, to fall in love at this particular time! And what was worse, almost to declare himself. He pulled himself together. 'We must be thankful that no one saw us.'

'Oh, but someone did,' she said and nodded towards another rider who sat quite still on another path, watching them.

He followed her gaze. 'Martindale!' he said as the man turned his horse and trotted away.

'Are you quite sure? He was too far away to recognise, surely?'

'I am sure.'

Her euphoria evaporated as suddenly as it had come, leaving her deflated and worried. She had no reason to believe he would not report what he had seen and what would the tattlemongers say about it, not to mention her mama?

He helped her to mount and they rode silently side by side towards Thomas, who was limping along beside his cob, apparently having been thrown in his efforts to keep up with them.

Chapter Three

It seemed to be tacitly agreed among the members of the *ton* that Miss Martindale would make her choice between Mr Devonshire and her cousin, and her other would-be suitors quietly faded into the background to watch developments.

Consequently, in the next few weeks, Juliette found herself escorted by one or the other gentleman to the theatre, to Bullock's Museum, to Vauxhall Gardens and Astley's Amphitheatre, to soirées and routs and afternoon tea parties, which she might have enjoyed if she had not been so conscious of the fact that each was trying to outdo the other, and that wherever she was taken by one of them, sooner or later, the other would appear as if by accident.

'You would think the fellow would take the hint,' James grumbled, when Philip arrived towards the end of a musical evening being held at Lady Grainger's house in Park Lane.

'Hint, Mr Martindale?' Juliette queried. 'What can you mean?' It was the supper interval and they had repaired to the dining room for refreshments. Juliette sat holding a plate containing a small pork pie and a plum tartlet in one hand and a glass of cordial in the other.

James was at her side, as he had been all evening. She wished he would go away so that she could converse with other guests about the music, which had been very fine. He, apparently, had been unimpressed and she wondered why he had bothered to attend.

'Well, I mean to say, the man should know by now he is not welcome.'

'Not welcome?' she queried, looking at her mother who sat across the room, apparently deep in conversation with one of her bosom bows, but Juliette knew she was keeping a watchful eye on her. 'I think Lady Grainger would hardly have invited him if he were not welcome.'

'Lady Grainger is an empty-headed goose and will do anything and invite anyone if she is told it is fashionable to do so. The gabble-grinders have made a meal of his mysterious background and she must needs see the man for herself. Look at her now, gushing all over him.'

'She is simply being a good hostess. Really, Mr Martindale, I wonder what you can have against Mr Devonshire that you dislike him so much.'

'Me?' he queried lightly. 'I have nothing personal against him, nothing at all, so long as he leaves you alone.'

He knew he had gone too far when he saw her eyes flash and her cheeks colour angrily.

'Mr Martindale, I shall be the one to say who is to leave me alone, not you. If you have elected yourself my guardian, let me remind you that I have a father who is very careful of me. Your services in that respect are neither required nor wanted.'

'Oh, I did not mean that. My concern is of a different nature entirely. It is simply that I am abominably jealous when I see the way he looks at you. . .' He paused. 'He is not half so rich as he would have you believe, you know, and what he has has been acquired through dubious means.'

'By that, I suppose you are referring to the story that he has made his money in trade,' she said. 'There is nothing wrong with honest work, Mr Martindale—I collect you work for the War Department yourself. And Mr Devonshire has not spoken to me of his wealth at all. Why should he? I hardly know him.'

'Oh, I don't know,' he said airily. 'You seemed to know him very well that morning you went riding with him in the park. When I saw you, you were certainly not riding. Unless my eyes deceived me, you appeared to be in his arms.'

'I most certainly was not!' she said, feeling her face burning at the remembrance.

Mr Devonshire had taken hold of her as if he meant to kiss her, but he had desisted. It might have been because he thought better of the impulse or it might have been because he saw James in the distance before she did, but either way, she had felt strangely empty when he had moved away from her, as if something pleasurable which she had been about to grasp had been snatched from her. 'And you should not have been spying.'

'Spying?' he reiterated, his voice suddenly cold with suppressed anger. 'I hope you will not repeat such an accusation in company, it might be misconstrued.'

She looked up at him, wondering about his sudden change of mood, but then decided she must have imagined it because he was smiling blandly at her, apparently perfectly relaxed.

In repose, he was a handsome man, Juliette acknowledged, but he was so rarely in repose that she did not think of him as especially good-looking. Against Philip Devonshire's languorous nonchalance, he was a firefly, always on the move. It was as if he was afraid to be caught doing nothing for fear that others might realise he had nothing of consequence to do.

'I think we have exhausted Mr Devonshire as a subject of conversation,' she said, holding out her empty glass to him. 'Would you please fetch me another lemonade?'

'Certainly, I will. Please forgive me. I will not mention the gentleman again.' He took her glass and went off to find a waiter to have it refilled, leaving her to nibble at the tartlet and look around the overheated room. Philip Devonshire had left Lady Grainger's side and was helping himself to a glass of punch from the bowl on the table. James passed him on his way back with her lemonade, but the two men did not speak.

James returned to her side and spent the remainder of the interval telling her amusing anecdotes of his time at Cambridge, where he had, as a result of the Viscount's generosity, spent three happy years. It was as if there had never been any discord between them; he did his best to be charming and attentive, but she was left with the impression that it was something of an effort for him.

She was glad when it was time to return to the music room for the rest of the concert, where Philip

Devonshire stood at the back, chatting to Lord Cavendish. She would have much preferred his company to that of James and wished he would come and talk to her, but all he did was to bow civilly across the room to acknowledge her and she solemnly inclined her head towards him in response. Grand passions were not made of such mundane gestures.

The following Sunday, a perfect blue and gold of a day, Juliette was one of a party of young people riding out to Richmond for a picnic. The ladies and their chaperons were in carriages, escorted by the young men on horseback.

Juliette and her mother went with Lady Carstairs and Lucinda in a barouche with Mr Devonshire riding alongside, clad most devastatingly for Juliette's peace of mind in close-fitting buckskins, top boots of shining brown leather and a riding coat of Bath cloth. Mr Boreton, on a chestnut, stationed himself on the other side of the carriage and set out to be agreeable to Miss Carstairs.

A second carriage followed with more picnickers and escorted by other outriders. Ahead of them—a long way ahead—was a lumbering town chariot carrying several hampers, two maids and a butler who were supposed to seek out a suitable picnic spot and have everything prepared by the time they arrived.

James Martindale arrived at the rendezvous driving a high-perch phaeton drawn by a pair of spirited bays and was keen to show off their paces. 'Miss Martindale, will you ride with me?' he asked. 'It is perfectly safe, you know.'

'I am sure it is,' she said. 'But if you do not mind, I will stay where I am.'

'Pudding-heart,' he said cheerfully and, whipping up the bays, he rattled off, taking the bend ahead of them at breakneck speed and was soon lost in a cloud of dust.

'I do hope he does not overturn that contraption,' Lady Martindale murmured. 'It looks decidedly dangerous to me.'

'Oh, it is safe enough in experienced hands, my lady,' Philip said. 'I do not suppose it is the first time he has taken it out.'

'Have you driven one?' Juliette asked him, her imagination conjuring up a picture of him sitting like a god high above ordinary mortals and ordinary carriages, the reins in one hand and a whip in the other, his fine figure outlined against a deep azure sky. It was a very disturbing image.

'Yes, on occasion, but the vehicle is not to my taste. It is too ostentatious by far.'

The vision faded. How silly of her to think he would do anything so exciting, so frivolous, as to drive a high-wheeled phaeton! No man had a right to look so dashing and behave so sedately; it upset all her preconceived ideas that a man's looks should mirror his character.

If he were to behave like he looked, he would have kissed her in the park. Was he afraid to? She would have been obliged to be outraged if he had, of course, but what was that to the point? He had not even given her the opportunity to be angry with him. Why she wanted to be angry with him, she had not the least idea.

'We shall find him in the ditch before we ever reach Richmond,' Lady Carstairs murmured as they continued on their stately way. 'What I cannot fathom is where he found the money to pay for it. Last week he was trying to dun Carstairs for his rent. That's the trouble with the slip-gibbets these days, they think buying horses is more important than paying for a roof over their heads.'

'He told me he had prospects,' Juliette put in. 'Perhaps they have materialised. A win at cards perhaps, or a profitable transaction on the 'Change.'

She heard a gentle chuckle just behind her and swivelled round to see Philip Devonshire smothering a smile. She could not think what he found so amusing, but she would not give him the satisfaction of asking.

Instead, she began a discourse with Lucinda on the merits of Miss Austen's second book, only just out, which she held was much superior to the first and they arrived at the picnic site in Richmond Park without incident to find James idly leaning against a tree and his horses, still in their traces, gently cropping the grass.

The servants had everything arranged, with rugs and cushions and tablecloths laid upon the grass and the wine bottles cooling in the brook. They feasted on capons and ham and pies and tarts, with green salad, washing it down with the wine and lemonade.

Afterwards, the older members of the party dozed on their cushions while the young men played cricket, watched by the young ladies, who spent much time comparing the relative merits of those close to their hearts, while pretending to be entirely indifferent.

Juliette, try as she might, could not be so light-hearted. Marriage was much too serious to be a subject for jest, especially if you felt you were being pushed one way when you most decidedly wanted to go the other. And the memory of her parents wrangling over it just would not leave her.

She watched the game for half an hour, then strolled off alone, taking the towpath beside the river. It was a warm cloudless day and very peaceful beside the lapping water. A pleasure boat full of young people was being rowed downstream; a small sailboat with a single occupant tacked its way towards Kingston; a dog snuffled along the grass beside the path followed by its owner with a sporting gun tucked under his arm, its barrel bent.

On the other side, a barge loaded with osiers was being towed by a single plodding horse; a skylark hovered, afraid to return to its nest while danger lurked. This was England at its best, she thought, and stopped to breathe deeply and lift her face to the sun.

The Season was well advanced, many of the unattached young people had already attached themselves, amid congratulations and wedding plans, but here was she with two apparent suitors neither of whom had yet declared his hand. She wished wholeheartedly that she were not an heiress, then she could marry for love.

She did not love James Martindale, who unsettled her with his swings of mood and flickering eyes, and Philip Devonshire had shown no sign of wishing to have her as his wife. She told herself he was a cold fish, ignoring the fact that he had almost kissed her. Almost.

Pierre *had* kissed her. Poor, defeated, humiliated Pierre, who had nothing to gain, had kissed her because his instinct had told him to. For the pleasure of it. He was not concerned with dowries and settlements, land

and buildings and the niceties of propriety and etiquette. And it had meant nothing to either of them, she knew that now. Beside Philip Devonshire, he was no more than a boy playing at being a man.

It was as if they were all being cold-bloodedly manipulated. But by whom? Her mother? Her father? By other considerations such as the size of her dowry? Or was it Fate who held the reins? Were they all waiting for something to happen that would make everything clear? Perhaps she ought to make it happen, then she could release the tension which seemed to be all around her, especially in her mother.

Mama was like an overwound clock. One day the spring would break and the works fall out. In all her life Juliette had never known Lady Martindale to lose her temper or to appear even a little ruffled. Now she started up at the least little thing, snapped at her husband and found fault with Juliette as if she had done something terribly wrong for which Lady Martindale could not forgive her. If only she knew what it was!

At the far end of the park, she turned to go back, striking out across the grass to cut off the corner and thus return to her starting place. Ahead of her she could see a group of trees and a white building surrounded by an overgrown garden that she needed to pass. She approached carefully, wondering if it were inhabited and if there might be ferocious guard dogs.

There were no dogs, but there were two men standing beside a large pond on which a family of ducks swam. The men had their backs to her and were deep in conversation, but she recognised James Martindale as one of them; the other she did not know. He was most assuredly not one of their party, being unshaven and dressed

in an ill-fitting greatcoat with torn flap pockets and
layers of shoulder capes. Beneath it she glimpsed
grubby blue trousers.

Half-afraid to be seen, she darted behind the shelter
of an oak and peered out to watch them. She saw James
hand the man a bundle of papers and receive in
exchange something that looked remarkably like bank-
notes which he stuffed into his coat pocket. They spoke
for a few more minutes, then James strode off and the
man scuttled away in the opposite direction.

Juliette waited several minutes before coming out
from her hiding place and following James, who was
undoubtedly returning to the picnic. That money had
changed hands she was certain, but for what reason she
could only guess—a gamble won, a debt repaid, though
it seemed inconceivable that James should gamble with
such a one, or lend him money; he had looked decidedly shifty.

She thought of bribery and blackmail and and spying,
and though she told herself such ideas were absurd,
they stuck in her mind. The idea of the picnic had only
been mooted three days before, so how had the man
known James would be at that particular spot at that
time? And then she remembered it had been James's
idea in the first place.

'Let's all go to Richmond on Sunday,' he had said,
when she and Lucinda, escorted by Philip, had met him
in Hookham's Library. 'I am advised it will be a fine
day and we could take a picnic.'

It had taken little persuasion and the party had soon
grown to include several of their friends. 'The more the
merrier,' James had said jovially. He had even refrained

from grumbling when Mr Devonshire had asked to be included.

According to Lady Carstairs, James had been trying to borrow from her husband a week ago and since then had acquired a top-of-the-trees equipage. Had he taken money from the man before? Was that how he had paid for it? It was all very curious and worrying. Ought she to tell someone? But who?

Philip Devonshire came immediately to mind, but that would seem as though she were playing one man against the other and she did not want anyone to think that. Besides, family loyalty forbade it. Or was she making something out of nothing? Just because she was not enamoured of her cousin, did not mean he was the kind to consort with criminals, did it? But deep inside her, she felt a quiver of apprehension and fear which she could not shake off.

Immersed in thought, she did not hear the footsteps behind her and the voice made her almost jump from her skin. 'There you are, Miss Martindale, I had thought you might have lost your way. I came to find you.'

She twisted round, her heart pumping at twice its usual rate. 'Oh, Mr Devonshire, you startled me.'

He fell into step beside her. 'I beg your pardon, but you know you should not wander off alone. There are some very unsavoury characters about these days.'

'Did Mama send you to look for me?' she asked, wondering if he had also seen the man with James and that had prompted his reference to unsavoury characters. She was tempted to ask him, but his next words drove all thought of her cousin from her head.

'No, I missed you.'

He had missed her! If there was ever a time to declare

himself it was now. Her heart missed a beat and she stumbled. He put out a hand to steady her, but did not speak.

'I have not been far,' she said, endeavouring to control the tremor in her voice. 'I wanted to walk and everyone else was otherwise disposed.'

'I would have accompanied you, had you asked.'

She gave a cracked laugh. 'You were busy hitting a cricket ball all over the place and if I had mentioned a walk everyone would have decided to come.'

'You did not wish for company?'

'No. I wanted to think.'

'Oh. A knotty problem to solve?'

'Yes.'

'And have you the answer?'

'The answer seems to be to go back to Hartlea and pretend we never came to London.'

'Have you not enjoyed your stay in town?'

'I might have done if. . .' She stopped. If he had obeyed his instinct and kissed her, instead of drawing back? If James was not so obviously after her dowry?

'Oh, I do not like the marriage mart. Marriage should come as a result of two people finding they have everything in common, a meeting of souls, a feeling in each that to live without the other would be unbearable.' She stopped and laughed in an embarrassed way. 'Now tell me again I have been reading too much fiction.'

'No, I would not do that,' he said softly. 'I find myself in agreement.'

She turned startled eyes on him. 'You are?'

'Oh, yes.'

'Mr Devonshire, you surprise me. I had thought you might be a man of the world.'

'And may a man of the world not fall in love?'

'Are you in love?'

'I think, perhaps, I might be.'

'Does the lady know of it?'

'There are reasons why I cannot offer for her. One day perhaps. . .' He stopped speaking suddenly. What in heaven's name was he thinking of? He had almost allowed his feelings to run away with him.

It was all very well to talk of a meeting of souls, but there were other things which must be taken into account, and not just wealth and position. The obstacles to declaring himself were of his own making, but that did not mean they could be easily thrown aside. It was a question of duty and loyalty and love of a very different kind.

She held her breath waiting for him to go on, wanting him to explain himself, to tell her why he escorted her so frequently when he could not make an offer. Could he possibly be acting under instructions? Was he part of what she saw as a conspiracy to keep her away from the French lieutenant? She could not imagine him agreeing to that; he was too independent to be coerced, too honourable to deceive a lady in that fashion.

She smiled inwardly, wondering what had given her that impression. Could it be that he had refrained from kissing her when he might have done? She had behaved badly herself and he could have been forgiven for thinking she had wanted to be kissed. And she had.

Was she falling in love with this enigmatic man? It was too soon, too soon after the incident over the portrait to unscramble her feelings, but of all the men she had met, he was the one she felt she could lean on, knowing he would not let her down. Was that the beginning of falling in love?

She wanted desperately to find something light to say, to diminish the huge knot of confused thoughts and emotions which constricted her chest, so that she could breathe easily again, but nothing came out of a mouth which had suddenly gone dry.

Neither spoke and the silence stretched between them like a tangible thing, a taut wire that, if it were stretched too far, would break and whirl about their heads, cutting them to pieces. She dare not speak and he would not. The moment had gone. Suddenly a cloud obscured the sun and made her shiver.

'You are cold, Miss Martindale?'

She pulled herself together. She was reading too much into what was, after all, a perfectly ordinary conversation. 'Only a little.'

He took off his jacket and put it across her shoulders, leaving him in his white linen shirt and kerseymere waistcoat. His touch was like fire, even through the cloth of the coat. How could she admit even to herself that the sign she had been waiting for, the knowledge that here was a man she could fall in love with, had come and passed like a flash of lightning and now nothing would ever be the same again.

He had found the woman he wished to marry and it was not her or he would have declared himself. She did not have two handsome men vying for her hand, only one. And it was the wrong one! She did not love James Martindale, could not even begin to think of him as a husband while this disturbing man was anywhere near her. All at once she felt tears prick her eyes and she had to turn away from him.

They returned to the picnic spot without exchanging another word. Juliette retrieved her shawl from her mother and returned the coat with a polite thank-you. The servants packed up the napery, the cutlery and the empty dishes and set off in the town coach back to London.

The cricket bat and ball were retrieved from under the tree where they had been discarded; coats, bonnets and hats were donned, shawls and reticules gathered up and everyone climbed into their carriages or saddles for the return journey.

Juliette, sitting beside her mama in the barouche, found herself watching the straight back of Philip Devonshire as he rode alongside, with a huge feeling of loss. Her stomach was tied into a hard knot of discomfort, which she could not persuade herself was anything to do with eating on the ground.

It was made up of disappointment and not a little anger that she should have allowed herself to believe that he was interested in her. His interest in her was no more than his way of executing the task her father had set him, to keep an eye on her. Well, he need not bother!

As the cavalcade drew up at the junction of Park Lane and Mount Street from where everyone would disperse to their homes, she noticed James had remained demurely with them the whole way. Perversely she smiled at him and he jumped down from his phaeton and strode over to her.

'Miss Martindale, a successful outing, do you not agree?'

'Yes, indeed.'

'Perhaps you would consider a ride in the phaeton. I would drive very carefully, I promise you.'

'If Mama consented, then I should like that,' she said, favouring him with a dazzling smile, which Mr Devonshire was meant to see.

'Then may I call for you tomorrow afternoon? We could take a turn in the park, very sedately, of course.'

'Mama?' She turned to her mother. Lady Martindale appeared to be daydreaming. Hearing Juliette's voice she pulled herself together.

'Yes, yes, but I think Thomas should ride alongside.'

There was no room in the phaeton for three people and agreeing to ride with a gentleman, even on a crowded carriageway where everyone could see them, almost constituted a declaration. It was not exactly an offer but it would be tacitly assumed that one was inevitable and would be accepted.

Juliette was aware of this and she had no idea why she let it happen. Thomas's presence on the cob would be no more than a fop to convention. It was folly to agree, but Mr Devonshire had just dismounted and was standing beside the carriage watching them, and she certainly did not want him to think he had upset her. It was an act of defiance, of self-defence.

'I shall expect you at two o'clock,' she told James, then turned to bid Philip Devonshire goodbye in the coolest voice she could manage, a gesture which apparently left him unruffled but caused a smirk of satisfaction on James's face.

James arrived with the phaeton in good time the following afternoon, boyishly eager, and in less than fifteen minutes they had turned in at the park gates. Juliette felt quite regal sitting in the phaeton high above everyone else; though the ride was not exactly comfortable, it was invigorating and James was at his charming best, keeping the horses to a walk and bowing and smiling to everyone they met.

'I am the envy of the *ton* today,' he said, turning to look at her. She was dressed in a gown that had a powder-blue bodice of jaconet and a skirt of white muslin over a blue silk slip. A little jacket of matching blue velvet and a bonnet whose underbrim was trimmed with tiny blue flowers, set off her pale complexion and silvery hair to perfection. Beneath her silk parasol she looked like a goddess.

'Thank you.'

'Would you care to drive?'

Juliette, who had been wondering if she dare ask him to let her take over the ribbons, turned to face him, her eagerness undisguised. 'Oh, may I?'

'Naturally, you may.' She closed her parasol and laid it on the seat beside her. He handed over the reins, though he kept his own hands over hers. 'Gently, see, they are high-spirited beasts and respond to the slightest pressure.'

'Yes, I understand. I had a pair like that once, at Hartlea, though I did not have a high-perch phaeton, but a curricle. I had no difficulty managing it and used to drive all round the estate until one of the horses injured himself in his stall and Papa was obliged to shoot him. Then we found the other would not go with any of the other horses and he was sold. I still miss them.'

'Then you shall have these.'

She turned to him in delighted astonishment. 'A gift?'

'Of course.'

Sanity returned almost instantly. 'No, it is not

possible. I cannot accept such a gift, it would be misconstrued and. . .'

'There is a solution, you know,' he said, noticing the colour flare in her cheeks. 'You could call it an engagement gift.'

'But . . .we are not. . .'

'That is soon remedied. You have only to say yes to make me the happiest of men.'

She took her eyes from the road to look at him. He was gazing down at her with every appearance of sincerity, his glance flickering over her face from eyes to lips to the top of her head and a throat which had suddenly become dry.

'Mr Martindale!' She affected surprise, which was dishonest of her and made her ashamed of herself. It had to come sooner or later and she should have had her answer ready. But after that first exclamation she found herself unable to speak. Her mind was filled with the image of another man, a tall, enigmatic man whose dark eyes seemed to see into the very core of her and yet had missed the most important thing of all; her love for him.

'You must have known I would ask you,' he went on. 'I have only delayed for propriety's sake.'

'I hardly know you,' she said, finding her tongue at last. 'And you know nothing of me.'

'Are we not cousins?'

'Yes, but that makes no difference. We are strangers to one another.'

'Miss Martindale—Juliette—I have spent several weeks trying to remedy that. You have to admit I have been most attentive. Everyone expects an announcement. . .'

'Do you think I am swayed by what everyone expects?' she demanded sharply.

'No, that was stupid of me. But your mama has been kind enough to look favourably on my suit.'

'And Papa?'

'I am not so sanguine as to imagine he favours me wholeheartedly, but no doubt he will be guided by her ladyship; after all, ladies know best when it comes to such matters, don't you think? He will come about. He has not forbidden you to see me, has he?'

'No, he would not. He has said I must make up my own mind.'

'And have you?'

'No. I cannot.' And that was certainly true.

'Cannot marry me or cannot make up your mind?'

'I meant I will make no decision until I am sure of my feelings. And of yours.'

'If you need more time, of course you may have it,' he said, so complacently she felt like striking him. 'But I beg of you, do not delay too long, there are arrangements to make, things to be done. I had planned a journey abroad in a few weeks' time, but if you do me the honour of accepting me, it will not be necessary.'

'Have you spoken to Papa about this?'

'No, but I will do so as soon as you tell me you wish it.'

'I do not wish it, not yet,' she said, relinquishing the reins to him.

He appeared to accept that and smiled. 'Shall we go a little faster? This pace is too slow for these cattle; they are bred for speed, you know.'

'I am not sure it is. . .'

Before she could finish, he had whipped up the beasts

and the walk changed to a trot that took them away from the main carriageway on to a little-used road. From a trot they moved to a canter, from a canter to a full gallop. The horses were fresh and obviously needed the exercise; they fairly flew over the ground, bumping her up and down in the high seat.

It was exhilarating and she had to admit she was enjoying the sensation of speed and the control he had over the horses. Folly it had been to come, folly it was to encourage him, but she was in no mood to be sensible.

She clutched at her bonnet to stop it flying off and turned in her seat to see Thomas, struggling to keep up with them. It was unfair on the poor groom who was undoubtedly terrified; if she was thrown out and killed or injured, he knew he would be blamed. 'Mr Martindale!' she cried. 'Please slow down, this instant.'

'You are afraid?'

'No, but my groom is.'

He laughed and the whip cracked again. 'I think I shall carry you off, then the decision will be taken out of your hands—the tattlers would see to that.'

'I beg of you, no!' She was truly frightened now.

He turned to look at her, then pulled the horses back to a walk, still laughing. 'No, it will not serve, will it? I must be patient.'

'I do believe you are a little mad,' she said, looking behind them. Thomas was once more in attendance, though his horse was blowing badly.

'Mad for you, my dear Juliette,' he said, turning to rejoin the promenade of carriages and resume their stately progress. She was convinced that everyone had seen them go and was busy with conjecture.

'Now you are being absurd,' she said. 'And I do not

remember giving you permission to use my first name.'

'But we are family already, soon to be even closer. . .'

His arrogance left her almost speechless. She should never have come, she should have known he would take it for granted that she would welcome a proposal. It infurated her. 'Mr Martindale, I never met such a conceited, overbearing man as you are. What makes you think I would consider such a proposal, if proposal it was meant to be? It was more an insult.'

His eyes flickered over her face, as if considering a rejoinder and then he smiled. 'I beg pardon. Please put it down to over eagerness on my part. I will not err again.'

Not wishing to give him a put-down in so public a place, she did not answer but sat stiffly beside him, not speaking, until Philip Devonshire appeared beside the rail and put her composure completely to flight.

His horse was standing quite still, but its lathered neck told them that it had recently been galloping. 'Miss Martindale, good day,' he said, then leaning forward, presented her with her own parasol. 'I do believe you dropped this.'

She stared at it. 'Yes, but where did you find it. . .?'

James understood how it had happened. Philip had been following them and seen the parasol fall from the carriage. 'Look here, Devonshire,' he said. 'Can you not see you are not wanted? If you follow us once more, I shall be obliged to call you out. It is insupportable. . .'

'Why should I follow you?' Philip queried. 'I was out for a ride and saw the parasol on the ground. I recognised it as the one Miss Martindale was using at the picnic.'

'Oh, please do not quarrel on my account,' she said,

accepting her property, but annoyed to think Mr Devonshire had witnessed what had happened. 'It is quite unnecessary. Thank you, Mr Devonshire.'

Philip bowed and took his leave, leaving a bad-tempered James to take her home.

Two days later, when Lady Carstairs and Lucinda called at Mount Street, Juliette was dismayed to learn that there were strong rumours that Mr Martindale and Mr Devonshire had quarrelled violently and a duel was to be fought.

This piece of information was conveyed to her as the two girls sat in Juliette's bedroom, talking about the gowns they were going to wear for her fancy dress ball the following week. Lucinda was to be escorted by Arthur Boreton who, not particularly handsome himself, had decided that there was more to a wife than a pretty face, and offered for her. Lucinda's joy was only matched by her mama's, who had been beginning to think she was unmarriageable.

'I do believe they are fighting over you.' Lucinda, whose appetite for romance was fed on novelettes borrowed from the lending library, was deeply thrilled. 'How romantical!'

'It isn't at all,' Juliette said, dismayed that James had been rash enough to carry out his threat. She had thought it was all bluster, meant to impress her. 'It is foolish in the extreme, besides being unlawful. If they are caught, there will be the most dreadful fuss. They could go to prison.'

'Fustian! Who do you suppose is going to get up at the crack of dawn to arrest them? It will all be over before any justice of the peace can be roused from his bed.'

'But supposing they kill each other?' Her mind was in a turmoil, picturing the scene so vividly, the two men, their jackets discarded, standing facing each other with loaded pistols, or perhaps drawn swords, prepared to kill or die. It was horrible, barbaric. It could not be over her, it just could not. She was not worth fighting over. 'Are you sure you have not made a mistake?'

'No, Arthur told me. He is to be Mr Martindale's second.'

'When? And where? Tell me quickly.'

Lucinda shrugged. 'I do not know. Arthur would not say.'

'Then you must find out. It must be stopped.'

'You are making a deal of fuss,' Lucinda said, peering into her friend's face. 'Which one are you concerned about? I thought at first it might be Mr Devonshire, but you have seen more of Mr Martindale this last week.'

'Neither. Both. Oh, don't you see, how impossible it is?'

'I think Mr Devonshire is the most handsome, but he has a brooding look about him, as if he were weighed down with troubles. But I suppose he would be, having no fortune but what he can make for himself, considerable though it seems to be. On the other hand, Mr Martindale is so amusing, so *galant*. You may insult him to your heart's content and he never minds it.'

'That's because he is too insensitive to mind.'

'Oh.' Lucinda was silent for all of thirty seconds before she added, 'It is Mr Devonshire you favour then?'

'No it is not,' she snapped. It was as if her friend

had touched a raw nerve. 'Oh, I do wish you would not refine upon it, Lucinda. I am too worried to play silly games.'

'I am very sorry, I am sure. I would not have told you about it if I had known you would be so crotchety about it.'

'Oh, Lucinda, I am not cross with you, it is those stupid, headstrong men who have angered me. Please forgive me.'

'Of course.' Lucinda was nothing if not good-natured. 'But what are you going to do?'

'I don't know, but I must do something. Do you think you could persuade Mr Boreton to tell you the details?'

'I will try.'

'Send me a note when you know when and where it is to be. Make sure whoever you send has instructions to hand it to me personally. I do not think Mama should know of this.' She paused, realising there were other ways that Lady Martindale might learn of a duel. 'Does your mama know?'

'I don't know. I shouldn't think so.'

'We had better go down and join them or they will wonder what we are up to.'

They stood up, straightened their muslin skirts and went down to join their mothers who were so absorbed in their plans for the ball and the things which had to be done in preparation they had hardly missed them. But Juliette could not stop thinking about the duel and was so silent after their visitors had left, her mother declared she must he sickening for something.

Two days later, Juliette was woken in the early hours by someone throwing stones at the window of her bedchamber. She lay for a moment, unable to tell what had wakened her, until the sharp patter came again. She rose, padded in bare feet across to the window and threw up the sash.

Lucinda, dressed in a riding habit, was standing on the flower bed below her, about to gather up another handful of stones. 'What on earth are you at?' Juliette called down to her.

'Come on,' Lucinda hissed in a loud whisper. 'Get dressed and come down. Or we shall miss it. Arthur left about half an hour ago.'

'Do you know where?'

'Hampstead Heath. Hurry, we have to be there by dawn. I left my horse tethered to the gate.'

'I'll meet you at the kitchen door.'

Juliette pulled her riding habit from her wardrobe, found underwear and stockings and scrambled into them. A quick comb through her hair, her riding hat jammed on top and two minutes later she was creeping down the stairs with her boots in her hand. Lucinda was waiting outside the kitchen door, where Juliette stopped to put on her footwear. Then together they ran across the yard to the stables and saddled Juliette's mare.

Five minutes later they were on their way, walking their horses between the houses, half afraid to breathe and ready to jump at the least sound. There were gas lamps at intervals along the main streets and flambeaux at the doors of some of the big houses, left to light the late-night reveller home, but as they moved away from the better-class districts, the lights became fewer, the shadows longer and deeper, making their flesh creep.

They had not been going very long before Juliette

wished she had not been so foolhardy as to come. Anything could happen; they could be beset by footpads, murdered, abducted, become lost. If she had been sensible she would have told her father of the duel and left him to deal with it. At the very least, she should have confided in Thomas and asked him to accompany them. But Thomas would never have agreed.

'Are you sure you know the way?' she asked her companion, still whispering.

'Yes, I have done it any number of times. We come this way when we travel north by coach.'

'Not in the middle of the night. Not on horseback.'

'No,' she admitted. 'But Arthur can't be far ahead.'

A cat sniffed a pile of garbage on the side of the road, a drunkard rolled homeward and stopped to watch their passage. Juliette held her breath until they were safely past. 'How did you find out? Did Mr Boreton tell you, after all?'

'No. He spent the evening playing cards with Papa and Lord Hart and I crept down to listen outside the door, thinking he might mention it.'

'And he did?'

'Yes, it got very late and they were still playing and then I heard Arthur say it wasn't worth going home to bed, he might as well stay until it was time to go. They asked him the time and place and he told them. I went upstairs and dressed and then I heard him leave. It took me ages to saddle my horse and then I couldn't find anything to mount from. But we shall catch him up soon, I am sure.'

They were riding in open country now. The moon, which had been lighting their way ever since they left the town behind, disappeared over the western horizon and a faint grey and pink light was growing to the east. A carriage passed them. 'How much further?'

'Half a mile or so.'

And then they were on the heath, making for a stand of spindly saplings where stood the coach that had overtaken them. Three men stood beside it, two of whom were holding the reins of riding horses. They looked up at the approach of the girls.

'Good God!' Arthur exclaimed. 'Lucy, what are you doing here?'

'We came to put a stop to this duel,' Juliette said, flinging herself off her horse and running over to them. 'It cannot take place.'

One of the other men laughed, a young man whom Juliette did not know. 'We thought it was the protagonists and it's nothing but a couple of petticoats. Have they sent you in their place? What sport, eh?'

'They are not here?' Juliette was so keyed up, she could not believe that frightening ride through the night had been for nothing. The seconds were here, to be sure, but the duellists were absent.

'No, but there is time,' the third man said. Although older and plump, he was dressed as they were in unrelieved black.

At that moment the sound of a horse's hooves sounded loud on the still air. They turned to see James Martindale riding into the clearing. Juliette's heart sank.

'Good God!' he said, repeating Arthur's exclamation at the sight of the ladies. 'What are you doing here?' Juliette took a deep breath. 'Mr Martindale, you must not fight. It is wrong. He may kill you. You may kill him.'

'That is the whole idea.'

'If you do, I shall never speak to you again, do you hear me?'

He laughed. 'Very well, for your sake, I shall not kill him, I shall merely give him a little sword prick he won't forget in a hurry.' He turned to the other men. 'Where is he?'

'Not arrived yet,' Arthur said.

The sky grew lighter as they stood about and waited, but no one else appeared.

'Well, well, it seems he is not coming,' James said, hiding his relief in joviality. 'The coward has failed to turn up. What are we to make of that, eh? What will they say in town?'

'He has more sense than you,' Juliette said, half-relieved and half-disappointed. She had not wanted the men to fight, but she had never thought Philip Devonshire was a coward. But it seemed he was. Why else would he fail to appear?

Already she was beginning to understand the implications. He would be ostracised. No one would want to know him. He would be invited to no more social gatherings. It would be the end of his career; he would not dare to show his face in society again.

Supposing something had happened to him to prevent him coming, something dreadful, like illness or death? Some would say that was the only acceptable excuse for an honourable man. But if he had come, he might now be lying dead at her feet. Which was worse? The thought that she might never see him again was too much to bear and she suddenly burst into tears.

'Come, come, my dear,' the older man said, taking her hand and patting it. 'It is all over and no harm done, for which I am truly thankful. Doctoring duellists is not something I do with any enjoyment.'

'We had better get the ladies home,' Arthur said. 'Though how to get them back in their beds before they are missed, I do not know. The morning will be well advanced before we arrive.'

The impossibility of hiding the night's adventure from her parents struck Juliette like a blow. Oh, there was going to be the most dreadful fuss and her punishment would be dire. She rode home in a very subdued frame of mind, her head tumbling with confused thoughts; what to say to her parents and wondering why Mr Devonshire had not arrived.

Could he have mistaken the time and place? Was he really a coward? Did she care what he was when to be with him, to have him beside her, laughing with her, teasing her, talking to her about all manner of things that interested them both, was all she wanted? At this particular moment it was unimportant whether he loved her or not.

And why was James grinning like a cat that had stolen the cream?

Chapter Four

Anne, going to wake her mistress at nine, had discovered the empty bed and the open window, and a search below it had revealed footmarks in the flower bed. It had been assumed that Juliette had been abducted—for what reason no one could tell. Servants were sent to scour the countryside in search of her, while her parents paced the house imagining all sorts of terrors.

Their relief on discovering that she had been indulging in a little adventure of her own and was unharmed, turned quickly to anger. Juliette wished fervently that James had not insisted on coming in and delivering her to her parents in person and thus witnessing her humiliation.

'Ungrateful wretch!' her mother said, as soon as they were assembled in the withdrawing room and Arthur Boreton had left to take Lucinda home. 'But then what more can one expect from someone so thoroughly indulged all her life? Your father is to blame, no doubt of it. I wish I had never. . .' Here she stopped because her husband's thunderous look quelled her.

'Now, what are we to do?' This to the Viscount. 'Her
reputation will be quite in shreds and ours too, for
allowing it to happen. . .'

'Oh, come, my dear,' his lordship said. 'You put too
high an import upon the escapade. No one need know.
I doubt Carstairs will want his daughter's involvement
noised abroad and we can rely on James, I am sure.'
He looked at his nephew, who nodded acquiescence.
'Besides, Juliette did not go alone and her intentions
were good, though I wished she had told me of the duel
instead of trying to stop it herself.'

'In the event it was not the least necessary,' James
drawled. 'The coward did not turn up.'

'No doubt he had his reasons,' his lordship said. 'And
I, for one, am glad of it. Duelling is a barbaric custom
that no civilised society should condone.'

'So it may be, sir, but the challenge was issued. Had
he been the gentleman he purports to be, he would have
been honour-bound to afford me satisfaction.' He sighed
heavily. 'But then, it is well known he is a nobody,
dragged up from nowhere and used to all kinds of trick-
ery to make his way in the world.'

'That is enough!' Lord Martindale snapped. 'I have
always found Mr Devonshire totally reliable.'

'What is that to the point?' Lady Martindale cried.
'I do not care two pins who did or did not turn up.
What I want to know is what we are going to do about
Juliette. Lucinda Carstairs can be forgiven, she is
already betrothed to Mr Boreton, but Juliette is not even
properly out. . .'

'Mama, I would like to go home to Peterborough,'
Juliette murmured. 'I would like to live quietly in the
country.'

'No! That would instantly become a talking point for all the tattlemongers in town with your own come-out ball only two days away and all the arrangements made. We must divert the gossips with something else to occupy their tongues.' She turned to her husband's nephew. 'James, I know it is asking a great deal, considering Juliette's behaviour, but do you think. . .'

'Certainly!' he said, understanding immediately. Then to Lord Martindale. 'May I speak with you in private, my lord?'

Reluctantly his lordship agreed and the two men retired to the library.

'Mama, please!' Juliette cried, her eyes full of tears. 'I do not want to marry James Martindale. I do not want to marry anyone. I am truly sorry I have displeased you, but it is not fair to punish me for the rest of my life for one small misdemeanour.'

'Now you are making a Cheltenham tragedy out of something commonplace, Juliette. There are half a dozen girls I can think of who would be ecstatic to marry Viscount Martindale's heir. You must think yourself fortunate that he does not hold your hoydenish behaviour against you and is still prepared to offer for you.'

'But I do not love him!'

'Heavens! What is that to the point? He is personable and charming and he is the Martindale heir. If anything happens to your father, it is the only way we shall be allowed to stay at Hartlea. You must see that.'

Juliette was suddenly alarmed. 'There is nothing wrong with Papa, is there? Oh, tell me he is not ill.'

'You know he works too hard and the government will not let him rest. I have said, time and again, that

it will be the finish of him. It is not helped by behaviour
from you such as we have endured today. It is a wonder
he did not have a seizure when he learned you had
disappeared.'

'I am sorry, Mama. I did not think.'

'No, you never do. Now we must do what we can to
contain the damage. With you safely settled, he might
relax a little.'

It was blackmail, even Juliette recognised it, but she
could not withstand it. She loved her father above all
people. It was to his lordship she had gone as a child
with all her troubles, grazed knees, broken dolls, school-
work that would not come right. He seemed to have
the cure for everything.

It was her father who had taught her to ride and
drive the curricle, who encouraged her to read and ask
questions, who explained the war in terms she could
understand. She loved her mother, of course she did,
but Lady Martindale was always a little distant, holding
her at arm's length, as if she were afraid to show her
feelings.

Papa had explained that it was because she had lost
three babies, one before it had even been born, one at
birth and the other who had lived three weeks before
being carried off, and all of them had been boys. He
said she was afraid to become too attached to anyone,
because whomever she loved, she lost.

Mama herself never mentioned the dead little ones.
She went about her household duties with a back that
was ramrod straight and suffered no slackness, either
in herself, in Juliette or the servants. If they were to
lose her father, how could they go on?

'Very well. If that is what Papa wishes, then I will

consider a proposal from Mr Martindale,' she said in a voice so low it was hardly audible.

The strange thing was that James left the house immediately after his interview with his lordship and did not return to the withdrawing room. Hearing him leave, Lady Martindale hurried to the library to speak to her husband, leaving Juliette to toil upstairs to her room, where she flung herself on her crumpled bed and wept. Now, too late, she realised the consequences of her escapade.

She had wanted to make something happen, but not this. She had no love for James Martindale, could not even like him, but he had to be her choice. She wished, with all her heart, they had never come to London, then she would not now be mourning a love that was lost. And all because of that portrait. It was nothing more than paint on canvas and yet it had ruined her life.

No one came to her, no one offered her any comfort, and eventually she fell into a troubled sleep in which she dreamed the duel had taken place, but she could not tell who had survived and who had not, but there was blood everywhere, even on her own hands. She tried to wipe it off on her clothing, rubbing them this way and that, but it would not go away.

She could hear sounds, voices, laughter, a drum. The drum was insistent, thump, thump, thump, filling her ears until she woke up screaming, to find herself kneeling up in bed and all the covers on the floor.

The door was flung open and Anne rushed in. 'Miss Juliette, whatever is the matter?'

'I had a bad dream,' she said, unable to shake it off. 'There was so much blood.'

'That comes of rushing off to duels, miss. It would

not surprise me if you have caught a chill. I'll bring
you a tisane and you had better remain in your room.
I'll tell her ladyship you are not well, shall I?'

'No, I am not ill, Anne. I have been very foolish and
must face the consequences. Keeping to my room will
not change anything. I will go down to dinner.'

So Anne helped her to dress and arranged her hair
and she took her place at the dining table with as near
a smile as she could manage.

James did not return to the house before the evening
of the ball and Juliette began to wonder if he really
meant to make an offer after all. The waiting was tearing
her composure to shreds and making her mother more
than usually brusque with her.

'You have no one to blame but yourself if he has
changed his mind,' she said, while busy directing cooks,
florists, maids and footmen.

The ballroom had been added to the ground floor at
the back of the house by his lordship's father, fifty years
before. It was not large by the standards of the day,
but it could accommodate fifty couples in comfort and
several more at a squeeze and Lady Martindale was
determined it would be a squeeze because that would
be a measure of the ball's success.

'He will bring another bride to Hartlea and then
where will we be?' She spoke as if her husband were
already dead and that upset Juliette even more.
'Banished to Scotland, that will be our fate.'

Although the daughter of an earl, Elizabeth had been
brought up in utmost hardship. Her father had not
believed in mollycoddling his multifarious brood and
had made them take cold baths every day and study in

an icy schoolroom in a castle on the rocky shore of the East Highlands. Hardy himself, he was determined that none of his children would grow up soft.

Elizabeth had been fortunate to catch the eye of Edward Martindale when he was invited to a hunting party on the estate. Married and brought south to the comfort and warmth of Hartlea, she would have been content, but for the fact that she had been unable to produce an heir. If Juliette married James, then she would be allowed to stay; James had promised her that in return for her support. He needed Juliette's dowry as much as Elizabeth needed Hartlea.

'Mama, Papa has assured me he is not ill and James cannot inherit until. . .'

'Have you ever known him to admit he was not in plump currant?'

'No, but. . .'

'Juliette, one must be practical about these things and not be selfish. James will be at the ball and I want you to make a push to engage him. We cannot have him backing out now. We will make the announcement after supper, when everyone has unmasked.'

The Countess of Wentworth had persuaded her to make it a *bal masqué*, saying fancy dress was all the mode. After much debate, Juliette had decided to go as Diana, Goddess of the Hunt. Her white crêpe gown was draped from her shoulders in soft folds, which hinted at the lithe figure beneath, but revealed nothing. It was decorated with garlands of greenery.

She wore Greek sandals, a circlet of greenery in her silver-blonde hair and carried a small crossbow. A tiny pouch across one shoulder contained half a dozen little arrows.

She dressed on the evening of the ball with little enthusiasm. What might have been a glittering occasion, to remember with pleasure, was something to be dreaded. James would be there and she would have to agree to link her life with his because there was nothing else she could do.

That Philip Devonshire would be absent, she was equally sure. He had not been seen in polite circles since the evening before the aborted duel, though she understood from Lucinda, who got it from Arthur Boreton, that he had returned to town. Even though he had been invited to the ball three weeks before, he would not have the effrontery to attend because he must know that everyone would cut him dead.

It was common knowledge that he had reneged on a challenge to his honour. Did that mean he had no honour? And no courage either? It would be easier to put him from her mind if she really believed that, but she did not and she could not stop thinking about him. And wondering.

Oh, if only it had been he who had turned up and James who had stayed away; it would have been more credible. And if she had not been so foolish as to dash off into the night, she would at least have been allowed the luxury of making her own decision about whom she should marry.

There was something about James's arrogance, his flickering eyes, that unnerved her, as if his manner were all a front to hide his own insecurity. But he must know he was secure in his inheritance, even if he had no money of his own to maintain it now her—dowry would see to that.

As for Philip Devonshire, she could not see herself

marrying him either, even if he were to ask. It was not his lack of background or family, or the fact that no one really knew how much he was worth, that would deter her. It was his ability to keep himself close, to hide within himself. He was completely self-contained and needed to lean on no one.

He apparently did not even care about being branded a coward. But most of all, it was his admission that he had found the woman with whom he wished to share his life and she knew it was not Juliette Martindale. He would have spoken if it were and he had remained silent.

It was that which hurt. It hurt because no amount of telling herself that he was totally unsuitable could alter the fact that when she was in his company, her heart beat faster, her limbs trembled and she wished more than anything to remain with him, to learn more about him, to be held in his arms as he had held her in the park, to have those deep eyes looking into hers, soft with love.

She brought herself up short. How romantical! And how silly she was being. It was unlikely she would ever see him again.

She sighed and, taking a last glance in the mirror, which revealed eyes a little too bright and cheeks a little too pale, put up her mask and left her room to descend gracefully to the ground floor to stand beside her parents and welcome her guests as they arrived. Her mama was dressed as Cleopatra, but her father had eschewed costume and was elegant in traditional breeches and silk stockings with a high-collared coat in rich burgundy.

The guests came in twos and threes: cavaliers, Roundheads, Greek gods, Roman soldiers, wood nymphs, Henry the Eighth, Queen Elizabeth, complete with enormous ruff and bright red wig, milkmaids, highwaymen, highlanders, courtiers of fifty years before, their coiffures so tall they had been unable to sit upright in their carriages. They lined up to be received and then, their cloaks and mantles taken from them, passed into the brilliantly-lit ballroom, where the laughter and gossip vied with the music and dancing for attention.

James was among the last to arrive. Dressed as one of many cavaliers, his fluttering eyes made him easily recognisable. He bowed before her parents, smiling and confident, and then took Juliette's hand and carried it to his lips. 'Miss Martindale, your obedient.'

She tried to smile, but it stuck somewhere between a grimace and a frown. 'Mr Martindale, welcome.'

'Oh, you have found me out! And I had hoped to flirt a little with you before we unmasked. No matter, we can pretend we do not know each other.'

He gave a silly laugh which betrayed the fact that he had already been imbibing freely. Juliette was disgusted. Did he have to make himself drunk before he could bring himself to propose to her? He turned to her mother. 'My lady, can you not release your delightful daughter from her station and allow her to accompany me into the ballroom?'

'I do not think there are any more guests to come,' Lady Martindale said. 'Juliette, you may go into the ballroom with James.'

There was nothing for it but to take his arm and do as she was bid. No one else was coming; no gallant hero would arrive to carry her off to some fantasy land where there was no hypocrisy, no equivocation, where truth and beauty reigned with love. Oh, how fanciful she was becoming! There was no such place, no such man. But the image of Philip Devonshire came to her mind unbidden and made her want to cry.

They joined an incomplete set and James bowed before her, smiling with satisfaction.

'You seem exceedingly pleased with life,' she remarked, rising from her curtsy and taking his hand to promenade between two rows of dancers.

'Do I? Perhaps it is because life has come up trumps at last and everything is going well, a pleasant evening to look forward to, and that to be followed by many more evenings, days, months, years, all to be spent in happy contentment with my delightful bride at Hartlea. What more can a man want?'

'May I remind you that Hartlea is not yet yours,' she said, sharply. 'Papa is in the best of health.'

'True, but I am a patient man.'

'And your bride?' she queried, wondering if it were possible he meant someone else.

'You, my dear Miss Martindale. You know that, surely?'

Her heart sank. 'I do not remember agreeing.'

They turned and circled round each other. 'Oh, that is only because I have not asked you yet.'

'Why haven't you? You spoke to my father two days ago, after. . .' She could not bring herself to mention that escapade.

'So I did. But I had a little business to see to first.'

She was suddenly reminded of his encounter with the stranger in Richmond Park. Was that where his business lay? 'And has it been successfully concluded?'

'It is well on the way to being so, I am glad to say.'

The dance came to an end and she was immediately

surrounded by young men, all eager to mark her card. James had perforce to relinquish her to others, but not before he had scribbled his name against the supper dance. 'I shall be back to claim you, my lovely Diana,' he whispered. 'And then perhaps we can find a little time alone. One must do these things formally, after all.'

She danced and smiled and flirted harmlessly, but all the time the gilded clock on the mantel ticked inexorably towards supper. And then he was bowing before her. She looked round wildly for a way of escape, but could see none. Her mother, who was sitting between Lady Carstairs and the Countess of Wentworth, saw them and nodded imperceptibly.

Her father was nowhere to be seen. He might have helped her, but he chose not to. She could not understand why. In every other respect he was a strong-willed man, but faced with the determination of his wife, he always gave in. She executed a deep curtsy and laid her fingers upon his arm. The time had come.

Philip Devonshire put the last touches to his costume and smiled at himself in the cheval mirror which stood at an angle to the window of the bedchamber in his lodgings in Haymarket. He was dressed in the all-enveloping white robes of a cardinal, complete with red cap and cape. And the mask he wore covered all but his eyes and mouth. No one would recognise him.

It was not that he was particularly afraid of recognition; he had nothing of which he need feel ashamed, but he did not want to upset his lordship's household by appearing at the ball as if nothing had happened.

He could imagine the covert looks, the whispers passing from one to the other of the guests, the more open stares and then the condemnation, the insults. Of all people, he admired and respected Viscount Martindale the most, but he wished he had not brought this disgrace upon him.

'I want you to go to Peterborough,' the Viscount had said, early on the morning of the day before the duel was to take place, a duel he had neither sought nor wanted, but James Martindale had goaded him so that there had been no alternative but to accept the challenge. 'It is most urgent.

'My information is that there is a man in the camp at Norman Cross who is arranging for prisoners to escape and passing on state secrets for them to take back to France with them. My information is that he will be at the camp tonight. I doubt he will stay once he has spoken to his contact there, but will return to his English master. It is that gentleman the War Department wishes to identify.'

'My lord, I have a very pressing engagement for tomorrow.'

'Since when have private matters taken precedence over the good of your country and mine?' his lordship had demanded. 'You know the conditions under which you are required to operate.'

'Indeed I do, my lord, but this a question of honour.'

'Do not tell me you have engaged to fight a duel?'

'Yes, my lord. It was. . .'

'I do not wish to hear the details. It would mean condoning it and, in my position, I cannot do that.' He paused. 'I thought you had more sense, Philip. If you were to be killed or even injured, the country will have lost one of its best agents.'

'I could not ignore the challenge, my lord,' he said,

deciding not to reveal the identity of the challenger. 'It would have been construed as cowardice. I had the choice of weapons and chose the rapier. It would have done less damage than a bullet.'

'I know you for a fine swordsman, Philip, but none the less your duty must come first, even at the expense of your reputation. You must know that.'

Of course he knew that; he had been foolish even to mention it. He had gone to Peterborough, hoping to complete his mission and be back in time.

He had left his horse safely housed at an inn just short of Norman Cross, joined a ragged file of new prisoners disembarking at the quay and marched with them to the prison barracks. The man he was seeking had not arrived and though he had waited and talked to as many of the prisoners as he could, he had discovered nothing of him.

When it became obvious he was on a wild goose chase, he had made himself known to the commandant and been smuggled out by the guards. Retrieving his horse, he had galloped all the way back to town, changing his mount whenever it showed signs of tiring.

He had arrived at the rendezvous half an hour beyond the agreed time to find the clearing deserted. He had cursed roundly in several languages, wishing they had waited, but he realised that James Martindale, who had no real stomach for the fight, would have been delighted to go home as soon as the appointed hour passed and crow over him. His reputation had suffered immeasurably as a result and he knew he could no longer expect to be received in polite society. And because it was not in his nature to protest about the injustices life dealt him, he could do nothing about it.

Since then he had discovered a little more of the man they were hunting and he needed to tell his lordship of it. The trouble was that they had not arranged to meet and he could not openly go to see him. He was quite sure he was being watched.

The ball it would have to be. With luck, he might catch his lordship's eye before his presence became known and he could leave as soon as their business was concluded. It was a great pity because he would have to forgo dancing and talking with Juliette.

He would have to put her from his mind. He could not tell her he loved her, could not ask her to wait, not when the waiting might be for years. Besides, she would not marry a man without a title, without a fortune, much less a known coward.

He would never marry now. The memory of her lovely face, her delightful laugh, her brightness, would have to be enough. But to relinquish her to James Martindale, of all people, twisted the knife in the wound. If only . . .

He pulled himself together; wishing for the impossible was a futile exercise and he did not have the time. He finished dressing and went out to the hired carriage that had been waiting at the door for the last twenty minutes.

He arrived at Martindale House just as her ladyship left her station in the vestibule to go into the ballroom. His lordship had turned away, intending to have a quiet drink and a cigar in the library before joining her. He turned back as his new guest arrived. 'Philip, is it you?' he asked, peering into the young man's face.

'Yes, my lord. I needed to see you and. . .'

Lord Martindale laughed. 'You make a fine cardinal, though I'll wager there are few churchmen of your height and build. Come, let us go up to the library, we will not be disturbed there.'

It was not until they were seated one on either side of the hearth, each with a cigar in his hand and a glass of brandy on a table at his side, that his lordship said, 'Now, what news have you?'

'I could identify no one at Norman Cross and the prisoners closed ranks as soon as I arrived. It was as if they were afraid to speak, though I was dressed as one of them and spoke only French.'

'How did you get away?'

'I saw the commandant and he arranged for me to escape.'

His lordship smiled. It was not like Philip to leave a job half-done. 'But there is more?'

'As you know, I have contacts among the *émigrés* in London. One of them speaks of an escaped prisoner of war, who instead of taking the opportunity to return home, has been organising safe houses and smugglers' vessels to help others escape. I am told he roams freely all over the eastern counties and frequently comes to London.'

'Do you know his name?'

'He calls himself *Le Merle*.'

'The blackbird.'

'Yes.'

'He cannot work without help. I need to know who he is and who is helping him. I think a longer sojourn among the prisoners is necessary, Philip. Will you go back?'

Philip sighed. 'Yes. I suppose it is not surprising that

Philip Devonshire should disappear. After all, he is a craven coward.'

'You refer to that duel?'

'Yes, my lord.'

'You did not tell me it involved my nephew.'

'No, my lord. I did not wish to upset you and I had no intention of killing him.'

'He would not have behaved so chivalrously towards you.'

Philip shrugged as if that fact were of little importance. 'As it was, I arrived too late.'

'You know my daughter heard of it and rode out before dawn to try and prevent it?'

Philip was taken aback. 'I had no idea. Why?'

'Like me, she did not want to see anyone hurt. I suspect she thought the quarrel might have been over her. Was it?'

'No. Why did she think that?'

'I surmise because you and my nephew seem always to be at daggers-drawn. And you have both been escorting her.'

'It was not over Miss Martindale.' He paused. 'I accused him of cheating at cards. He took exception to it and challenged me.'

'And was he cheating?' His lordship smiled a little grimly. 'You need not spare my feelings. His father was just the same.'

'Yes. I am sure of it. I was angry because his friends backed him against all the evidence and I accepted the challenge in the heat of the moment. I could not afterwards back out.'

'So that is how he has been able to buy new horses and carriages. Three weeks ago he had pockets to let.'

'I am sorry, my lord, and even sorrier that Miss Martindale should have been upset by it. She took no harm, I trust.'

'No. James escorted her home. And now Lady Martindale is convinced it is necessary for her to marry her cousin to save face. What have you to say to that?'

Philip's heart sank. 'Has she agreed?'

'The announcement is to be made after supper tonight.' His lordship paused, while Philip struggled with his emotions. 'Why were you not a little quicker off the mark, m' boy? You know I would have been delighted.'

'My lord, you know how little I have to offer your daughter. Besides, I have sworn not to marry while I do the work I do. I would be very vulnerable if I were forever worrying about my wife while I were away. Besides, I own no estates and the money *Maman* and I were able to bring out of France in '94, bought only a small annuity. I am thankful the British government pays me well for the work I do, but when the war ends, which I believe it must do soon, I shall not even have that.'

'My friend, that is what your head might be telling you, but what of your heart?'

Philip grinned ruefully. 'That, my lord, is another matter entirely.'

'Sometimes,' his lordship said softly, 'it is better to be ruled by the heart. And so I have told Juliette. But against Lady Martindale I have no weapons.' He paused and then appeared to change the subject completely. 'There is another matter, I would like you to investigate while you are at Norman Cross. There is a Lieutenant

Veillard confined there. I want you to find out all you can about him.'

'You think he might be *Le Merle?*'

'No, this is a private matter. He was engaged as a gardener at Hartlea, but while he was there he painted a portrait of Juliette. It was a very strange portrait.' He paused, wondering how much to reveal to the young man. 'He depicted her as a French aristocrat loaded with jewels. Lady Martindale was particularly distressed.'

'His notion of a joke, perhaps?' he suggested, deciding not to reveal that Juliette had already confided in him.

'Perhaps. But you see, I recognised the jewels. They once belonged to the Comte de Carrone.'

'But he and his family were guillotined in '94.'

'Yes, I know. I want you to find out all you can about this lieutenant and how he came to know about the jewels.'

'I will do my best.'

'You are not to put it before matters of state, you understand. Finding this blackbird fellow and his informant must take precedence.'

'I understand.'

His lordship rose. 'Now, I must join my guests. Will you come?'

'No, my lord. I might be recognised and that would cause you embarrassment. With your permission I will finish this excellent cigar and leave unnoticed.'

'Very well.' His lordship drained his glass and stood up. 'We shall soon be returning to Hartlea. You may reach me there when you have something to report.'

Philip stood and watched him go, noting how he seemed to have lost the spring in his step and looked very tired. The energetic, courageous man he had known as a child seemed to be weighed down with cares and his heart reached out to him. It might help if he cracked the nut he had been given as soon as possible. He rose and left the room.

At the bottom of the stairs he paused. Then, unable to resist the temptation, he slowly made his way over to the ballroom door and stood for a moment watching the dancers, looking for one in particular. Just a glimpse would be enough and then he would take himself off. The room was packed to bursting and with everyone in costume he could not see her, and then she danced into view, partnered by James Martindale.

She was a vision of delight, but one that was marred by her expression. She wore a small mask that covered only the upper part of her face. He could see her mouth, smiling up at her partner for all the world as if she were enjoying herself.

But the eyes! Those expressive eyes, outlined by the silk of the mask, were bleak, as if she had just been dealt a devastating blow from which there was no hope of recovery. Had Martindale proposed? Had she accepted? He had to know.

The dance came to an end and the pair began to walk towards the open doors to the garden. Before they reached them, she turned and saw him. Recognition lit her face momentarily and then disappeared as if she thought her eyes were deceiving her.

He pushed his way through the throng and intercepted them, bowing before Juliette. '*Mam'selle*, will you do me the honour of dancing with me?' He spoke like a French *émigré*, whose accent had never quite disappeared. It was aristocratic and precise.

'No, sir,' James put in and Philip was certain he had not recognised him. 'The lady is with me and she wishes to be taken into the garden.'

Juliette laid a hand on his arm. 'We can go into the garden later, James. I must not neglect my guests.' She held out her hand to Philip, who took it in his and turned to lead her back to the dancers, leaving James hardly able to conceal his fury.

'My Lord Cardinal,' Juliette said with a glint of mischief in her eye, 'is it fitting for an eminent churchman to waltz?'

He was glad to see the sad look go from her eyes and whirled her into the dance, feeling her slim body under his hand and wishing he dare hold her closer than the stipulated arm's length. 'Oh, this churchman is not all he seems.'

'That I realise.' He was a superb dancer and her feet were carrying her as if they had wings, following where he led, just as if they had been practising the steps for years.

'But I collect you were going into the garden.' And with that he whirled her, still dancing, out through the doors and on to the terrace, where it was cool.

'Mr Devonshire!'

'You know me?'

'Of course I know you. Did you think you could disguise yourself from me? It was very unwise of you to come. You know what they are saying, don't you?'

'That I am a coward. Is that what you think of me, Miss Martindale?'

'Does it matter what I think?'

'It matters a great deal. I have heard that you rode out in the middle of the night to try and stop the contest.'

'Oh, I have no doubt that my disgrace is all over town.'

'The disgrace is surely mine.'

She smiled suddenly. 'Then we are in it together, don't you think?'

'Together,' he murmured, looking down at her. The fixed smile was still there, but he sensed her tension beneath his hand on her waist. 'Would it were so. But why did you do it? You must have known it would cause the most dreadful fuss.'

'I did not think of that. I was only concerned with preventing you from fighting. I could not bear the thought of you. . .' She stopped, confused by what she had been about to say. 'Of anyone being hurt. But I could have saved myself the bother. You did not keep the appointment.'

'No, I was unavoidably detained.'

Her smile was more relaxed now and there was a hint of a twinkle in her eye. 'That, I suppose, is as good an excuse as any, and I am glad. There is enough fighting going on between nations without individuals putting an end to each other.'

'Amen to that. So, no harm has been done?'

'None except. . .' She could not go on.

'Except?' he prompted.

Her steps faltered and she stumbled against him. He caught her in his arms. and before she could cry out, had enfolded her in his arms and was kissing her.

She pushed at his shoulders with her hands and tried to protest, but the only sound she could utter was a little grunt. A strange sensation in the pit of her stomach swept away her resistance and she found herself leaning into him, her mouth hungry for his. She forgot where she was, forgot her parents, the music, James Martindale, forgot everything in the pleasure of his embrace. Here was her love.

He came to his senses first and let her go, dropping his hands to his sides. 'I beg pardon. That was unforgivable of me.'

Her breast was heaving and her mouth slightly open, as if she could not breathe properly. Then, realising slowly that some reply was expected of her, she said, 'I am glad you realise it, for I shall not forgive you.'

That was untrue and the colour in her cheeks betrayed her. She had wanted the kiss to go on and on, though the sweetness was tinged with bitterness.

He was simply playing with her, proving, if any proof were needed, that her recent behaviour obviously led him and everyone else to believe she would not demur at any liberties they might take. Any young lady who could creep out of the house at dead of night and gallop about like some highwayman, deserved all she got. No wonder her mama had been so shocked. 'Please take me back inside.'

'Of course. I am profoundly sorry I distressed you.' He encircled her waist once more and waltzed her back into the ballroom, as if they had done nothing but take a turn about the terrace.

As the music came to an end, they both became aware that they were the subject of speculation. The mothers and chaperons ranged around the room had left off their gossiping and were peering through quizzing glasses at them.

Their host's daughter, the tabbies knew, but the man they did not recognise. He was very tall and danced superbly, but who was he? And by the look of him, he was putting James Martindale quite in the shade. Juliette Martindale was nothing but a little flirt and the sooner her mama and papa took her in hand and married her off, the better.

'I think it would be expedient to disappear,' he whispered to her. 'I am afraid I have to go away for a while, but do not let yourself be forced into this marriage, if that is not what you want. Wait. Play for time. I will be back.'

But she knew they would not let her wait, not James, nor Mama, nor even her papa who could not, or would not, stand up to his wife. 'I am not being forced,' she said, unable to explain how confused she was. She only knew that for five heaven-sent minutes she had been happy, five minutes of a lifetime. How little that was to hold on to for the rest of her life. 'It is my wish.'

'Then I bid you *adieu, ma petite.*' He left her side and all eyes, complete with quizzing glasses, turned to watch him go. Then they swivelled back to where she stood a little to one side of the dancing area, alone and apparently not quite composed. There was a collective sigh that was audible all round the room.

James was striding towards her, determination etched on his face. She moved towards him, her face stiff with trying to smile when all she wanted to do was weep.

Philip returned to his apartment to discard his robes and change into rough blue breeches and a coat of drab cloth that had certainly seen better days, a low-crowned hat and scuffed French army boots. Then he hurried down the steps and mounted his horse, walking it slowly down the length of Piccadilly before turning north into

Park Lane, which would take him past the end of Mount Street.

It was almost dawn and the ball must have long-since ended, the guests departed. What had happened after he left? Had she succumbed to persuasion?

Sitting upright in his saddle, he relived the few short minutes they had danced together. He dreamed of having her in his arms again, kissing her again, of telling her he loved her. Because he did love her; it was no use denying it. 'Wait,' he had told her. 'Play for time.' But had she understood? He doubted it.

Without knowing why he did it, he turned into Mount Street and down a narrow lane beside Martindale House that led to the stables and garden. Here he dismounted, tethered his horse and walked forward. He was creeping about like a thief in the night and to what purpose? Miss Martindale would be curled up in her bed fast asleep and even if she were not, he had no right to intrude again, even if he had been suitably dressed to go calling.

All there was to say had been said and it was not in his power to change either his circumstances or hers. He glanced up at the back of the house. Everywhere was in darkness.

And then he saw a shadow flitting between the bushes, which was there one moment and gone the next. He was not the only one slinking about. A real thief? Or someone who intended to harm Lord Martindale? His death would cause a furore in government circles and would certainly please his country's enemies.

Philip crept forward silently, making for the spot where he had last seen the shadow. He was momentarily taken aback when the figure came into view. She was wearing a long black burnous that covered her almost completely, but he knew those eyes, even in the poor light of a moonlit garden, and the way she held herself; they were imprinted on his heart.

Startled to find someone else in the garden, she turned to face him, but recovered quickly when she recognised him. 'Mr Devonshire, what are you doing here?'

'I was riding by and I thought I detected an intruder,' he said. 'I did not know it was you. I am sorry if I startled you.'

'I needed a breath of fresh air.' She was doing her best to keep her voice light, but she was only too aware that she was trembling uncontrollably. 'I did not expect to find anyone else taking a moonlight stroll in our garden.' It was then she noticed his strange garb. 'Mr Devonshire, why are you dressed like that? The masked ball finished hours ago.'

'I am simply playing the part that Society has cast for me, a mountebank, a social outcast.'

'You are bamming me.'

'Not at all.'

'Then is it to do with your work for Papa or James?'

'James,' he asked in surprise. 'Why James?'

'I don't know. Except that you seem to be enemies and he has some curious acquaintances, one of them dressed very much as you are now.'

'How do you know that?' He tried not to sound too curious, but he had to know.

'I saw them together in Richmond Park when I was walking alone the day of the picnic. I wondered why the man was wearing a greatcoat on a warm summer's day. And money changed hands, I am sure of it.'

'Perhaps it was a beggar who accosted him,' he said,

levelly. 'There are so many about these days.' He
paused. 'But why are you not in your bed? You were
not planning to ride away into the night again?'

She smiled a little wanly. 'No, I could not sleep.'

'Too much excitement, I'll wager.'

'Perhaps.'

He peered into her face. There were tears glinting on
her lashes. 'Has the announcement been made? Are you
officially betrothed?'

'Yes.'

Inwardly he cursed. 'What has become of the young
lady who told me she would only marry for love?'

'I am persuaded that it will come. Mama told me she
hardly knew Papa when she married him, but theirs has
been a very happy union.'

'Do you believe you will come to love your cousin?'

'Oh, don't you see?' she cried. 'I have to believe it
or. . .' Her words trailed away and she choked on a sob.

He reached out and took her into his arms, realising
as he did so that she was wearing nothing but a night-
shift under the all-concealing cloak and her feet were
clad in the Greek sandals of her earlier costume. He
did not speak, for what could he say? He simply held
her close until she quieted.

'I am sorry,' she said at last. 'You were right. I have
had too much excitement. I had done better to take a
little Godfrey's Cordial to make me sleep than a walk
in the night air.'

'Perhaps. But I am glad you did.' He put his finger
under her chin and tipped it up so that he could look
down into her eyes. The hood fell from her hair, which
cascaded free like a shining silver river. For a long time
neither spoke. Words seemed superfluous.

If she had been anyone but Viscount Martindale's daughter, he would have carried her off there and then and been damned to the consequences. But he could not and because he could not, it would have been thoroughly reprehensible of him to tell her how he felt about her. That must remain locked in his heart. He could give her no comfort and had no right to expect comfort from her.

If there is ever anything I can do for you, it will be my privilege to do it,' he whispered. 'You have only to ask.' Then, very gently, he lowered his lips to hers in a featherlight kiss and seconds later he had gone, melted away into the shrubbery, leaving her to make her way slowly back to her bed, so bemused she hardly knew what to think.

Chapter Five

'You mean you took a walk in the middle of the night dressed in nothing but a nightgown and a cloak? Miss Juliette, whatever possessed you to do it?' It was almost midday and Anne, coming to help her mistress dress had found her curled up in a ball in the middle of the bed with the covers heaped up round her. Her face was flushed and her body hot as fire.

'Now, you've caught cold. Whatever will your mama say? There will be dozens of people calling this morning to offer congratulations, not to mention Mr Martindale, who will expect you to be radiant. And there will be arrangements to make.'

'What arrangements?' Juliette, eyes watering and nose blocked, peered over the edge of the sheet as if she really did not understand.

'For the wedding, miss. You can hardly have forgotten that.'

'Oh. Yes, but we have not set a date. It won't be for ages yet.'

'Anyone would think you did not want to marry Mr

Martindale. You are not behaving like a happy bride-to-be at all.'

'Aren't I?' Juliette said dully.

'No. You should be laughing and full of energy and busy making plans. . .'

'I don't feel well enough.'

'And whose fault is that? Of all the cork-brained things to do, that was the most foolish.'

'But the night was so warm.'

'So it might have been, but you had been dancing in an overheated ballroom and drinking more wine than you are used to. To go out half-naked. . .'

'I was not half-naked,' she protested feebly, wondering if Mr Devonshire had been aware of how little she had been wearing. Whatever had he thought of her? She had all but thrown herself into his arms. But oh, how comforting it was there!

He had appeared like a wraith, almost as if he had been waiting for her. But he could not have been, could he? He could not have known she would suddenly decide she needed to get out of the house, away from its cloying atmosphere, where the smell of stale perfume, wine and faded flowers did battle with that of snuffed candles, oil lamps and honest-to-goodness sweat.

But he had been there, like a guardian angel, large and warm and tender. That was what she had needed most, tenderness, to feel that she mattered as a person in her own right, not someone to be married off for expediency's sake.

She closed her eyes a moment, reliving his kisses. The first, out on the terrace, while they had been danc-ing, had been powerful and urgent and aroused in her a flood of warmth that seemed to have as its source, that most private of places, between her thighs. It had made her cling to him in a kind of desperation which, she told herself, was purely physical. It both repelled and attracted her, a contradiction she could not understand.

The second kiss, out in the moonlit garden, had been very different, gentle, undemanding, as if he really cared what became of her. But he could not have done or he would have offered for her himself. And now the decision was made and her fate was sealed. Looking radiant was the last thing on her mind.

'I really do not know where you get your hoydenish ways, Miss Juliette.' Anne's voice broke her reverie. 'It is certainly not from your mama. Now, I had better make you a restorative and go and tell her ladyship.'

'You won't tell her I went out, will you? I don't think I could bear her ringing a peal over me. It is bad enough having you scolding me. I want to go back to sleep.'

'No, I shall not tell her. I shall say I think you took a chill when you went riding on the heath in the middle of the night. It will have to serve, though that was two days ago and on that occasion you did have the sense to dress properly. Now, you stay there. I shall be back directly.' She went off still grumbling, but Juliette knew she would say nothing to her mother of how the cold had been caught.

'You are to stay in bed today,' she said, returning ten minutes later, carrying a glass full of steaming liquid. 'Her ladyship will be up to see you soon. She is entertaining Mr Martindale.'

'Oh.' The voice was muffled by a pillow.

'He sends his regards to you and hopes you will soon recover.'

'I don't think I shall.' But she was not referring to her illness.

'Now, don't be silly, miss. It is nothing but a catch-cold. You are a little feverish to be sure, but it is not serious. Now drink this, it will make you feel better.' Anne helped her to sit up and drink the bitter liquid.

She pulled a face at the taste. 'I do not want to be better if it means I have to start thinking about my wedding.'

Anne sat down on the edge of the bed and looked searchingly into Juliette's face. It was clear that it was not only the cold which had made her eyes red and swollen, but a paroxysm of weeping. 'Child, whatever is the matter? Surely you want to marry Mr Martindale?'

'No, I do not. Oh, Anne, I am so m. . .miserable.' And she flung herself into the maid's arms and sobbed.

'Hush, my dear, hush.' Anne held the girl in her plump arms, stroking her hair and murmuring to her. When Juliette had become calmer and only the occasional sniff betrayed her distress, Anne went on. 'Why did you agree to marry him? You could have refused. Your papa would have understood.'

'Papa would, but not Mama. She says it is my duty to marry Mr Martindale. He is the heir and she says Hartlea and its fortune should be kept together. It will mean that Mama can live with us at Hartlea after. . .'

If Anne had been a cursing woman, she would have had some choice words to say about Lady Martindale, but she remained silent on the subject. It was not for her to criticise her employer. 'But you would like to be mistress of Hartlea one day, would you not?'

'Yes, but. . . Oh, Anne I do not love him. He. . .he frightens me a little.'

'Frightens you! Now you are being fanciful. Why, he is nothing but an overgrown schoolboy. You will have him eating out of your hand in no time at all, you will see.'

'Do you think so? Do you really think so?'

'Of course. But it won't hurt him to wait a little. I shall tell him, and your mama too, that you are not at all well and it would be much better if you were to return to Hartlea to recuperate.'

'Can you do that? Oh, Anne, if only I could go home.' She had brightened a little but then became sombre again. 'Mama will not be deceived. She will send for a physician.'

In the event it was easier than they had expected. The physician, prompted by a private word from Anne, declared that country air might be more beneficial to the patient, and before her mother could argue, Lord Martindale announced that he had business to look after in Peterborough.

'The Season is all but over,' he said. 'Juliette is betrothed, which was the whole reason for coming, so we may as well all go home to Hartlea.'

Juliette's happiness was marred only by the fact that Mr Devonshire had disappeared again and her mama had invited James to come and stay for a few weeks. He was due to arrive two weeks after they returned. She began to look on it as her last two weeks of freedom.

They arrived back in Hartlea to find the harvest in full swing. Men were out with scythes cutting the corn under a cloudless sky, their movements fluid and rhythmic.

The women were there too, their heads protected by
floppy cotton bonnets, gathering up the golden sheaves,
tying them and standing them upright in stooks. Bare-
foot children ran around chasing the rabbits who ran
before the glinting blades.

Laden carts made their way slowly along the narrow
lanes to the barns where the corn would be threshed
during the winter months, catching their overhanging
loads on the hedges as they passed, so that wisps of the
cereal clung to them, like tiny fluttering banners.

Juliette began to feel better immediately and a week
later was pestering her mama to allow her to go out.
She wanted to ride, to clear her lungs with a good
gallop. Permission being given, she put breeches on
under her riding skirt and hurried to the stables.

Diablo seemed pleased to see her. He snickered and
rubbed his head against Juliette's shoulder while one
of the stablelads saddled him. That done, the boy held
out his hand for Juliette's boot-clad foot and threw her
up. She settled herself astride in the saddle and set off
across the home park.

As soon as they reached the open meadow, Juliette
put the horse to the gallop and away they went, thun-
dering over the turf. It was gloriously exhilarating,
especially as her papa did not insist on her being accompanied while she was on home ground; there was no
Thomas plodding behind and she could please herself
where she went.

She rode all round the estate, stopping now and again
to watch the harvest workers and exchange pleasantries.
She had known most of them all her life and they
rewarded her with a cheerful smile and a wave. Later,
when all was gathered in, she would attend the early

part of the harvest supper in the barn of the home farm to celebrate the successful bringing in of the harvest. It was a tradition in his lordship's family.

Viscount Martindale was a good landlord and employer and popular among his people. Juliette sincerely hoped that James would continue in the same way when his turn came. She could not bear it if he spoiled it all.

Thinking of James made her feel miserable again, but the day was too splendid to allow thoughts of the wedding to ruin it. And besides, she told herself firmly, being married to James might not be so bad. Many young ladies had far worse to contend with. Some were married off by their parents to old men simply for a title or a fortune, while some found themselves mistresses of crumbling old mansions with everything threadbare.

Others became step-mamas to motherless children and even more were expected to be nothing more than breeding machines. If you were a woman, you did as you were told and that was that. If she could stay at Hartlea, then she could learn to live harmoniously with James. In spite of his insensitivity and his unbounded conceit, he was not an ogre.

She pulled up on the far side of the estate where a group of prisoners of war was helping with the harvest. The number of prisoners had risen since Wellington had completely routed the French at Vittoria in June, and forced Napoleon's brother, Joseph, to flee from Spain into France. She watched them, remembering Pierre. What had happened to him? Surely he had not been punished for painting that portrait?

She had intended to find out why her mother had

reacted so violently to it, but she had been too preoccu-
pied to do anything about it. Now she was back, perhaps
she could. The first thing to do would be to find
Lieutenant Veillard.

She rode forward, pausing at the edge of the field.
One of the prisoners, who had been gathering up the
stooks ready to load onto a cart, looked up when her
shadow fell across him.

'Good day,' she called.

'*Bonjour, mam'selle.*'

She dismounted and walked her horse forward. 'Do
you know Lieutenant Veillard?'

'Pierre Veillard? *Oui, mam'selle.* 'E 'as been 'elping
with the 'arvest at the farm of Monsieur Golightly.'

She thanked him and rode on. So Pierre was working
on Anne's father's farm on the other side of the estate.
It was too late to go there today, but tomorrow she
would set off in that direction. She could pretend she
had come to see Mrs Golightly and then contrive to
waylay the French lieutenant. She turned for home.

The ride had brought the colour back to her cheeks
and the sparkle to her eyes and the prospect of a little
adventure, to take her mind off a bridegroom-to-be for
whom she had no affinity, and another man whose handsome features and soft voice were forever etched on
her brain and heart, served to enliven her so that her
mama commented that the country air had indeed
effected a cure and she was pleased to see she had
thrown off her Friday face.

'Oh, it is so good to be home,' Juliette said, to which
her mama responded by saying, 'Quite', a single word
that spoke volumes. She meant she was thankful she
did not have to repeat her arguments in favour of James,

that she was glad Juliette had understood at last and
she hoped there would be no more dissension.

Because the ride had so obviously been beneficial,
neither of her parents raised any objection to it being
repeated and the next afternoon found Juliette trotting
towards the Golightly farm, her hands not quite steady
on the reins and her heart pounding.

She rode along the lane that bordered the harvest
field, glancing over the hedge as she did so, pretending
not to be searching out a particular figure. There were
several prisoners working alongside the local men; their
mutilated uniforms were easy to pick out from the
smocks of the locals and the fact that they, being soldiers, did not have the same grace of movement when
swinging a scythe.

She spotted him as he straightened up to wipe his brow
with the back of his forearm. He saw her and strolled over
to speak to her from the other side of the hedge.

'Mam'selle Martindale. You are well?'

'Yes, yes, I am well. How are you?'

'Well enough for a prisoner, many miles from his
'omeland and made to work like a peasant.'

'I am sorry about that, indeed, I am.'

'It is not your fault.' He waited, knowing she had
not come simply to pass the time. She remained silent,
unable to frame the words to ask her question. Her
horse moved restlessly and she dismounted and led it
towards a gap in the hedge. Pierre slipped through it
into the lane and came towards her. '*Mam'selle*, is there
something I can do for you?'

She had almost forgotten what he looked like. He was
young, only a year or two older than herself; his features

were beautiful rather than handsome, a colt rather than a stallion, a comparison that reminded her forcefully of Philip Devonshire. Now, there was a stallion; dark, powerful and independent. She really must try to put him from her mind, but oh, how very difficult it was!

'I have been away,' she began.

'I know. It was because of that portrait, yes? I am sorry it displeased your *maman*.'

'But why did you paint me like that? It is so alien to me.'

'*Au contraire, ma chérie*, it is exactly like you. In another life, you must have been *une française*.'

She gave an embarrassed little laugh. 'I am more concerned with this life and why the portrait upset Mama so much. Do you know why?'

'No, *mam'selle*, I do not. Your parents wished to know why I painted you with all the jewels. They asked where I 'ad seen them before.'

'The jewels? Not me or my gown?'

'No, *ma chérie*, the jewels. 'Ave you never seen jewels like that, Juliette?' He pronounced her Christian name in the French way.

'Indeed, no. Where had you seen them before?'

'I do not know. They are so unusual that I think I must 'ave seen them and not imagined them, but where. . .' He shrugged. 'It must 'ave been long ago in France.'

'I do not think Mama has ever been to France,' she said thoughtfully. 'Perhaps Papa has. Oh, I wish you could remember where you saw them! I do so hate mysteries, especially ones that make people unhappy. And Mama is very unhappy.'

'I will try to remember, but I 'ave not the portrait.

It is *difficile* to recall *exactement*. . .'

'I believe it has been put up in the attic. Mama said she never wanted to see it again.'

'Such a waste! It is the best I 'ave ever done. I was aided by a most beautiful subject.' He looked earnestly at her. 'If I 'ad it to look at, I could perhaps remember. . .'

'Then I shall bring it to you.'

'Do not bring it 'ere. I will meet you. In the little house in your garden.'

'The summerhouse where we. . .' She stopped, blushing at the remembrance of a kiss that had meant so little. It had not repelled her as James's betrothal kiss had done, when he had forced his tongue into her mouth and bruised her lips, nor turned her limbs to a quiver of longing, which was what had happened when Philip Devonshire had kissed her.

Pierre's inexpert embrace had left her unmoved and yet it had been the beginning of her troubles. He had asked to paint her. If he had not done that, there would have been no portrait, no mystery, no journey to London, no betrothal to a man she could not even begin to like, and no meeting with Philip Devonshire. If she had never met him, she would not now be longing for him with every fibre of mind and body. 'If Papa or Mama were to see you, there would be a dreadful fuss.'

'Come at night, when everyone is asleep.'

'Do you not have to go back to camp at night?'

'Oh, it is easy to slip out. The guards are not very efficient.'

'When?' Already the prospect of doing something positive was making her eyes bright. Not for a moment did she consider she was playing with fire.

'Tomorrow.' He laughed, holding his cupped hands to help her mount. 'At midnight.'

'Very well.' She pulled the horse round and rode off down the lane, remembering to call on Mrs Golightly and enquire about her rheumatics before returning home.

She smiled to herself as she scrambled out of bed a little after eleven-thirty and dressed by the light of the moon coming through her window. She would not risk taking another chill and made sure she was warmly clad. Then, throwing her burnous over her shoulders, she crept along the corridor to the narrow stairs that led to the attics, found the painting standing with its face to the wall, picked it up and crept noiselessly down to the first floor again.

Here, instead of going down the main staircase, she descended the back stairs, used by the servants, and out past the butler's pantry to a small door beside the kitchen. There was no one about. She darted across the cobbled yard into the kitchen garden and from there, by a roundabout route that kept her out of sight of the house, to the flower garden and the rose arbour.

'Lieutenant,' she whispered breathlessly, as she approached the summerhouse.

''Ere, *ma chérie*.' He was standing leaning nonchalantly against the door jamb, smiling. ''Ave you brought it?'

'Yes.' She thrust the painting at him. 'But we cannot see it properly in the dark.'

'I shall take it back with me and look at it later. My comrades, they can per'aps throw light upon the mystery, *n'est-ce pas*?'

'Y . . .yes,' she said doubtfully. She hadn't considered that he might want to take it away. But then Mama had said she never wanted to see it again, so she would hardly go looking for it. 'But you will bring it back?'

'I do not see why I should. I 'ave not been paid for it.'

'Oh, you cheated me into bringing it!' she cried, trying to snatch it back. 'I did not think you were so mercenary. . .'

'No, no, *ma petite*, I was only 'aving what you say, a tease.' He took the picture from her and leant it against the wall before taking both her hands in his. 'Do not be upset. I will bring it back. I should not like to think of my beautiful Juliette being punished for removing it. I shall make a leetle copy, one for my pocket. 'Ow is that?'

'Oh, that is a good idea. How long will it take?'

'Two days, three per'aps.' He paused, smiling down at her. 'Then you will 'ave to meet me again, and of all things that will be the most pleasant.'

'You must not flirt with me.'

'Why not? There is no 'arm in it. And I like you very much. If you were *française*. . .' He sighed dramatically.

'But I am not and I am betrothed.'

He was not in the least put out. 'Then I must offer my felicitations, no? I envy 'im.'

'I must go.' It sounded weak, when she ought to have been strong, but the moonlight and the strange quality of the air, coupled with the clandestine nature of the meeting, seemed to have acted like a drug. She could not think decisively.

'Go, *ma petite*,' he said, releasing her hands. 'I will see you here two nights from now.'

* * *

Two nights later he told her the copy was not yet ready and he needed more time. She suspected he was using it as an excuse to continue to see her. She knew she ought not to agree to meet him again, but she had to retrieve the portrait before it was missed and there was no other way.

'Tomorrow,' he murmured. 'And per'aps I shall 'ave the answer to the mystery too.'

'You will? What is it? What have you found out?'

He laid a finger on her lips and laughed. 'Do not be impatient, *ma petite*. Tomorrow, eh?' And then he was gone, melting away into the shadows, leaving her with a feeling of frustration that made the next twenty-four hours a trial of patience in which she tried to behave as if nothing at all was happening and made Anne absolutely sure she was sickening again.

He was late for the rendezvous and Juliette was kept waiting nearly half an hour before she heard his stealthy step on the gravel of the path and he came into view, carrying the painting wrapped in a piece of cloth. He put it down to take her into his arms.

'Ah, *ma petite comtesse*.' He held her at arm's length to study her face. 'Yes, yes, I do see it.'

'See what?' she demanded, pulling herself away from him. 'And you are late. I was on the point of leaving.'

'Ah, then you would not have learned what you above all wish to know.'

'And what is that?'

'Who you are.'

'Who I am? Do not be silly, Lieutenant. You know I am Juliette Martindale, daughter of Viscount and Viscountess Martindale of Hartlea.'

'No, *ma petite*, you are not.'

'Oh, I have no time for your silly jests,' she said, exasperated by his superior air.

'So, you do not wish to know why your lady mother is afraid that I 'ave uncovered the truth and am about to tell it to the world.' He laughed; it was a brittle sound that made her shiver. He pulled the cloth from the picture and jabbed a finger at the necklace. 'Do you know where I saw that before?'

'You said that you could not remember.'

'Ah, but now I 'ave. Those jewels belonged to the dowager Comtesse de Caronne—in the days before the Terror, *naturellement*. There was once a famous portrait of her as a young girl, which I saw hanging in the Louvre when I was very young and learning to be an artist. My mind must 'ave stored the details, but more than that, it stored the likeness of the lady, so *exactement* like you.

'The same light eyes and silver hair, the same small mouth and eyebrows arching, so.' He smoothed a finger along one of her brows, making a shiver pass through her. 'The same way of 'olding your 'ead.'

'So?' She was intrigued, in spite of herself.

'I 'ave a friend in the camp,' he went on. 'And 'e told me a story about the Caronne family which is *très interessant*. They were all guillotined, except one, a baby girl. She escaped. 'Ow no one knows. She would 'ave, let me see, nineteen years now. It is a strange story, *n'est-ce pas?*'

'What are you trying to say?' She was bewildered. It sounded as if. . . She shook her head. 'No, it cannot be true.'

'It is true, *chérie*. What we cannot be sure of is

whether you are the only surviving Caronne. If you are, you would be an heiress. The estate is very large.'

'No, it is not possible,' she cried. 'There has to be another explanation. I have lived here all my life with Mama and Papa. I am English and I've never heard of the Comte de Caronne.'

''Ave you no early memories?' he asked, watching the changing expressions on her face, incredulity, dismay, even a glimmer of doubt. 'Little things, favourite toys, names of people and places, things that 'ave been said. . .'

'Yes, but they are all of Hartlea. I have known no other home. We have a town house, of course, and I've stayed there and we've been to Scotland, which is Mama's home. There is nothing unusual about me, Lieutenant, nothing out of the ordinary at all.'

She desperately wanted to believe that, but her heart was thumping and her limbs were shaking and all she could think of was her mother's strange reaction when she had seen the portrait. Something had caused that.

He could see that the story had taken a hold on her imagination and took her face in his hands so that he could look into her eyes. 'You 'ave been cruelly deceived, *ma petite*. The people who call themselves your mama and papa are not your parents. They rescued you or stole you, I am not sure which, but they are using you.'

'I do not understand.' It was all too much to take in and she felt confused and light-headed, as if she had drunk too much wine. 'I love them both. They are my dear mama and papa. Why would they use me?'

'To keep 'Artlea. Lady Martindale 'as no children of her own and by marrying you to the heir. . .'

'How do you know that?' she cried. That part was only too painfully true.

'It is known.'

She was silent. There were a thousand questions on her tongue, but none she could voice. If he had told her the story before her mother had seen the portrait, she would have angrily refuted it, but she could not help remembering her parents' strange reaction to the painting and her conviction at the time that there was something havey-cavey going on.

She recalled the conversation she had overheard between her mother and father and her mother's reference to 'the truth', as if there were something to hide. Supposing the lieutenant were right? Was she living at her beloved Hartlea under false pretences?

If his lordship had saved a little French aristo from the guillotine, why had he passed her off as his own? Should she feel love and gratitude or anger and resentment? Strange, she felt nothing at all. She was numb.

'Try and find some proof,' he went on, gently. 'There must be papers, even jewels. It is better to know than to go on living a lie.'

'I am not living a lie!' she cried, stepping back and facing him, her chest heaving. 'And you are abominable to confuse me so. Why did you have to tell me?'

'You wanted to know and the truth is often unpalatable.'

'I do not believe it is the truth. I shall ask Mama. She will tell me.'

'You will tell 'er ladyship that you 'ave been meeting me secretly in the garden?'

'No.'

'Then 'ow will you explain where you learned the story?'

'I'll think of something.'

'You would do better, *ma chère comtesse*, to look for proof. If you are Juliette Caronne, you are a French aristocrat, even more lofty than Viscount Martindale. Think about that. Think about *un grand château* and a thousand 'ectares of vineyards in Hautvigne and jewels like that.' And again he stabbed at the canvas.

'They are your in'eritance. And I have heard there are other treasures hidden about the *château* and they all belong to you, being the only direct descendant of the *comte*.'

'Oh, you are despicable!' she said and turned on her heel to escape him, though escape her whirring thoughts she could not.

'I shall come again tomorrow night,' he called after her. 'You may 'ave need of me.'

The remainder of the night was a waking nightmare. Pierre's words went round and round in her brain, until she thought she would lose her sanity. How could she go on living at Hartlea, when, if Pierre were correct, she had no right to be there, that not only the estate but all the money set aside for her dowry rightfully belonged to James? And James was being deceived too. How could they do it to him?

How could they have hidden from her every detail of her birth, never even hinted, never let slip with the tiniest word, that all was not as it seemed? Of course, they could not. It was all a lie, a figment of Pierre's imagination. But why did she not take after her parents? Why was her hair so fair and her mother's so dark, why was her complexion pale when Lady Martindale was olive-skinned?

Why had that portrait upset her parents so much if they had nothing to hide? Apart from her parents, did anyone else know the truth? James's late father, for instance. It would be enough to cause a quarrel between brothers.

She had hardly begun to doze when Anne woke her. 'Come, time to rise, my little one. It is a lovely day. Are you going to ride again?'

'No, I do not think so,' she said lethargically. 'Where is Mama?'

'She took the carriage into Peterborough. Some shopping, I believe.'

'And Papa?'

'He is in the library. I believe he is expecting a visitor, so do not go disturbing him.'

'I won't. I think I shall look round the attics. There might be something up there, a desk perhaps, that James would like to have in his room when he comes.'

But it was not James she was thinking of as she searched the attics later that day; she was following Pierre's advice and looking for proof of her identity. She didn't want to be a little French aristo, a little orphan, an *émigrée* brought home to England because his lordship felt sorry for her. Was that how it had been?

No! No! She wanted to be Juliette, her papa's beloved daughter. And how could that be proved? Not by rooting around in the dust of the attics, turning out old drawers, pulling old clothes, bonnets and boots out of cupboards, shaking out the pages of musty-smelling books. She made her way downstairs, wondering where to look next.

'Look for the jewellery,' Pierre had said. And where would that be kept?

She turned along the first-floor corridor and made for her mother's boudoir. Pausing outside to make sure there were no servants nearby, she passed inside and shut the door behind her. She crossed the room and opened the drawer of the chest where her mother kept her jewels but the padded box which lay inside it was locked. Where was the key? Last time she had seen it, it had been on her mother's chatelaine.

Her misery and frustration made her less than careful; she began pulling out drawers, rifling through their contents, crying in desperation. She found a duplicate key, at last, tucked away at the back of the escritoire. She sat on the bed with the box on her lap and the key in her hand and did nothing. It was a wicked thing she was doing, a deceitful, wicked, disloyal thing and she could not bring herself to insert the key in the lock.

But she did not intend to take anything, so it wasn't stealing, was it? And besides, it was all a hum and there would be nothing there. Better to get it over and be done with the uncertainty. Slowly she inserted the key and turned

The box contained a collection of necklaces, brooches, armlets and rings, some set with precious stones, others not so valuable, but none resembled any in the portrait. There was certainly no great ruby pendant.

She breathed a huge sigh of relief and began putting them all back. What a ninny she had been! How Pierre must be laughing at her! Then, right at the bottom, she found a little velvet bag closed with a drawstring. She loosened the neck and tipped it up.

Into her lap fell the ruby in its silver filigree heart; not the whole necklace, but enough of it to be unmistakable. She picked it up and laid it on her palm, twisting it to catch the light.

It was so beautiful it made her catch her breath, now the rich colour of blood, dark and a little menacing, and now light, transparent as wine was transparent, winking up at her, telling her. . . what? That Pierre had told the truth? Could there be any other explanation? She was so engrossed she did not hear the door open and close again.

'Juliette! What are you doing?'

She looked up to see Lady Martindale standing over her, white-faced with suppressed anger. 'I. . .' She swallowed hard, then found the courage to tell the truth. 'I was looking for this.'

'Oh, I see.' Her ladyship's voice was perfectly controlled. 'And why were you looking for it? And what are you going to do now you have found it?'

'I. . .I don't know. I thought. . . Oh, Mama, I knew you were angry when P— Lieutenant Veillard painted me wearing all those jewels and I could not understand why. He said you were afraid. . .'

'And when have you seen him to speak to him about it?'

'I met him at Mrs Golightly's. He was helping with their harvest. He asked me if you were still angry about that portrait. . .'

'I had forgotten it, as you should have done. You have disobeyed your papa's express orders not to speak

to that young man again and now you have made the
situation far worse.'

'What situation, Mama? The lieutenant told me such
a Banbury tale. I don't know what to believe.'

'Did he, now?' Her ladyship seemed lost in thought.
Even her anger had evaporated. 'He told us he could
not remember.'

'But he has now. He saw all those jewels on a portrait
of the Comtesse de Caronne in the Louvre. He said the
whole family had been guillotined, except one. He said
I was that one.' She paused, gazing up at her mother's
implacable face. 'Mama, tell me it isn't true. I am not
French, am I? I am yours and Papa's. Your daughter.'

Elizabeth sat on the bed beside Juliette and took the
ruby from her unresisting fingers. 'I had hoped that you
would never have to learn the truth, Juliette, but fate
has decreed otherwise.' She gave a little twisted smile.
'But the lieutenant is only half right.'

Juliette waited, hardly daring to breathe.

'You were born in France, Juliette. And you are the
daughter of the Comtesse de Caronne, as the lieutenant
suggested, though not of her husband. When the
Caronne family went to the guillotine, you were saved
because. . .' she gulped once and then went on
'. . .because your father was English and he
claimed you.'

Juliette looked up at her in shocked disbelief. 'You
mean Papa?'

'Yes.'

'But that means. . .' She could not go on. Her heart
was thumping against her ribs and her limbs were shaking visibly.

'Yes.' The one word was repeated firmly, without any effort to soften the blow.

'Oh, no, no! I cannot believe it. I won't. It is even worse than I thought.'

'I had lost three infants,' her ladyship went on in a matter-of-fact voice, while she relocked the box. Her upright posture did not relax for a minute. 'I could not give your father a legitimate heir. He persuaded me I should come to love you.'

Juliette was silent; there was nothing she could say. She looked back on her childhood and realised there had always been an aloofness in her mother that she had not understood at the time. Always she thought it was something she had done to displease her, some childish mischief that must be punished. And she had tried all the harder to be good.

'I tried to love you.' For the first time there was anguish in her ladyship's voice. 'It is not your fault, child, and so I tell myself every day of my life. I have tried to think of you as my daughter and, as far as the world is concerned, that is what you are.' She paused. 'I did my duty and now you must do yours.'

'Marry James, you mean. Is that why Papa did not oppose you over that?'

'Yes.'

'I cannot believe he could be so cruel. It is not like him at all.'

'Juliette, it will not be so bad. We have been over it again and again and you agreed.'

'Oh, I did not mean about James, I meant about making you bring me up as your own. Does anyone else know?'

'No.'

'But how did you keep it from the servants?'

'When my last little one was due to be born, your papa was in France on a diplomatic mission. I was lonely and afraid and your grandmother persuaded me to visit her in Scotland. It was thought the bracing air might be good for me.

'Only Anne came with me and she was there at the birth of a boy. He lived only three weeks. If I had remained at Hartlea, where it is comfortable and warm, he might have survived.' The bitterness was there in her voice, though she tried to conceal it.

Even in her own misery, Juliette could feel for her. 'I am so very sorry.'

Her ladyship did not appear to hear. 'I stayed in Scotland until your papa returned. When he came to fetch me, he had you with him. Later we returned to Hartlea and everyone was allowed to think. . .' She stopped speaking, stood up and returned the jewel case to the drawer before turning back to Juliette, her voice once more brisk. 'Nothing has changed, nothing at all.'

'Oh, but it has!' Juliette cried. Her whole world had been torn apart; everything was ruined. She was a by-blow, a nobody, someone who should never be seen in polite Society. What would everyone think when the truth came out? James? He would reject her and demand his birthright and who could blame him? The thought of James being put off marrying her lightened her spirits for the space of a heartbeat, no more.

Her thoughts flew to Philip Devonshire. If she had been harbouring a faint hope that James's rejection of her might bring about a change of heart in that young man, it died before it could flicker into life. He would not have her. No one would, not when the truth became known. She would be an outcast. 'I must talk to Papa. . .'

'No!' her ladyship almost shouted. 'You will not speak of this to your father at all, do you hear? It will never be mentioned. I do believe he is ashamed of what he did and we have been happy in our way. I have no wish to reopen old wounds. In a few weeks you will be married and it will no longer matter.'

'Is James not to be told?'

'No, there is no need.'

'He would not want me if he knew.'

'You will say nothing, child. Think of the scandal if such a thing became public. We should never be able to show our faces in Society again. It is one thing to have a skeleton in the cupboard as long as you keep it there, quite another to let it loose for every tattlemonger to rattle. I should be ostracised, you would never marry and your papa would lose his position in the government. Think of him, if you can think of no one else.'

She paused to let her words sink into Juliette's benumbed brain. 'Now, please go back to your own room and change for dinner. We have a guest.'

At Hartlea they kept country hours; dinner was at three and supper at eight. 'James has arrived?' He was the last person she wanted to see.

'No, James is not due for several days, you know that. Mr Devonshire is in the area and your papa has invited him to dine with us.' She paused to look at the young girl who still sat on the bed as if she did not have the strength or the will to rise. 'You are looking exceedingly pale, so wear your blue jaconet, it will give you a little colour. I shall tell Anne to put a little rouge on your cheeks too.'

Philip. Philip, who had told her to play for time, Philip who had kissed her and whom she loved. How could she face him? 'I cannot sit and eat and pretend nothing has happened.'

'Yes, you will. Even though the man is no longer acceptable in Society on account of that duel, that seems not to count with your father, so you will act with dignity and good manners.'

Juliette returned to her room on leaden feet and said nothing at all while Anne helped her dress and arranged her hair. 'I do not believe you have quite got over that cold,' the maid said. 'You are white as a sheet.'

'Am I?' She could not pay attention to Anne, her head was swimming. Today she had died a little. Today she had learned that she was an imposter; not only that, but a bastard. The dreadful word rang round and round in her brain, along with 'duty' and 'dignity' and 'good manners'. Was that all there was to her life?

'You had best tell me why you are having such a fit of the dismals,' Anne said, dabbing Juliette's cheeks with safflower powder.

'You deceived me too,' Juliette said. 'You knew. . .'

'Knew what?'

'That I am not who I seem.'

'Who told you that?'

'Mama. But she is not my mama, is she?'

'Oh, I see.' Wondering why her ladyship should have chosen this moment to speak, Anne put the rouge pot down and took Juliette's hands in her own. 'Listen, my love. Her ladyship did not give birth to you, but in all other respects she has been your mother.

'She has loved you in her fashion, brought you up, guided you, taught you how to behave. In fact she has been a better mama than many I could name who have little time for their children and consign them permanently to the nursery until it is time to bring them out and marry them off. You have had a happy childhood and you cannot deny it.'

'And now I must grow up.'

'And now you must grow up.' She smiled reassuringly. 'You are what you are, not who you are. Can you not understand that?'

'Do you know who I really am?'

'No, and I do not want to know. And neither should you. There is nothing to be gained by prying into the past.'

She took a last look at her charge. 'There! You look very charming. Off you go and see if you cannot bewitch Mr Devonshire. I have just seen him and he is looking as handsome in country clothes as ever he did wearing the latest fashion in town.' She had either forgotten, or chosen to ignore, the fact that Juliette was engaged to marry James Martindale.

Not even the thought of seeing Philip Devonshire again could bring Juliette out of her gloom. If anything, the prospect of having his searching eyes delving into her soul, revealing all the pain and misery there, made matters worse. She had never been able to hide her feelings from him; he could read her like a book. And he would turn the pages until he had found out all he wanted to know.

Would it make any difference to him? No, she decided. Although he had kissed her and comforted her, he had never said a word about loving her. And he knew she had accepted James.

'Nothing has changed,' her mother had said. But

Lady Martindale was not her mother. Her mother was a French countess who had lost her head in more ways than one. And everything *had* changed. No matter what her mother said, James must be relieved of his obligation towards her. She could never marry.

She took a deep breath and went downstairs, holding her head high and feeling for the steps with her toes. She was almost at ground level when her parents came out of the library accompanied by Philip Devonshire. She paused, clinging to the bannister until she could make her trembling limbs obey her, then forced herself to smile, and completed the descent.

'Mr Devonshire, how nice to see you again.' Her voice was clear and brittle as ice.

'Miss Martindale, your obedient.' He returned her smile as he inclined his head, but his mind was asking himself what was wrong with her. She looked as pale as death. 'I trust I find you recovered.'

'Recovered?' she queried, her head so full of the revelations of the last few hours she could think of nothing else. He couldn't know, could he?

'I collect you were unwell in London and that is why you curtailed your Season.'

'Yes, of course. I had quite forgot it. I am quite recovered, thank you. The country air, you know. There is nothing like it for effecting a cure. I have been watching the harvest. . .' She was prattling now, babbling like a lunatic, and he was looking at her with those dark penetrating eyes and even at the distance of two paces, she could feel the warmth of him, the power in him, and it was all she could do not to faint at his feet.

Lady Martindale inadvertently rescued her. 'Come, let us go into the dining room,' she said and led the way.

Chapter Six

There was something wrong with Juliette, Philip thought, as he picked at the bones of the fish on his plate. She not only looked ill, but desperately unhappy. She was toying with her food and taking gulps from her wine glass as if the answer to her problems lay in its ruby liquid.

And though she answered when she was spoken to, there was a brittleness in her voice and no life in her eyes, which was strange because if he had been asked to describe her he would have said that, of all things, she was vitally alive, a personality in her own right, not the sterile product of an over-protective mama who had taught her not to say boo to a goose.

Now she looked as though she had been dealt a mortal blow and Lady Martindale was doing her best to cover up her daughter's shortcomings by talking too much. And that, in itself, was unusual.

He listened and answered, but he could not take his eyes off Juliette. For the second time in as many weeks, there stirred within him an overwhelming urge to comfort her, to take her in his arms, to kiss her as he had done before, to make her smile, but she would not meet his gaze.

'Boney's mistake was to march on Moscow last year,' his lordship said, helping himself from the dishes on the table. Whatever was troubling his daughter had not been communicated to him, Philip decided. But how could he not see something was wrong? 'He should have known the Russian winter would beat him.'

'Do you think the war will soon be over?' her ladyship asked. 'Now that Lord Wellington is at last turning the tide, Napoleon cannot hold out, can he?'

'We must not underestimate him, my lady,' Philip said. 'He is cunning and persuasive. While the French continue to believe in him, he will fight on. It is necessary to undermine their faith in him. It will be his own supporters who will bring him down in the end.'

'Then we shall have peace at last,' his lordship said. 'France and Britain will become friends again and we shall be able to resume trading and make visits. You should ask James to take you to Paris, Juliette. It is a magnificent city. If peace is signed by the new year, you could make it your wedding trip.' He stared in astonishment as Juliette sprang to her feet and rushed from the room. 'What is the matter with her?' he demanded of his wife.

'Nothing,' Elizabeth answered calmly. 'James is due to visit soon and she is a little nervous, that is all.

'Then go to her, my dear. I do not want her to be unhappy. I had rather cancel the wedding. Tell her that.'

'No.' Her ladyship's voice was sharp. 'It is simply nerves, nothing more.' She stood up and turned to Philip. 'Please excuse me.'

Philip watched her go, pondering on the single-mindedness of a woman who could see her child unhappy and remain so cool about it.

'Well, young man, have you cracked it?' his lordship asked, pouring himself a glass of port and handing the decanter to Philip.

'Cracked it?' He was filling his own glass but his mind was still on Juliette. Had she been coerced into accepting James Martindale? It might account for the tears she had shed in the garden after the ball, but she had denied it when he questioned her. And Lord Martindale undoubtedly loved his daughter; surely he would not force her to marry against her will?

'The identity of *Le Merle*.'

'Oh, yes.' He forced himself to pay attention. 'He is Captain Michel Clavier, one of Napoleon's Old Guard. He was captured at Fuentes d'Onoro in 1811 but escaped soon after arriving in England.'

He gave a faint smile. 'One of the few who managed to return to France and fight again. He was taken again at Cuidad Rodrigo the following January, possibly on purpose. He has been engaged ever since on escorting escaped prisoners on to fishing vessels held off the coast for the purpose, taking vital information with them.'

'And his British contact, the traitor?'

Philip hesitated. He would say nothing until he was sure. 'I have not yet discovered his identity, my lord, but I will, I promise you.'

'And that other matter? Lieutenant Pierre Veillard?'

'Apparently he had seen a similar portrait in Paris and simply copied it. A coincidence, no more.'

At that point Lady Martindale returned to say that Juliette had decided to retire and begged to be excused from bidding him goodnight. He took his leave, to ride the four miles back to Peterborough where he was to resume his disguise as a prisoner of war and allow himself to be recaptured. It had all been arranged with the commandant, including the punishment he was to receive for attempting the earlier escape.

His contact inside the camp had told him of furtive comings and goings, whispers, sidelong glances that betrayed the fact that something was afoot, a mass break-out perhaps, and though he wanted to be there when it happened, he was reluctant to leave Juliette. If only he could have had a few words alone with her he might have discovered what was wrong.

From her bedroom window Juliette watched him ride away, her heart torn to shreds and her eyes red from weeping. The startling disclosure of her origins had felled her like the kick from a horse; she had been, and still was, winded by it. From anyone else she would have dismissed the tale as fabrication, but coming from someone she had always trusted, someone who rated truthfulness as one of the foremost virtues, she had to believe it.

Mama—it was difficult to break the habit of calling her that—would have had no reason to lie to her. But now she knew the truth, she could not carry on as if nothing had happened. Her whole life had been a sham.

Who would want her now? Certainly not any of the young bloods who had courted her so assiduously in London, believing her to be the legitimate daughter of Lord and Lady Martindale. Nor James, who expected to marry an English heiress not a French bastard. He was entitled to the Martindale inheritance, money and all, without recourse to marrying her.

As for Philip Devonshire, he had sat at the dinner

table making polite conversation, totally unaware that she was not the sort of person with whom anyone of note should be conversing at all.

Or did he know already? Was that why he had held back, deciding it was easier to intimate he had another love than admit it? But why then had he kissed her and spoken so softly to her, telling her to wait and he would be back? He had come back, but now he was riding away again, sitting tall and upright in his saddle and taking all her love and hopes with him.

Pierre had said he would be in the summerhouse again that night if she should have need of him. And she did need him because there was no one else.

As soon as the house was quiet, she flung her burnous over her shoulders and left the house by a side door, making for the summerhouse.

To give the lieutenant his due, he accepted that she could not go on living at Hartlea and put forward a plan of his own. 'We will go to Hautvigne and find the surviving members of your family,' he said. 'There must be cousins, uncles, aunts. You are so like your *grandmére*, they will recognise you at once.'

'But how can we go to France? We are at war.'

He tapped the side of his nose and laughed. 'Oh, there are ways, *ma petite*. Leave it to me.' Still she hesitated. It was such an enormous step to take and once taken, she could never return. It meant turning her back forever on the man she loved, but she was beginning to realise that love was not and could not be a consideration. What right had she to expect love? Her girlhood dreams were just that. Dreams. And now came the awakening.

'I will look after you,' he added, as if reading her

thoughts. 'I will not hurt you, as others have hurt you,
I promise. When you are with your own people again,
then we can think of the future. Until then, you may
be as chaste as you wish.'

It was that promise as much as anything that decided
her. No doubt he would expect his reward when he had
delivered her safely to her family, but she would deal
with that when the time came. 'When do we go?'
she asked.

He kissed her lightly on the cheek. 'Go back to the
house and fetch the ruby,' he said. 'We may need it to
convince your family of your true identity. I shall wait
here for you.'

If she had not been so distressed, if Pierre had not
been so persuasive, if Philip Devonshire had not come
to dinner and fixed his dark eyes on her so that she felt
uncomfortably exposed, if she had felt able to trust
anyone else, she might have stopped to consider what
a dangerous game she was playing. But all she could
think of was distancing herself from all that had hurt
her and finding a welcome somewhere else.

And perhaps her French relatives would be pleased
to see her, as Pierre had said they would. She had not
told him that she was a love-child; she was too ashamed.

Reluctantly she returned to the house. Her parents
were still in the drawing room, she could hear their low
voices as she passed the door. Resisting the temptation
to listen at the keyhole, she crept up to her ladyship's
boudoir and retrieved the jewel.

Then she went back to her own room and scribbled
a letter to them, saying she could not go on living a lie
and intended to go where she would be accepted as
herself. Having signed and sealed it, she packed a small

cloakbag with a change of clothing, her personal jewellery and five sovereigns his lordship had given her for pin money.

She had no idea how they would make the journey to France, but she realised it would hardly be in luxury, so she dressed in a simple homespun skirt, linen blouse and sturdy half-boots that she wore when helping out in the stables. Leaving the letter on her pillow, she threw her cloak about her shoulders and left the house, not daring to look back.

Philip was at his lodgings, putting on the shabby clothes of a prisoner of war when a message arrived asking him to return to Hartlea at once.

He threw the old uniform back in the cupboard and, unshaven though he was, dressed in buckskins, top boots, linen shirt, waistcoat and riding coat, not ostentatious but far removed from the ragged filth of a prisoner of war, and rode back to Hartlea, fuming at the delay but hoping that he might yet find an opportunity to speak to Juliette.

He found Lord Martindale pacing the library, and her ladyship sitting rigidly upright in a winged chair by the hearth, stony-faced. His lordship turned as Philip was announced. 'Juliette has disappeared,' he said without preamble.

Philip's heart missed a beat and he felt a constriction in his throat. He coughed to try and clear it and give himself time to sound calm. 'You mean she has been abducted? Surely your enemies would not stoop so low. . .'

'It is possible, but unlikely. My wife tells me Juliette

learned something yesterday which may have upset her. . .'

So, there *had* been something wrong!

'She has run away,' her ladyship said, and this time he detected a crack in her iron control; her voice was hoarse. She had never seen her husband so angry as when he discovered what she had told Juliette. All those years of misery and resentment, all so unnecessary. 'She always was impetuous and I. . .'

Lord Martindale turned on her, momentarily forgetting the presence of the young man. 'You should not have told her, especially you should not have filled her head with half-truths. How did you expect her to react?'

Philip looked from one to the other. 'You think I can help? I assure you, my lord, my lady, I have no idea where she may be.'

'We think she may be trying to go to go France,' his lordship said.

'France? But why? How?' He looked from one to the other. His lordship looked angry and her ladyship aggrieved and neither seemed disposed to enlighten him. And all the time they prevaricated, Juliette might be in danger.

'She has been seeing the Frenchman,' her ladyship said. 'She admitted that to me yesterday.'

Something clicked in his brain, like a piece of puzzle finding its place. 'You mean Veillard?'

'Yes,' his lordship said. 'We think he means to use Juliette to help him escape.'

'Oh,' he said, his mind working furiously. If Veillard was involved in the break-out being planned, he did not need Juliette to help him. In fact, she could very well be a hindrance.

On the other hand, he might know nothing of his countrymen's plans, in which case he might put them in jeopardy by acting alone. The men would not hesitate to rid themselves of both Veillard and Juliette if it served their purpose. How much of the secret work he did was known to Lady Martindale? How much did Juliette herself know?

'Have you told James Martindale that Miss Martindale is missing?' he asked.

'No. I do not want him to know,' her ladyship said. 'If it became common knowledge. . .the scandal. You do see, don't you?'

'Yes, I understand.' The sooner he returned to the camp the better. Lord Martindale would understand that better than anyone. He turned towards him. 'You need my help?'

'Yes,' his lordship said, then to his wife, 'Will you excuse us, my dear? I need to speak to Philip privately.'

'Do you really think Veillard is involved?' Philip asked as soon as they were alone. 'If he is part of the plot to break out, why take Miss Martindale? The others would see her as nothing but an encumbrance.'

His lordship smiled wryly. 'She may not have given him a choice. She must have been feeling very let down and unwanted and she would think he was the only one who understood.'

'You mean she had formed a *tendre* for the Frenchman?' The idea was insupportable. 'They have eloped?'

'I had better tell you the whole, my boy, then you must use your own judgement on how to act.'

His lordship rose and began pacing the room again. 'I was in Paris in '94,' he said. 'A diplomatic mission, though why we should have wasted our energy on being diplomatic with that bloodthirsty regime, I do not know.'

'I know, my lord. You rescued my mother and me and I shall be eternally grateful. *Maman* said so until the day she died.'

'What? Oh, yes, but this was six months earlier. On the day I speak of, *Madame Guillotine* was having one of her busiest days. The streets were so crowded there was no hope of getting through with a carriage, nor even a chair. I was on foot and pressed so close by the throng I found myself almost touching a tumbril taking the Comte de Caronne and his family to their execution.

'The Count was standing looking straight ahead with his arm about his ten-year-old son. His wife stood just behind him clutching a baby.' He shuddered suddenly. 'I shall never forget that lady's anguished face if I live to be a hundred. She was weeping pitifully, though her tears were not for herself but for the child in her arms.

'That the beasts should stoop to slaughtering little children sickened me and I was close enough to see she was a beautiful child. She could not have known there was any reason to be afraid and smiled at me. I raised my head and found myself looking directly into the eyes of the *comtesse*. The cart rumbled by me, with the crowd pressing round it baying for blood and the guards kept busy holding them off.

'I stepped forward and held out my hands. "Give me the child," I called to her. "I will care for her." She hesitated only a second and then handed her over. I grabbed her, hid her quickly beneath my cloak and melted into the crowd.'

'A risky thing to do, my lord.'

'I did not stop to consider it.'

'No, you would not. The child was Juliette?'

'Yes. I took her to the Embassy, where she would be safe. Then began the difficult part, getting her out of France to safety. The family had had what passed for a trial, and I, as an envoy, could not be seen to flout the law of the land. The only solution I could think of was to pretend that the child was mine, that her mother, my mistress, had died and left her to my tender mercies.

'I made a great show of being angry at being saddled with her. My friends advised me to leave her in an orphanage, but though I pretended to consider it, I finally said I could not do it, she was my flesh and blood. I brought her back to England.'

'You brought her here?'

'Yes. While I had been away, Lady Martindale had borne a son who did not survive beyond three weeks, though I did not know of the tragedy until I returned. It was a trying time and I wondered if I had done right to ask her to take the child on, but it seemed to help her. We brought her up as our own.'

'Is Juliette her real name?'

'Yes, her mother whispered it when she handed her over.'

'And the rest of her family, they really were executed?'

'Yes, apart from some distant cousins who had embraced the new regime. I returned to France six months later to find out what had happened. That was when I met you and your mother.'

'For which I thank you and the good Lord. But did you not tell Juliette who she was?'

'I always meant to. I was simply waiting for an opportune time, but it never seemed to come. And everyone believed she was ours. . .' He paused. 'And then that Frenchman painted the portrait and Elizabeth recognised the ruby. It had been sewn into Juliette's petticoat. I assumed it was put there in the hope of bribing a gaoler or the executioner.'

'And you still did not tell Juliette the truth?'

'No, to my shame I allowed myself to be dissuaded by Elizabeth. She was worried about the scandal, though I could not see that it mattered. We had done no wrong and might even be applauded for taking the child. But Elizabeth could not see how we could suddenly tell the world the daughter we had said was ours, was not ours at all. And she wanted Juliette to make a good marriage, preferably to James, for reasons you can guess.'

He stopped pacing suddenly and sank into a chair opposite the young man and put his head in his hands. 'If only I had known what had been smouldering in her heart for years. . .'

For a moment he could not go on and Philip waited impatiently. The tale was long in the telling and he wanted to be on the move, to be doing something positive to find Juliette, but good manners dictated that he must hear him out.

His lordship looked up at last. 'I had no idea my acting all those years ago in Paris had been so convincing. It was only intended to deceive the French authorities and I saw no reason to tell Elizabeth of it. How I wish I had! My brother heard of it by chance four years later and he told Elizabeth that Juliette was my natural child. It was done maliciously, I know that, meant to ruin our marriage and put paid to any chance of my begetting an heir.'

He smiled wryly. 'He did not know that Lady Martindale could have no more children and his inheritance was safe. What he did not bargain on was that my wife would say nothing to me of what he had said; the idea that I had once had a French mistress simply festered inside her until she told Juliette two days ago.'

'Oh, *ma pauvre p'tite*,' Philip murmured. What a shattering blow she must have suffered! Her safe, comfortable, predictable world, her English world, had suddenly been turned into a nightmare. She was not who she thought she was and her home was only her home because Lady Martindale had condoned her husband's infidelity and harboured his bastard.

What it must have done to Juliette he could easily imagine. She would have felt let down, abandoned, deceived by those she had revered and trusted. And she would have felt unable to face the man she had promised to marry. Flight would have seemed the only option, the French lieutenant her only hope.

'We have to find her and stop her before she leaves the country. Tell me what you know of the escape route.'

Philip stood up. 'I know nothing of value. I can only learn more by returning to the camp. And you must not think of rushing after her yourself, you are needed here. Your wife must be suffering for misjudging you. I will find Miss Martindale, even if I have to go to France to do it.'

'Thank you, my boy. I had hoped you would say that.'

'It is the least I can do for someone who has been a second father to me,' he said, omitting to add that he would go to the ends of the earth, through any danger, if it meant saving Juliette. 'I will do my best to communicate with you, but if I cannot, rest assured I have not given up the search.'

'And if I have to recognise that scapegrace of a Frenchman as a son-in-law, so be it,' his lordship added, as Philip made for the door.

The young man did not answer. It was something that he did not even want to think about. He rode at a gallop all the way back to his lodgings, changed into the garb of a prisoner of war, dirtied his face and prepared to give himself up.

A north wind blew across the Wash in opposition to the outgoing tide, making the sea choppy. The little boat rose and dipped so that one moment the flat marshes could still be glimpsed on the horizon behind them and the next they had disappeared behind a wall of water. Ahead of them, now clearly to be seen, now hidden by the waves, a fishing smack lay at anchor. Juliette was already feeling sick and longed for stability and warmth, even that provided by a fishing smack. Her fingers and toes were frozen. Beside her Lieutenant Veillard sat staring straight ahead, as if he, too, were having trouble controlling his heaving stomach. There were eight others in the boat, all French, all from the camp at Norman Cross. They had escaped and, given a little luck, would soon be on their way home.

She wished she could feel like they did, optimistic, looking forward to seeing loved ones, rejoining compatriots, but try as she might, she felt as though she had taken a great leap in the dark and below her there was nothing but an abyss which would swallow her, leaving nothing behind, not even an identity for some-one to mourn.

It was only two days since she had left the home she loved and yet it seemed like a lifetime. From Hartlea, she and Pierre had walked to the river and gone on board a barge. Aware that his French accent would give him away, he had pretended to have a sore throat and left her to negotiate payment for taking them to Lynn. From there they had walked for miles across the marshes.

As if in a dream she had stumbled after him, putting one aching foot in front of the other, hardly aware that both were wet because her boots leaked. Nothing seemed real, neither the river, nor the marshes, nor the extraordinary sunset, which tinged the whole sky with orange and vermilion and purple, nor the crying of the hundreds of seabirds that drifted down to feed as it grew dusk.

At last they had stopped at the door of a hut, set beside a deeper channel, miles from habitation. 'We stay here tonight,' he had said, pushing open the door and ushering her. 'Tomorrow, we will be on our way.'

She had been too tired answer. Huddled in her cloak, she had sat on the floor with her back propped against the wall and dozed fitfully.

Just before dawn the others had arrived one by one, dirty, dishevelled and weary, but buoyed with hope. They had not been at all pleased to see her, shouting at Pierre for being a fool and threatening to kill them both. The arrival of their leader, a big man in a drab overcoat with three capes and huge pockets, put and end to the arguments, though she guessed it might only be a temporary reprieve.

The side of the ship loomed above them and their leader, whose name she had learned was Michel, reached out to grab the net that had been flung over the side for them, then turned and pulled her to her feet. 'Up you go.'

She looked up at the deck outlined against the night sky and recoiled at the height of it. 'I can't. I'll fall.'

'You climb or you fall, it is of no importance to me which you do,' Michel said.

Reaching up, she grabbed the net with her hands and placed her feet in the mesh. It swayed out with the movement of the ship and then flung her back, banging her against the hull. She cried out, but hung on grimly and then began to climb, hauling herself up a few inches at a time.

Behind her, she could hear Pierre's laboured breath and behind him the others, urging them both to make haste. She reached the rail at last and hands came over and grabbed her shoulders, hauling her unceremoniously on to the deck.

'A wench, by God!' a voice said as she straightened up. 'No one said anything about taking women.'

'She came with me,' Pierre told them as he scrambled over the side to join her, followed by the others. 'And she is not a wench but a *comtesse*, so you will treat her with respect.'

'A froggy countess, eh? Valuable cargo, indeed.' The man was apparently the captain, for the rest of the crew stood behind him, gaping.

'You have been paid,' Michel told him. 'Set sail, if you please.'

'Not until we have negotiated a new price. Or overboard she goes.'

Juliette turned her back on them, delved into the pocket tied about her waist under her skirt and produced a single string of pearls that her father had given her for her come-out. 'Will these do?' she asked, holding them out. 'They are very fine. Enough for my fare and a cabin.'

He took them and examined them, holding them up to the light. 'Cabin, eh? This ain't the cross-channel packet, you know.'

'But you do have a cabin?' Pierre queried.

'Naturally, there is a captain's cabin.'

'Then you will not mind putting it at the disposal of the countess, will you?' He paused and looked round at the motley collection of crew and prisoners of war. 'Can you sail a ship when its crew are paying more attention to a lady's limbs than their work?'

'Oh, very well,' the man conceded. 'I'll take the mate's cabin and he can move in with the crew. As for the rest of you, get below and stay there until we are safely out of reach of the revenue cutters. We'll be taking on another passenger at Lowestoft, but that needn't concern you.' To the crew he yelled, 'Weigh anchor and let's be away.'

Five minutes later there was no sign on deck that the ship was anything other than an innocent fishing vessel. The crew were busy trimming the sails, the erstwhile prisoners were confined in the hold and Juliette was sitting on the bunk in the cramped cubbyhole that the captain graced with the name of cabin, wondering what she was doing there.

From beloved daughter to fugitive, from a mansion to an evil-smelling boat, from dry land to heaving sea, all in the space of two days. Her carefree childhood, her growing up, were behind her and she could never return to them. They must be forgotten.

She had thrown in her lot with the enemies of her adopted country and the penalty for that was death. The fact that she was travelling unchaperoned paled into insignificance beside it. And any one of these men could rape her and she would be unable to do anything about it. She doubted if Pierre would be much help, even if he chose to try.

In the last two days she had lost all her illusions about him. He was not the romantic figure her imagination had painted. He was irritable and selfish and grasping and it was only the prospect of her supposed wealth that would protect her.

But she had another protector—the sea. Within an hour of setting sail she was struck down by seasickness and the cabin became her prison. One of the sailors came in now and again to take away the bowl and replace it with a clean one. Twice a day he brought a jug of water. It was supposed to be clean drinking water, but it tasted bitter and made her feel worse.

She ate nothing but still her stomach heaved. The room and her clothes began to stink, but opening the porthole let in cascades of water and soaked her bedding. It was shut again. She doubled over the basin, praying to die.

Then, as her stomach emptied and there was nothing more to bring up, she sank back on the smelly bunk and dreamed of the sunlit gardens of Hartlea. The scent of roses filled her nostrils and she could hear laughter, her mother's and Anne's.

There was someone else there too; a man. Not her father, not James Martindale, whose features she now found difficult to recall, but Philip Devonshire. He was standing so close she could feel his warmth, the strength emanating from him and enveloping her like a cloak. He was smiling so that the dimple in his chin deepened.

'Time,' he was saying in aggrieved tones. 'That was all I asked of you.' And then she was awake and weeping, tears she had not been able to shed before. Every pore of her longed for the time she had denied him, had denied herself. Now there was no time. She slept at last, through sheer exhaustion, and when she woke the storm had passed and the ship was on an even keel.

She had to get out of that stinking cabin and go on deck, even if it meant mixing with the men. She would just have to behave with the dignity of a countess and hope for the best.

She scrambled to her feet, stripped off the clothes she had been wearing and washed herself, using the clean basin and water from the ewer. Then she found her cloakbag, which had been thrown into a corner, and pulled out a plain woollen gown and a shawl. Thus clad, she left the cabin and went up on deck.

It was a bright sunlit day, the water was calm and sparkling. Above her the sails were filled with the breeze taking them southwards. She could not see land and wondered how long she had been confined to the cabin, how far they had come. There were men about, working or simply leaning over the side contemplating the water. One of them turned as she approached and she found herself looking into the amused eyes of James Martindale.

At first she thought she must still be dreaming, but then he laughed. 'Surprised to see me, are you, my dear wife-to-be?'

'How. . .? W-what are you d-doing here?' she managed to stutter at last. 'How did you get on board?'

'I came aboard at Lowestoft. You were too ill to notice.'

'Have you taken over the ship?'

'Now why should I do that?'

'To arrest these men, take them back to prison. Though how you knew. . .' She paused, suddenly remembering James's encounter in the park with the man in the long coat. It had been Michel! He was not an escapee, he was an informant and had betrayed the other prisoners to James. She was almost sorry for them. 'What are you going to do with me? Will I be arrested too?'

'Why? Have you done something illegal? According to Lieutenant Veillard, you are merely returning to your homeland.'

'He told you?'

'Yes. Now, thanks to you, I have had to change my plans. I was to visit Hartlea, or had you forgot?'

'I am sorry. Will you take me back?'

'I do not see how I can do that, my dear, not immediately. We are very close to Calais.'

She turned to look over the bows. A flat coastline was clearly visible and even a few houses and a church could be seen. One of the crew lowered the British ensign and hoisted a French one in its place. 'I had no idea we were so near.'

He turned as Pierre joined them. 'Lieutenant, I have just been telling Miss Martindale. . .' he smiled and corrected himself with a bow to Juliette. '. . .Mam'selle Caronne, that I have taken over her welfare. You may leave her in my care.'

'But I promised. . .'

'I absolve you from all promises, Lieutenant. The

lady is betrothed to me; I do not recall the engagement being broken. When we dock, you may take your leave. Your task is done.' His manner brooked no argument and the young Frenchman moved away to join his compatriots.

'There now,' James said, when he had gone. 'I shall look after you from now on.'

'But you do not know the whole truth. . .'

'Oh, but I do. The trouble is that you have been hopelessly compromised, even if the truth about who you really are is suppressed.'

'Then you will wish to break off our engagement. I understand that. You need not spare my feelings.'

'You do not understand.' For the first time his lazy voice was raised. 'His lordship wishes to recognise you and if that is so, nothing has changed, except your precipitous flight. What a ninny you were not to wait.'

'That is exactly what. . .' She stopped. She could not mention Philip Devonshire, it would only anger him. 'What I could not do.'

'No, or the lieutenant would have gone without you. It had all been arranged weeks beforehand.'

'You knew?'

'Of course.'

'Michel told you.'

'Indeed he did. How clever of you to see that. But now, my dear, you are up to your pretty little neck in intrigue and only I can save you.' He paused and put a finger under her chin to lift her face to his.

'Our story goes like this: Pierre Veillard inadvertently let slip to you the information that there was to be a break-out and, once he had done that, he could not let you go to raise the alarm. He forced you to go with him. I heard about it through Michel and followed in order to rescue you, but I could not bring it about before we arrived in France. Consequently, we had to go along with the prisoners until an opportunity arose to escape and return. I shall be a hero.'

He smiled and bent to kiss her lips, though he put no pressure on them, aroused no response beyond bewilderment. 'We were married at the earliest opportunity, of course.'

She should have felt relieved at so simple a way out of her dilemma and one that meant she could return to Hartlea with her reputation almost intact, but there was something about his smug self-satisfaction that repelled her. 'Why are you doing this? Why are you putting yourself at risk to save me?'

'Hartlea,' he said. 'You know what it means to me and I will not insult you by pretending otherwise. Oh, I know it will be mine one day; his lordship cannot break the entailment, but I need money to run it and the pay of a government clerk is a mere pittance. I need a dowry and yours is the most generous of any among this year's debutantes.'

'It won't be now.'

'Oh, I think his lordship will be magnanimous, you know. He loves you.'

Did he? Then she had let him down very badly. If only she had been told the truth a long time ago, she might now have come to accept it; there would have been no need to flee. That was the coward's way. 'How soon can we go back?'

'I really cannot say. But since we are here, we ought to go to Hautvigne.'

'Why?' She was puzzled.

'My dear Juliette, it is your birthplace. Are you not a little curious? After all, you have rights. . .'

'I am not at all interested in claiming those.'

'Why not? There are lands and buildings, a château full of furniture, not to mention hidden treasure, so I am told. And when the war is over and we are at peace again, they will be added to your dowry.'

'Lieutenant Veillard is only guessing.'

'Perhaps, but he seems well-informed. We cannot risk losing it for the sake of a few days' travel.'

'But the risk of being captured must be greater. And besides, we would be unchaperoned.'

He flung his head back and laughed until the tears ran down his face. 'My dear Juliette, how illogical you are! You left home with a gaggle of common French soldiers. Anything could have happened.' He stopped to look closely into her face and, for once, his eyes, were still. 'Perhaps it did, perhaps Pierre has already enjoyed your favours, perhaps they all have. . .'

She was so astonished, all she could say was, 'How dare you!'

'Oh, I dare. I dare anything as far as you are concerned, because the rewards I expect to receive outweigh my natural repugnance. I shall be your husband and, for the purposes of our journey, I shall need a new name. Yes, I will be a Scotsman with a grudge against the English. James Stewart, how does that sound?'

'No!'

'You do not like the name?'

'I care nothing for names. I meant no to marrying you.'

'But we are already betrothed, my dear, we have

made a sacred promise to each other. I realise it cannot be the wedding of your dreams, but a wedding there will be.'

She did not want to marry him, even to save herself. 'How can you go to a priest in France? You will be arrested at once.'

'There is that possibility, of course.' He paused, enjoying tormenting her. 'We could be married at Hautvigne, surrounded by your family, though it would not do to let them know you really intend to return to England.'

'You are so sure of yourself,' she said. 'When did you plan all this?'

'Only since I came on board and found you here. Veillard supplied me with the details, which is what I meant when I said you had made me change my plans. I had intended to stay on board only a short time and then go to Hartlea as arranged.'

They had entered a river estuary and were moving so slowly that the people on the towpath were able to walk alongside and call out to them. The Frenchmen on board called back, laughing at the realisation that at last they were free and among their own people.

The side of the ship jolted against the bank, almost throwing Juliette off her feet. The sails were let down, a line was thrown out and caught and they had arrived. She watched the men swarming down the gangplank, laughing and joking in voluble French.

She envied them; they were coming home. She felt no sense of homecoming. She didn't feel French at all. And all she could think of was what she had left behind, her home, her father, and the man she so dearly loved.

If only it had been Philip instead of James who had come aboard!

James was infuriatingly sure of himself and apparently not in the least concerned about her feelings at all. How had she come to accept him in the first place? He was rapidly becoming repugnant to her. And yet he was her only hope.

'Here we are!' he said heartily. 'And no one stopped us.'

'But they might still do so. You will be taken prisoner.'

He laughed. 'No, I do not think so, but there are enemies all around us, so we must take care. Have you seen Philip Devonshire of late?'

The question took her completely unawares and she stared at him, wondering what had prompted it. Enemies and Philip Devonshire's name spoken in the same breath, how significant was that?

He smiled, aware of her reaction. 'He was at Hartlea the day before you left, wasn't he?'

'There is nothing out of the ordinary in that,' she said, wondering how he knew. 'He is my father's friend.'

'And yours too, I collect.' He paused, watching her face carefully. 'Though how you can entertain as a friend someone so lacking in honour, I do not know.'

'I did not entertain him. We hardly spoke more than a few polite phrases. Why are you so interested? Surely you do not still consider him as a rival?'

'Not at all. But do you think, being a friend of Viscount Martindale, he might be persuaded to come after you?'

'To France?' She attempted to laugh but it sounded forced. 'Why should he do that? Why would a coward like Philip Devonshire risk his life for me? He could not even find the courage to fight a simple duel. I despise him.'

He seemed to accept the lie and grinned easily. 'Yes, you are right, of course. He would never dare cross the channel. It would be certain death. Let us forget him and go ashore.'

He took her arm to escort her down the gangplank on to French soil. She wished James had not mentioned Philip because now she could not stop thinking about him.

She lived again every encounter she had ever had with him, dancing at her ball, waltzing her out onto the terrace, the meeting in the garden when he had hinted at. . .what? He had asked for time and that might have meant he had hopes of being able to unravel some problem that stood in the way of him declaring himself.

Had she imagined the gentleness of his voice, the soft look in his eyes, the pressure of his lips on hers? And that last time, at Hartlea, when she had been so confused and unhappy—if they had been alone, would he have offered her any comfort?

It was all too late now. She had been tried, found wanting and condemned, that was how it felt, and all she could do was to serve her sentence. Exactly what that would entail she did not know.

Philip, at that moment, was cursing the rough weather that had delayed his crossing. His ride to Hartlea and back had made him late into the camp and the prisoners had already escaped. He had gone after them, but had wasted time trying to discover the name of the vessel they had boarded; by the time he had the information, it had already sailed.

He had requisitioned a cutter in the name of the War Department and set off after them. The last time he had been in France a month before, he had almost been caught and he knew he was risking life and limb to return there, but that was no consideration now.

He had a legitimate reason for going; Lord Martindale had asked him to find Clavier's British contact and, if his information was correct, the man was on that boat. But that task dwindled into unimportance beside the overwhelming need to find Juliette.

Was she still with Pierre Veillard, or had he handed her over to his bloodthirsty companions? His blood ran cold at the thought. Would they stay in Calais long enough for him to catch up with them or move on immediately? But where? Oh, where was his darling? That he loved her had never been in question. Whether she loved him was more debatable, but he would not rest until he found her.

He paced the deck in a fever of frustrated impatience, his imagination painting lurid pictures of the fate that might befall her. Instead, he forced himself to think of the pleasure of their reunion, when he would, once again, hold her in his arms, when he could tell her of his love. But before that could happen there were other matters to resolve, not least the question of *Le Merle* and his informant, because they were all bound up together.

Chapter Seven

It was no good sighing for what might have been, Juliette scolded herself, as they journeyed through France, using several modes of transport, all of them exceedingly uncomfortable and furtive and matched only in unpleasantness by the inns and taverns in which they lodged.

And though she cried herself to sleep each night in the privacy of her room, she faced each new day with stoic determination to put the past behind her and make what she could of her future. One day James would take her back to England as his wife but, judging by the danger of travelling in enemy France, that might not be until the war ended.

She was surprised to discover he spoke very good French, better than she did, and he had some official-looking papers that ensured their safe conduct, but not their comfort. She was filthy, verminous and exhausted by the time they arrived at Hautvigne in the last of a succession of hired conveyances, a dilapidated one-horse carriage with no springs.

The chateau sat on a hill just above the town,

surrounded by what had once been a prosperous vineyard. Now it was neglected and overgrown. The vines
still producing fruit had not been tended and the grapes
were small and rotting.

The building itself was made of mellow stone and
beautifully proportioned, with a tall round tower at each
of its four corners, though many of its hundreds of
windows were broken and the great oak door, at the
top of a sweep of steps, was damaged as if it had been
attacked by a battering ram. It was nothing like the
splendid picture Pierre had painted.

She turned and surveyed the grounds surrounding the
house. The gardens had once been well laid out, but
were now a tangle of creepers, overgrown shrubs and
long grass, though she could see that one corner had
been cultivated recently for there were rows of cabbages
and potatoes.

James ran up the steps and hammered on the door.
The sound reverberated through the house, but no one
came. Juliette joined him as he pushed open the door
and together they stepped inside.

They were in a vestibule with a marble-tiled floor
and a vaulted roof. A magnificent wrought-iron staircase curved up to a first-floor gallery. The walls were
bare, but they could see by the darker patches that they
had once been hung with tapestries or pictures. Half a
dozen rooms led from the vestibule, some of which had
lost their doors.

'Anyone here?' James called. 'Is anyone at home?'

He moved forward into a salon, followed by Juliette.
It was an elegant room with a high plaster ceiling intricately carved, and long casement windows that looked
out over the terraces of vines to the valley below, where

nestled a group of houses, two churches and the town hall.

The road by which they had travelled could be seen at intervals as it wound its way down to the valley floor and then alongside the river, to disappear behind an outcrop of rock two or three miles away. The château, Juliette realised, was very strategically placed to command a view of the surrounding countryside. If there was anyone in or near the building, they must have seen them arriving.

She turned back to survey the room. There was a threadbare rug on the floor, a battered sofa, a couple of chairs, a cabinet and a table, miserly furnishings for a room at least fifty feet square. She went back to the hall and in at the next door. It must have been the library for it was lined with shelves, but all were empty. Other rooms were equally sparsely furnished

'So, this is my inheritance,' she said with a wry smile, as they returned to the vestibule. 'Hardly worth the journey, was it? We would have done better to have turned back at Calais.' A noise made them spin round. An old man had appeared from the gloom at the back of the stairs and stood facing them with a musket of immense length. 'Who are you? What do you want?'

'This,' said James, indicating Juliette, 'is Countess Juliette de Caronne.'

'Never heard of her.'

'Oh, I am sure you have,' James went on pleasantly. 'You are old enough to remember the *comte* and *comtesse* who were guillotined in '94. This was their home, as you must know. Their son died on the same day, but their daughter. . .' He paused. 'Their daughter survived, and she has come home.'

The old man stared at Juliette for a long time and then burst into a cackling laugh that echoed round the empty hall. 'Oh, that's a fine one, that is. The best yet. Do you think I am a fool?'

'No, but it would help to know who you are.'

'Me? I am Henri Caronne, cousin to the late *comte* and I would surely know if this one was his daughter.' He indicated Juliette with the barrel of the muzzle, making her step back in alarm.

'Would you? How close were you to the family? It is my guess, knowing how unpopular your kin were with the regime, you kept your distance. It is how you survived.'

The old man yelled over his shoulder, 'Jean! Anne-Marie! Come and see what the wind has blown in.'

A man and a woman appeared from behind him. They were in their forties and roughly dressed. The man was almost bald and had a rough stubble on his chin, but the woman's hair, beneath the grimy cap she wore, was pale gold, rather like Juliette's, or would have been if it had been clean and brushed. And her eyes, beneath fine winged brows, were clear blue. If Juliette had had any doubt about her identity before, it vanished now.

The younger man peered at the newcomers. 'Who are they?'

'The wench claims to be Juliette Caronne, daughter of the late *comte*, no less, with her head back on her shoulders and near twenty years older. As for him—' he indicated James and shrugged his shoulders '—perhaps he thinks he is Antoine.' And he cackled with laughter again.

'No, he is nothing like him,' the woman said. 'But the girl, there is something about her. . .'

'Superficial, that's all. You don't think I am going to take their word for it, do you? Why, she cannot even speak French properly.'

'That is because she was taken out of the country as an infant,' James put in quickly before Juliette could answer, though she had no wish to.

Over the last two weeks, she had become almost numb to sensation, either of pleasure or pain, fear or irritation. If thinking and feeling hurt, then it was better not to think or feel. Like a puppet, she allowed James to dictate her movements, to speak for her.

'She was saved from the guillotine and brought up by foster parents. She has only recently discovered who she is.'

He had been carrying Juliette's bag and delved into it to produce the copy of the portrait that he had had the foresight to buy from Pierre with a fistful of gold coins. 'Look at this. The artist was a French prisoner-of-war and recognised her.'

The older man took it and peered at it short-sightedly. 'It is the old lady, the *comte*'s mother. I have seen a portrait exactly like it.'

'Whoever painted this could have copied it,' Jean said.

'If you were to compare it with the original, you would notice the difference,' James said, while Juliette stood looking from one to the other, wishing she had never come; here was no welcome. Pierre had been wrong about that. 'The portrait you have in your hand is not of the old *comtesse*, but of the young lady standing before you now. It was painted this year in England, not Paris. See, it is signed and dated.'

'So what does that prove?' Jean demanded.

'She was—is—one of the innocents, an orphan of the Terror.' He turned to Juliette. 'Show them the ruby, my dear. Maybe that will convince them.'

Juliette hesitated, but they were all looking at her, waiting expectantly, and so she fetched out the jewel from the pocket round her waist, holding it on the palm of her hand, where it winked wine-dark in the gloom of the hall.

'Where did you get this?' the old man asked, reaching out for it.

Juliette closed her hand over it. 'I have always had it.'

'The rest,' he demanded. 'Where is the rest of it?'

'Shut up, old man, and put the gun away,' Jean said.

James gave a grin of triumph. 'I was right. You moved in and denuded the house, sold all the good furniture, the paintings, the ornaments, everything you could find, but you have not found the real treasure, have you?'

'Oh, so you have been listening to gossip, have you? That story is a fabrication, a myth, invented by the old servants. There is nothing here or we would have found it. Go back where you came from before we hand you over to the authorities. You have the look of an Englishman. Too much the aristocrat to be a citizen of France.' He stepped forward and fingered James's coat. 'And I have not seen woollen cloth like that since the war began.'

James laughed. 'Not all Englishmen are enemies of France. I would hardly have travelled so far into the country without being stopped and imprisoned, if that were the case. We have been asked for papers at every town we passed through and nowhere were we so much as delayed by a minute. The countess will tell you that. Here, look for yourself.'

He reached into his inner pocket, making the old man raise the musket again, but James ignored him and drew out a sheaf of papers. Juliette had seen them before. He had used them time and time again on their journey through France.

Jean examined them and laughed. 'So you have a letter signed by the Emperor himself. What does that prove?'

'It proves that I am not lying to you. The letter states quite plainly that I am to be given every assistance. I have orders to take over this château in the name of the young *Comtesse de Caronne*. His Majesty is desirous of seeing the lady reinstated here and the château restored. You may stay only if you wish to serve her.'

He was an accomplished liar, Juliette realised, and a forger too, for there was no way he could have obtained genuine papers. Her three relatives had already lost their bombastic attitude and were cringing slightly.

'Now, if you do not mind, we are both weary and need refreshment,' James said. 'Later we will talk of it.'

'Yes, *monsieur*,' Jean said, suddenly becoming affable. 'Anne-Marie, make a room ready.'

'Two rooms,' Juliette put in quickly.

'The two large rooms at the front,' Jean went on, addressing his wife. And then to Juliette, 'By the time you have washed and changed, refreshments will be ready.'

Suddenly all was bustle and eagerness as Jean yelled for someone called Gerard, Henri returned to the kitchen and Anne-Marie disappeared up the stairs. Another old man, even more bent and gnarled than Henri, plodded in at the front door, not even bothering to wipe the mud from his boots.

'Gerard, we have guests,' Jean shouted as the old fellow cupped a hand round his ear. 'Bring in the luggage and see to the horse and then wring the neck of one of the hens.' All of this was reinforced by descriptive hand signals, for the benefit of the deaf man.

The ruby and the prospect of finding more jewels had ensured their welcome, but Juliette was under no illusions; heaven help them when her relatives found out that she had no more.

Not that James seemed perturbed; he was exhibiting remarkable coolness, when all she wanted was to turn tail and run. If it had been Pierre, they would have been relieved of the gem and thrown out on their ears long before now. But how long could they keep it up? How long did James intend to stay?

When they were shown to their rooms, she took the opportunity to question him. He was maddeningly unforthcoming but she did learn that he was calling himself James Stewart because he was pretending to represent rebellious factions in Scotland who were hoping to revive the French-Scots connection, though what that had to do with the Caronnes and Hautvigne she did not know. He surely did not believe there was treasure hidden about the château?

But in the days that followed she was forced to the conclusion that he did believe it. Watched in wry amusement by the rest of the Caronne family, he proceeded to search every inch of the building, from attics to cellars, and the latter were extensive and full of old wine-making implements, barrels and hundreds of bottles, though all but a few dozen were empty.

When that produced nothing he ripped out whatever wood panelling still remained in the reception rooms, pulled up floorboards, poked about up chimneys and covered himself with cobwebs and soot. All in vain.

'Do you think we have not done all that already?' Henri laughed. 'Twenty years we have been searching. . .'

'Then you were not thorough enough. Fetch me another bottle of wine, this is thirsty work.'

Juliette watched him with growing dismay. He was not interested in her; all her efforts to persuade him to give up and take her home as he had promised were met with drunken anger. Occasionally he struck her, shouting at her that if she wanted to go home so badly, the least she could do was to help him search.

'It is a foolish waste of time,' she told him one day when they were alone in the salon. 'Why can't we go back to England? I realise you no longer wish to marry me, not after I ran off with Pierre, but to tell the truth, I do not think we should suit, but Hartlea would still be yours when the time came.

'I would be happy to live a simple life, working to earn my keep. But not here, not in France. Juliette Caronne died with her parents, she should never have been resurrected.'

'It is too late for regrets, my dear. I am afraid you have burned your boats. Now, I have a mind to search the library. There might be something hidden behind the bookshelves.' And with that he turned and strode away.

If she had been miserable before, she was doubly so now. She would retire to her room, or take long walks between the rows of vines or in the pine woods to the back of the château where the ground sloped up to the mountains. Again and again her thoughts turned to England, to the happy childhood she had had, even to the summer just gone when she had been fêted as the debutante of the Season.

But most of all she thought about one man in particular, tall and powerful, with dark all-seeing eyes and a dimple in his chin. Thinking about him set her whole mind and body longing for him, for his gentleness and understanding, his warmth and she recalled his words to her at the ball, *play for time*, and she could not stop the tears.

She was returning home towards dusk one evening when she saw a lone rider approaching the château; for one heart-stopping minute she was reminded of Philip Devonshire, simply because of the way he sat in the saddle, head up and hands relaxed on the reins so that it appeared as if the horse were guiding itself.

Ever since leaving England, she had had a dream, a vision: he would coming riding up on a white charger, like St George slaying the dragon, and carry her off, heedless of the obstacles that stood in their way, taking her to a land far way where no one knew of their past, where they could be happy. Without realising it, she began to run, her heart singing with joy. She reached the door as he dismounted and then came to a sudden stop, breathing hard.

The man who stood before her was not Philip Devonshire. This man was not, after all, so tall and he had a decided stoop. His hair was reddish, he had thick eyebrows, wore an untidy beard and there was a new scar across his cheek, as if he had been caught by the tip of a sword. He wore the faded uniform of a French cavalry officer, its epaulettes torn and its silver tarnished. His breeches were baggy, as if he had once been heavier than he now was.

He turned and stared at her, drawing his gaze up from her boot-clad feet, over the rough wool dress that Anne-Marie had lent her, to her face, sun-tanned and freckled. And there it rested. There was a flicker of humour in his eyes that made her catch her breath in remembrance, because Philip had sometimes looked at her like that, as if they shared a secret joke. But what could she and this stranger have in common to laugh at?

'*Bonjour, mam'selle,*' he greeted her.

She was still breathless. 'Who are you?'

'Captain Philippe Devereux. I am on my way south to rejoin my regiment in Spain and come to pay my respects to the Caronne family.' His accent had the heavy patois of the region; she recognised it as the same as that of Gerard, the only servant they had. At first she had found it very difficult to follow, but she was slowly becoming used to it and even her French had improved so that now she rarely had to ask James to translate.

'There will be a bed for the night,' he said. 'Henri Caronne will not turn the son of his old friend from the door.'

'Come in and I will see if I can find him.'

At that moment, Henri himself appeared, wandering round the corner of the house carrying a pitchfork. James's quest for treasure had infected everyone else and he had been using it to clear out one of the lofts in an outhouse.

'Henri, this is Captain Devereux,' Juliette said, indicating the man by the horse.

'Devereux?' the old man queried, peering into the soldier's face. 'Devereux? Do I know you?'

'You knew my father, sir. Antoine Devereux. The *comte*'s young son was named for him.'

'Oh, that Devereux! Come in. You can tell us about the progress of the war.' He turned to Juliette. 'Fetch a bottle of the best, girl, and be quick about it. And tell Gerard to see to the captain's horse.'

Juliette was glad to turn away and do as she had been bid. The soldier had hardly taken his eyes off her since he arrived, staring at her as if he could not believe what he was seeing, making her feel uncomfortable. As she moved away, she heard him ask, 'Who is that?'

Henri laughed. 'Her name is Juliette, or so she says. She claims to be the dead *comte's* daughter. . .'

Juliette heard no more as they went in the direction of the salon and she hurried through the door into the kitchen, where she found Gerard toasting his stockinged toes by the fender of the kitchen fire. Above it hung a blackened pot which steamed gently. 'We have a guest,' she shouted in his ear. 'Henri says you are to see to his horse.'

Grumbling he pulled his boots back on and shambled out into the yard, while she went down to the cellar and selected two bottle of red wine. Knowing nothing of wine and assuming they ought to use up the old bottles first, she chose those with the thickest layer of dust. If they turned out to be undrinkable and gave the men a bellyache, then she would shed no tears. She returned to the salon where Henri and his guest had been joined by Jean and Anne-Marie.

'Will this do?' she queried, holding out the bottles.

Henri took them from her. 'Where did you find these?'

'At the back of the cellar. Why?'

'The best year we ever had. I thought they'd been drunk years ago.' He turned to the captain. 'She calls herself a Caronne and yet she knows nothing of wine. What the Caronnes don't know about wine-growing is not worth troubling about.'

'True,' the captain said, as Henri looked about for a corkscrew. 'It is common knowledge they have wine running through their veins instead of blood.' He laughed harshly, looking under his thick brows at Juliette. 'They do say that when their heads came off, it was wine that spurted into the basket and the executioner got so drunk on it he missed one of them.'

Juliette shuddered. How could they be so crude? But was it generally held to be true that one of the family escaped? 'It is a pity you don't put your knowledge to better use,' she said sharply to Henri, who was busy uncorking the first bottle. 'Even I can see the whole place has been allowed to fall into ruin.'

'We can't get the workers. They've all been conscripted. The captain will bear me out on that, won't you, sir?'

'Yes, war has a voracious appetite for young men, there are only women, boys and old men left. And even the boys are being taken now.'

'Then you should put the old men and women to work,' she told Henri. 'And work yourself. I have never seen you do anything except eat and drink and. . .' She stopped suddenly. She had been about to add, 'and search for non-existent treasure', but if she admitted she did not think it existed, then they would throw her out, might even harm her.

She looked up, wondering how to finish her sentence and found herself looking into the captain's eyes, where there was a gleam of amusement as if he knew what she had been about to say. Again she was reminded of Philip, who seemed to be able to divine her thoughts almost as soon as they came into her head. This constant comparison was foolish, she told herself. It was all wishful thinking, her own longing making her see things that were not there.

'And sleep,' she added, at which the soldier threw up his head and laughed. It was so different from the coarse laughter of a moment before and so full of merriment that it transported her back to a meadow beside the river at Richmond.

She heard again the sound of bat and ball, the polite clapping of the ladies and the noisy applause of the men. Mr Devonshire had laughed like that when he had been run out, she remembered; it was the laugh of a man who did not have a care in the world.

And at that time neither had she, except that of deciding whether she preferred James Martindale or Philip Devonshire. Now she knew the answer, it was too late. Far, far too late. And thinking about it did nothing to help her to accept the life she was now forced to live.

'My, she is a spirited filly, this young cousin of yours, Henri,' the captain said, accepting a glass of wine from him. 'If I had the time, I might enjoy taming her.'

'How long do you have, Captain?' Anne-Marie asked.

He shrugged. 'I was sent to Paris with despatches for the Emperor, but I had to follow him all the way to

Dresden. He was in a foul mood over the treachery of the Austrians and his defeats at Grossbeeren and Katzbach. Fortunately those setbacks were followed by victory at Dresden. I left with instructions to make sure the country knew of it.

'I assumed from that I was to take my time spreading the good news on my way back to Spain. I am in no hurry to return to that hellhole, I assure you. I decided to visit my old home and pay a call on the château on my way. It is many weeks since I slept in a comfortable bed.'

'He can have the Englishman's bed,' Henri said.

'Englishman!' The new arrival, who had been idly studying the colour of the wine in his glass, sat up suddenly. 'What's an Englishman doing here?'

'She brought him,' Jean said, indicating Juliette.

'Her husband?'

'No, my escort,' Juliette said and was surprised by the change in the captain's expression. The tension in his features vanished and he looked at Juliette and smiled. There seemed to be a message in his eyes, though she could not read it.

'A strange sort of escort for a French *comtesse, n'est-ce pas?*'

'He says he is a friend of France and on the Emperor's business,' Jean said.

'So he is,' said a voice from the open door.

Everyone turned to see James leaning drunkenly against the doorpost. Juliette thought she heard the captain's quick intake of breath, but decided she must have been mistaken, for when she looked at him, he was sipping his wine.

'James, where have you been?' she asked. 'We have a guest.'

'So I see. Are you going to introduce him?'

'Captain Philippe Devereux.' And to the captain, 'This is Mr James Stewart.'

She thought she imagined a twitch of a smile to the corners of his mouth as if he understood the joke in the name, but then decided it was unlikely. He did not bother to rise, but smiled over the rim of his glass. It stretched the scar on his cheek and turned the smile into a grimace. She wondered idly if it gave him any pain. 'I am pleased to make your acquaintance Monsieur Stewart.'

'I might return the compliment if it did not mean giving up my bed,' James said.

'Oh, do not concern yourself, I will find another. Perhaps the lady will not be averse to sharing hers.' He spoke in a lazy drawl with an accent so thick, Juliette did not, at first, take in what he had said. It was only when Jean laughed and slapped his knee that she realised what he meant.

'The lady is very averse,' she snapped, going to pass him in order to leave the room. 'Please excuse me. I have work to do in the kitchen.'

He caught her wrist and pulled her down onto his knee. 'Oh, no, *ma petite*, you do not escape so easily. I have been starved of female company for a very long time and you have a fire about you that attracts me. . .'

She struggled in his arms, but he held her fast. In spite of his unprepossessing appearance, she could feel his strength, his animal power. He seemed strange and yet familiar, as if she had woken from a dream to find her fantasies had come to distorted life.

He repelled and attracted her at the same time. It was such a strange feeling that, for a moment, she ceased to fight him. She could feel his warm breath against her ear, and it sent a shiver running through her body.

'I do believe she is an imposter,' he said. 'If I were you, Henri, I should send her packing. I'll take her off your hands, if you like.'

'I shouldn't do that, if I were you,' James drawled, as she pulled herself free and stepped out if his reach. 'She is protected by the Emperor himself.'

The captain turned to look at him. 'How so?'

'Through me. I am his Majesty's agent. It is his wish that Juliette Caronne be recognised as the true owner of the château and its lands.'

'His agent, eh? Then you must be privy to a great many state secrets.'

'Naturally, I am.'

'Prove it.'

'I have papers. . .'

'So, *monsieur*, have I.'

Juliette listened to this exchange with growing alarm. Henri and Jean had accepted James's story because they were greedy for the jewels, but the captain was a little more astute. If he succeeded in sowing the seeds of doubt in her relatives' minds, she and James would be in serious trouble.

'It is not for you, a mere soldier, to question a Caronne,' she said, putting on her countess's imperious voice. Sometimes it worked, sometimes it produced nothing but merriment. 'And you,' she added, forcing herself to look him in the eye, 'are probably a deserter, so we will hear no more of papers and proof, or you might find the boot on the other foot.'

She was taken aback when he flung back his head and laughed so much the tears ran down his face and into his beard. 'Oh, you are a countess, no doubt of that. But where did you learn to behave like one?'

'With an English viscount,' James said. 'It is no secret. He stole her from her true parents.'

Losing patience with all of them, Juliette took herself off to the kitchen to see to the evening meal. Taking the pot of stewed hare from over the fire, she stood it on a trivet and expended her seething anger in stirring it.

James was useless as a protector and her relatives made no secret of the fact that they were only interested in finding the rest of the pendant and did not care what became of her once they had it in their hands, and Anne-Marie, who might have befriended her, was so influenced by her husband and father, she would do nothing to annoy them. And the stranger was no help.

For one fleeting moment when she first saw him, she had thought that here was her saviour, that a kindly Providence had sent someone to rescue her. But that was only because of his superficial likeness to Philip Devonshire and her own wishful thinking. She would do better to concentrate on the differences between the two men; the Captain's rough appearance, his crudity, the way he had pulled her on to his knee and the fact that he was French.

She put the pot back over the flames and set about laying the kitchen table. They did not eat in the dining room for the simple reason that it had no table and chairs, and besides, the food stayed hotter if served in the kitchen. Then she went down to the cellar and fetched up another two bottles of wine.

She was just putting the finishing touches to the meal

when Anne-Marie sauntered through to see if it was ready. The woman was dirty and lazy and did nothing beyond the absolute minimum of work. 'Taking your time, aren't you?' she sneered. 'We could die of hunger waiting for you to produce a meal.'

'Then you should do it yourself,' Juliette snapped, as the men trooped in behind the woman and seated themselves at the table. 'You did before I arrived.'

'I see no point in keeping a dog and barking myself,' Anne-Marie said, laughing. 'And it's the only way you are ever going to earn your keep.'

'Yes,' the captain agreed in a lazy voice. 'The days of the aristo have long since passed. That was the trouble with the old *comte*; he was dyed-in-the wool nobility, expected everyone to bow and scrape and lick his boots. He never turned his hand to anything useful. Parasites, all aristos. We are well rid of them. I don't understand why you are harbouring one under your roof, my friend. . .'

'It is not his roof, it is mine,' Juliette snapped.

He seemed not at all perturbed. 'Then it is you I must thank for this hospitality.'

'It is a matter of indifference to me whether I am thanked or not,' she said. 'No one else takes the trouble.'

'Not even Monsieur. . .' He paused, his mouth twitching in a smile. 'Monsieur Stewart? I understand you are betrothed.'

Unwilling to admit that she was, she looked up and found herself gazing into the captain's eyes, deep, dark eyes which seemed to be asking her more than the simple question his tongue had framed. She covered her confusion by fetching the stew and tureens of vegetables and putting them on the table.

Henri began helping himself immediately, followed by Jean and Anne-Marie, while James sat back twirling the stem of his wine glass in his hand. The newcomer sat and watched them, a smile of wry amusement on his face.

So, James had not recognised him, Philippe thought, but he was not so sure of Juliette. Once or twice she had looked at him with a strange expression on her face, as if wondering to herself where she had seen him before. But that last speech of hers and the forthright way she had met his eyes had convinced him she had no suspicion of the truth.

He was thankful for the lessons in disguise he had learned from Lord Martindale who had made more than one clandestine visit to France, not only during the Terror when he had saved many an aristocratic head, but since the outbreak of war. But older now and one of England's foremost ministers, he had forsworn active service in favour of directing operations from the Horse Guards in London.

From his lordship Philippe had learned not only how to use paint, false hair and padding, but how to change his character in the way he wore his clothes and the timbre of his voice. He had learned how to *be* the character he was portraying and he was a master at it.

Except where Juliette was concerned. It was almost impossible to be harsh with her and he hated himself for attempting it, but he did not want to reveal himself until the time was right, until he could safely spirit her away. And that took careful planning.

And there was James Martindale. Had he anticipated the wedding he was so confident would take place? The idea filled him with an anger he found hard to control.

The man was a drunkard, a gambler and a parasite and, what was worse, a traitor. It was Juliette herself who had planted the first seed of suspicion in his mind when she told him of James's meeting with the man in Richmond Park, but even so, it had been a shock to have his suspicions confirmed when he finally caught up with Pierre Veillard in Calais and extracted the truth from him.

The lieutenant was hardly more than a boy and he felt almost sorry for him. He had lost the girl and the fortune he was so certain she had inherited and now, instead of spending the rest of the war in the comparative comfort of a prison camp, he was left to rejoin a defeated army or become a deserter, always on the run. But Pierre was not the threat, James was, and what to do about him, he did not know.

If he had been anyone but Viscount Martindale's heir and betrothed to Juliette, it would have been easy. The man would die. He could try to take him back to England to stand trial for treason, but that would hurt Lord Martindale and damage his lordship's credibility and, in any case, would not be easy to accomplish because James would not return voluntarily. He could make some sort of bargain with him, but what? Could he trust the man to keep any promises he made?

How much did Juliette know? Had she condoned it on the grounds that she was a French citizen now and had severed all ties with England? Until he knew the answers to at least some of these questions, his real identity had to remain a secret, even from Juliette, and this was helped in some measure, by his recently acquired scar.

But, oh, how he longed to tell her, to hold her in his

arms and reassure her that she was not without friends, that if she wished to return to England, then he would do his utmost to grant that wish.

'English!' he sneered, helping himself from the tureens. 'What do they know of the *haut monde*?'

He was very hungry, having begrudged the time needed to look for sustenance on the way. His whole aim had been to reach Hautvigne as quickly as possible. Good food was scarce and very expensive, which was why there was only jugged hare on the menu at the château, but it was well-cooked and made tasty with onions, herbs and vegetables and he did justice to it, wiping his plate with a crust of bread to take up every drop of gravy.

The conversation turned to the conduct of the war, the battles won and lost, how life had changed since Napoleon had introduced conscription and taken the best of France's manhood for cannon fodder. Henri spoke nostalgically of the old days when the vineyards were thriving, of the wonderful furniture and textiles, the pictures and ornaments which had once graced the chateau.

'I inherited a museum,' he said. 'You cannot eat pictures and ornaments, so. . .' He spread his hands in an expressive gesture. 'Now all that's left is a pile of stone and rotting vines.'

'Unless we find the rest of the jewels,' Jean added.

'You inherited nothing,' James said. 'What was here, you stole.'

'Oh, not again!' Juliette exclaimed. 'Can't you stop quarrelling for two minutes together? I am sure the captain is not interested in your squabbles.'

'Oh, but I am,' he said. 'The idea of hidden treasure

fills me with curiosity. I think I shall take you up on your invitation, Henri, *mon vieux*, and stay and help the search. The Army can do without my assistance for a few days.'

It was a very strange household she was living in, Juliette decided as she made ready for bed that night. Three French civilians, living in poverty but dreaming of riches, an Englishman who was claiming, with some measure of success, to being an agent of the Emperor, and a French cavalry officer who seemed to have lost his taste for fighting.

And there she was in the middle, a lost, lonely young woman who did not know where she belonged, a love child pretending to be a countess. There was no one she could love and no one who loved her, no single human being who cared what became of her. If she was going to get out of this mess, she was going to have to do it by herself.

They did not know about her bastardy; she had told no one, not even James, of that, and if they accepted she was a Caronne, then she ought to be behaving like the countess she said she was, giving orders for the cleaning and restoration of the château, taking on workers to clear the vineyards, learning how to tend the vines and make wine. In the absence of a cache of jewels, it was likely to be her only income.

If her destiny was here, then she should make the most of it. But oh, how difficult it was to accept that!

It was a warm night, warmer than it would have been in Hartlea in autumn, and she went to throw open the window and lean out to breathe the night air. There was an overgrown jasmine climbing up the crumbling stonework to her window and she could smell its heavy scent just below her. The garden with its untidy shrubs and overgrown roses was bathed in moonlight.

Over to the right she could see the deep pewter gleam of the river and beyond that the outline of the distant hills. Somewhere, down in the town, a dog barked and immediately below her she heard the crunch of footsteps on the gravel.

She leaned a little further out and looked down. Captain Philippe Devereux was strolling under her window, smoking a small cigar. Its aroma drifted up to her and reminded her of her father.

He had had his cigars specially made in London and they smelled just like that. He had been smoking one the day before she left, the day Mr Devereux had come to supper, the day she had learned who she was. Or, rather, who she was not. Were such cigars obtainable in France? And if they were not, how had a French cavalry officer come by one?

She must have made a slight noise for he looked up and saw her at the window. '*Bonsoir, mam'selle*,' he called up to her. 'It is a beautiful night, *n'est-ce pas?*'

'Yes. You are enjoying a cigar, I see. It has a very distinctive aroma.'

He cursed himself under his breath. Of all the fools! Edward Martindale had given him a box of them before he left, and he should have had more sense than to smoke one here. It was well-known that scent was more evocative than any of the other senses and would remind her of home. He looked up and smiled.

'You do not like it? I will put it out.' He dropped it and ground it out under his heel. 'There, I shall not offend again.'

'It did not offend me,' she said. 'But, forgive me, I

have noticed so many shortages since I have been in France, I did not think good cigars were easy to come by.'

She did not know why she continued to talk to him; she ought to shut the window and retire to bed, but he intrigued her. One minute he seemed to enjoy shocking her and the next his voice had softened until she felt she could almost trust him. Or was it simply that the smell of the cigar and her nostalgia for Hartlea had imbued him with the same sterling qualities as her father? And that was nonsense.

'Oh, it is not especially good,' he said, realising he had almost forgotten the character he was supposed to be playing. 'I took it off a dead soldier, an English colonel.'

'Ugh.' She shuddered; he was nothing like her father, after all. 'How could you?'

'Oh, very easily, *chérie*. He had no further use for it and I did. One must take one's opportunities where one finds them. Is that not a sensible maxim?'

'Does war make everyone so callous or were you always like that?'

He laughed and again she was reminded of happier times and she wished he would not confuse her so. 'Why don't you come down and join me?' he suggested. 'We could take a stroll and discuss it.'

'Certainly not!'

'Then I shall have to come to you. I am getting a crick in the neck looking up at you.' He grabbed a thick strand of the creeper and began climbing. 'I think that you, my lovely Juliette, have taken a grave risk coming to Hautvigne. You might have been killed, might still be if those cousins of yours decide there is no treasure.

Why don't you persuade James Stewart to take you home?'

His head was on a level with the window sill now. 'You do not really belong here, do you?'

'I do not know where I belong.'

'Then the story of being Juliette Caronne is a fiction?'

'No. That is true.'

'Do the others believe it?'

'Yes, or they would not have given us shelter.'

He smiled knowingly. 'Or they fear that Monsieur Stewart is really who he purports to be and his papers are genuine. They are simple people accustomed to bowing down to authority and looking on the Emperor almost as a god. They dare not disobey what they see as his orders.'

'Perhaps, but they also know I am who I say I am, and blood is thicker than water.'

'So long as the jewels remain unfound. They are motivated by greed, not family feeling.'

'Are you always so cynical, Captain?'

'That is not cynicism; it is facing up to reality,' he said. 'It is a dangerous game you are playing.'

'No more than yours, for now you have to climb down again.'

He laughed. 'Now who is unfeeling? For one moment I felt like Romeo, reaching out towards his Juliet and you have spoiled it all.' He gave a melodramatic sigh. 'Ah, well! "Good-night, good-night! Parting is such sweet sorrow that I shall say good-night till it be morrow."'

In spite of her misery, in spite of her confusion, she found herself laughing. A French soldier who could quote Shakespeare was the last thing she expected.

'Oh, that's better,' he said, then let go of the creeper and disappeared. She gasped and leaned out of the window, expecting to find him laid out on the ground, but he knew how to fall and was standing below her, brushing down his overlarge breeches. It seemed to her at that moment that he looked taller, less bent, but it was an illusion, she realised as he walked away. He was as unprepossessing as ever, certainly no handsome Romeo.

Chapter Eight

In the following days, Juliette thought she must have imagined the soldier who quoted Shakespeare. Captain Devereux was there, to be sure, lazing about the house, grooming his horse, riding out to explore the countryside surrounding the château, playing cards and drinking noisily with the other men.

But he was as far removed from the romantic man who had intrigued her the night of his arrival as James Martindale was from the gentleman she had once believed him to be. There was something about him she could not fathom and, as the days went by, she began to wonder why he had come to the château. His story of being on his way to rejoin his regiment in Spain did not ring true.

She was convinced he was a deserter and yet she could not quite believe he lacked courage. He would laugh and joke with Henri and Jean and treat James with thinly-veiled contempt, but there was about him a watchfulness, a way of moving which reminded her of a cat, a large and powerful cat, a lion or a tiger. The claws were sheathed for now, but she knew they could be deadly.

But if that were so, who at the château was his prey? Had it anything to do with the pendant? Or the war? It was like living on a knife edge.

And then one day, when they were alone in the kitchen, he began talking to her, asking her about her life in England and treating her with a deference he had never shown before. Although his accent did not lose the patois of the region, his voice softened, its cadences became sympathetic to her ear and she was almost lulled into believing he was a friend.

She longed for someone to confide in, someone who would not laugh at her as the others did, finding amusement in her mistakes with the language and her ignorance of viticulture, someone who was not heartless as James was heartless, and so she sat at the table opposite him and told him of her childhood, of the portrait and her come-out, of James and Philip Devonshire.

'They arranged to fight a duel,' she said. 'But Mr Devonshire did not turn up. James said he was a coward.'

'There is a little of the coward in every man,' he said, resisting the temptation to reach across and take her hand. Already it was becoming work-worn. 'And a little of the hero, too. Circumstances dictate our actions; one man's honour might be another's shame and there may have been mitigating circumstances.'

'I should like to think so, because nothing he had done before indicated he was anything but an honourable man.'

'Do you miss your old home?' he asked softly.

She looked at him sharply, wondering if he were trying to trap her. She must not let him think she was yearning for England, in spite of what she had said. 'I am a Frenchwoman, Captain,' she answered carefully. 'And this is now my home.'

'And you are determined to make the best of it,' he said softly. 'I admire your courage, *mam'selle*.'

She was not afraid of him, was not intimidated by anyone, but he knew that underneath that brave exterior was a young girl who had been dreadfully hurt. Why had Lord Martindale not told her the truth long before and not left it to his wife? Why had he not explained to Lady Martindale how he had brought the tiny child out of France? It would have saved a great deal of heartache for all of them.

But there were compensations. If that had happened, he would not be here with her now, learning to love her all over again, not as the pretty daughter of an English aristocrat, but as the wonderful, resourceful, delightful young woman she was when the gloss was stripped away.

The change in his manner confused her. He was no longer the crude soldier, but a gentleman making reasonable conversation, paying compliments, and what was more, making them sound genuine.

It would be easy to forget he was almost ugly with his untidy red beard and heavy eyebrows. What did he hide beneath all that facial hair? She tried to imagine him without it, but gave up when all that came to mind was the image of another man, taller, straighter, with a dimpled chin, a man she would never see again, a man who had touched a chord in her emotions that had never had the chance to develop.

'It is not courage, it is necessity,' she said. 'The vineyards must be made to flourish again, it needs only a little ingenuity and hard work.'

'You cannot do it alone.'

'I am not alone. I have my family.'

'Yes, I have noticed how affectionate they are and how ready to share the work with you,' he said with studied irony.

She smiled suddenly and he was reminded of the girl she had once been, carefree and loved. Who was there to love her now besides himself? He was certain James did not. His anger at the man darkened his eyes for a moment and his expression became grim.

'We have to get to know each other,' she went on. 'You cannot blame them for mistrusting me.'

'Your loyalty does you credit. But what about Monsieur Stewart?'

'What about him?'

'Are you still going to marry him?'

She looked at him sharply, wondering what had prompted the question. 'Of course.'

'Because you love him or because you see no alternative?'

She did not answer, but he seemed unperturbed. 'Why have you not married him before now?'

'It is none of your business.'

'No more it is, but it seems a strange way to go on. You have come all the way from England and halfway across France with him. Surely his protection would be more effective if you were married?'

'His protection!' Her lovely mouth twitched into a hint of a smile, proving that, through all her troubles, she had not lost her sense of humour. 'I sometimes wonder who is protecting whom and why.'

'You have a point,' he said, glad that she did not seem as enamoured of James as he had feared. 'Without you, Henri or Jean might turn him over to the authorities as a spy.'

'That's nonsense and you know it.'

'Oh, come, *mam'selle*', think about it. He says he is Scots and he has a letter supposedly signed by Bonaparte himself. He claims to be the Emperor's agent. Either that is true and he is a traitor to the country where he was born, or it is false and he is playing a very dangerous game of counter-intelligence. Which is it?'

She decided against telling him she thought the letter was a forgery. 'I think he is more interested in treasure than in spying,' she said.

'Oh, I do not doubt that,' he said amiably. Her answers convinced him she did not know the truth. What he could not decide was if she was safer not knowing. On the whole, he thought she was. Her safety was paramount. His mission for the British Government was becoming insignificant beside that, although he could not afford to neglect it altogether. 'But have you wondered what he will do if there is no treasure?'

She did not dare tell him that she hoped James would keep his promise to take her back to England, though that was becoming increasingly unlikely. 'I have no idea.'

'If he has been wasting his time here when he should have been elsewhere doing whatever he came to France to do, then his masters, whoever they are, will not be pleased. They will seek to punish him. Have you thought of that?'

'Would you denounce him?'

'To whom? If he is working for Napoleon, I, a French soldier, can have no quarrel with him, can I?'

She got up to fetch a broom from the cupboard and began sweeping the floor, sending up a cloud of dust and cursing herself for a gullible fool. He wasn't interested in her, after all, he had simply been trying to find out what he could about James. She had been deceived once again by soft words.

She told herself she wasn't very good at judging the characters of men. Her father, James, Mr Devonshire, Pierre and now Captain Devereux, she had misjudged them all.

He could say no more because they were interrupted by Jean coming in and demanding his dinner, and no further opportunity for private discourse came their way. Her relatives did not trust her and were afraid she might be telling him things she had not told them and so they rarely left them alone together. Whether she would have told him more or learned any more about him if they had continued the conversation she did not know. But he had set her thinking.

If James was a spy, who was he working for? He had told the Caronnes that he was sympathetic to France, but what if he had been sent by the British government, even by her father, to gather information? Until the captain had started to question her, she had been so wrapped up in her own problems, she had not given it a thought. Now he was making her think.

She could not believe that a Martindale, a nephew of an English peer with an impeccable reputation, could ever be a traitor. It was easier to think of him as a patriot and the more she thought about it, the more the facts fitted that conjecture.

But all this business of spying and counter-spying was doing nothing to help her confused emotions. She was, she realised, a pawn in their game and she was expendable.

If only there was someone she could trust, someone to confide in, to lean on. Someone who could put everything right. But that was asking too much of anyone, especially Captain Devereux; however, occasionally she caught him looking at her from across a room and then his mouth would lift in a faint smile and his eyes convey a kind of empathy, as if they shared a secret.

She spent some time cleaning the château and when that was done, started on the upper slopes of the vineyard, clearing the weeds that strangled the vines. It was a far more productive exercise than yearning for what she could not have or looking for treasure.

'It is a waste of time,' James said, one morning when they were having breakfast. So far, only he and the captain had put in an appearance; the rest of the family were still abed, though she could hear Gerard out in the yard clucking at the hens as he fed them.

'Those vines will never amount to anything, they have been neglected too long. You'd have to grub them out and start again. And where's the money coming from to buy fresh rootstock? Unless you think there is a cache of gold buried out there on the slopes.'

'Oh, for pity's sake, can't you forget about gold and jewels and buried treasure for two minutes together?' she demanded in English. 'It would be more to the point to try and do something to make the château pay.'

'I know nothing about wine-making and neither do you.'

'We could learn. And if you don't want to do that,

do something about the house, it is falling down about our ears.'

'No, why should I? As soon as we find what we're looking for, we'll be leaving, you know that.'

Juliette became aware of the captain watching them from beneath his beetle brows and wondered if he understood English, but Jean and Anne-Marie came into the room before she could put him to the test. Jean sat down at the table and poured wine for himself from the carafe, while Anne-Marie fetched a pan and eggs from the cupboard to cook his breakfast.

'What were you saying?' Jean demanded, picking up his knife and fork in readiness. 'Speak French, why can't you?'

'I was talking of organising a new search,' James said. 'I might have overlooked something.'

'We have already looked everywhere,' Anne-Marie said, putting a plate of fried eggs in front of her husband and ignoring everyone else who had to make do with bread. 'If the little vixen does not come up with some ideas soon, we shall turn her over to the town mayor, see what he makes of her.'

'I heard her telling the Englishman she thought there was a cache buried on the upper terrace,' Philippe said, tearing at a piece of bread and spreading it liberally with butter from a crock on the table. 'It is why she has been working there.'

'Is that so?' Jean mumbled, egg yolk running down his chin.

'Yes. Something her foster parents said about a map.'

'A map!' Jean stood up and waved a fork at Juliette. 'You never said anything about a map.'

'There is no map,' she said. 'The captain made it up.'

'Now, why should I do that?' he queried. 'I have no reason to lie. I am simply an onlooker. Tell them where you were digging yesterday and save us all a lot of trouble.'

She could not understand what he was playing at. No mention had ever been made of a map and no one had thought of digging outside until James had taunted her with it that morning. The captain might have imagined he understood something of what they had been saying in English, but if he had, he was far off the mark. 'It is nothing to do with you,' she said. 'Shouldn't you be leaving to rejoin your regiment?'

'Oh, but I am disposed to help in the search—for a consideration, of course.'

'You had better get on with it then. I wash my hands of it.' She had been avoiding his eye, but now she turned to look at him and wished she had not. He was smiling in that lop-sided way of his, which stretched the scar on his face and pulled the side of one eye down, but the eyes themselves were clear and bright.

It was almost as if he were saying, 'You cannot hide from me, I can read your thoughts.' He made her feel weak when it was imperative she should appear self-assured. She stood up and began clearing the table. 'I have better things to do with my time.'

'I know where she was digging,' Jean said, then turning to James, 'Come on and bring a spade.' And to the captain, 'You keep an eye on her. She's tricky, is that one. And tell the old man to join us when he decides to put in an appearance.'

'I never heard of a map,' James complained irritably, as he got up to follow. 'She would have told me...'

'You are a sly one,' Anne-Marie said, addressing

Juliette. 'Thought you could deceive us all, did you?'

'This is a madhouse.' Juliette took her shawl from the hook on the back of the door. 'I am going for a walk.'

'Then I shall accompany you,' the captain said, getting to his feet.

She turned back to him. 'I prefer to be alone.'

'Can't allow it. Jean said not to let you out of my sight.'

She did not favour him with an answer but left the château and made for the pine-clad hills behind it. She knew he was following her but pretended to ignore him. It was all too silly for words and if she had not felt so homesick and miserable she would have laughed. As if she knew the location of precious jewels! As if she had anywhere to go if she left!

'Where are you going?' he asked, coming alongside her.

'Nowhere.' Determined not to let him see into her face, she continued to look straight ahead, though she was all too aware of him beside her, matching her stride with his own. 'Anywhere, away from those people.'

'But they are your family, you told me so yourself not a week ago. And James will soon be your husband. Or have you changed your mind about that?'

She did not answer and he went on, very softly, so as not to startle her. 'Do you regret promising yourself to him, little one?'

She turned to look at him, wondering what had prompted the question. From beneath those heavy brows, his eyes were probing hers, gently, inviting confidences. She opened her mouth to answer him and then closed it again. She must be on her guard, always on her guard.

'If you were going to offer an alternative, Captain, I should save your breath. I have no wish to become a camp follower. I assume they have such things in the French army as well as the English.'

He laughed. 'Yes, they do, but what gave you the idea that I was about to suggest such a thing?'

'Weren't you?'

'Supposing you do find valuables, what then?' he prompted, ignoring her question. 'Do you imagine Henri and Jean will allow you to keep them?'

'No doubt you expect your share,' she snapped. 'It is why you stayed.'

'I have made no secret of it.'

'Then why aren't you down there, helping them to dig?'

He laughed. 'You and I both know there is nothing there, don't we?'

'Why did you tell that silly story about a map?' she demanded. 'I never mentioned one. I have only been working on the vines to pass the time and do something useful.'

He chuckled. 'It is one way to have the weeding done for you, isn't it?'

In spite of everything she laughed. 'Yes, but now I suppose you are going to ask me where the jewels really are? It was a trick to gain my confidence.'

'Of course.' He was maddeningly self-assured.

'You have been wasting your time. I do not know the whereabouts of any jewels. If there ever were any.'

'Oh, I think there must have been. The *comte* was a wealthy man before the Revolution; he would have showered his wife with jewels and there would have been family heirlooms like that pendant.'

'What do you know of that?' she demanded.

'I have seen the portrait.'

She was instantly alert. 'When? Where?'

He cursed himself for his slip, then recovered quickly. 'Here, at the château, before the war, where else?'

'Oh, you mean the one of my grandmother?'

'Yes. It showed the jewels clearly enough. If they are not here, where have they all gone?'

'I do not know. If the pendant was broken up, it was surely done to make it more easily concealed. The *comte* and *comtesse* would have tried to take any valuables with them, probably hidden in their clothing, to help them to escape or to bribe a gaoler. And wasn't it common practice to give something to the executioner to ensure, a quick and merciful death? What was not used would have been found by those disposing of the bodies. They could be anywhere by now.'

'I should keep that notion to yourself,' he said quietly, jerking his head towards the slope where Jean and Anne-Marie were helping James to dig. 'While they continue to search, you are safe. But if Henri, or more particularly Jean, were to conclude there is nothing to find, you would be in great danger.'

She turned to look at him, wondering why she had told him what was in her mind. Had she been won over by a soft voice? How foolish of her! He could relay their conversation to the others whenever he felt like it. 'No doubt you are going to tell them?'

'No, why should I? Your family squabbles are of no interest to me. I am a simple soldier.'

'Then why risk a charge of desertion by staying here?'

'You would like me to leave?' His steps had slowed and now he stopped and turned towards her.

'I. . .' She stopped speaking, not knowing how to go on. She could hardly tell him that she wanted him to stay and protect her. The idea that he might do so was so absurd as to be laughable, but there was something about him, something she could not quite pinpoint, that told her she could trust him. Or was she simply grasping at straws? 'It is a matter of indifference to me what you do,' she said stiffly.

'Is that so?' There was a hint of amusement in his voice. 'Now, do you know, I had thought you might wish to escape from here, that I might be of some service. . .'

She stared at him. There was an expression on his face she could not fathom. And the message in his eyes was confusing too. There was softness there along with a steeliness that told her he did not easily bend, warmth with a cool appraisal, as if he would never let his feelings run away with him.

'This is my home and the Caronnes are my family,' she said, trying not to let her agitation show. 'Jewels or no jewels, we have to learn to live together in peace.'

'Peace,' he said, his voice so gentle, it was almost a caress. 'Now, there's a word to savour. It cannot come too soon for me.'

He had surprised her once again and she did not bother to hide it. It was strange how his moods changed so quickly. One minute he was harsh, laughing at her discomfiture, making drunken jokes at her expense, the next he was behaving like a true gentleman. He came from a good family so perhaps it was soldiering that had coarsened him.

'But you are a soldier,' she said. 'You are paid to fight. What will you do when the war ends?'

'Go home, if I am spared.'

'Are you married?'

'No, *mam'selle*. I could not ask anyone to share the life I lead.'

'But after the war is over?'

'I prefer not to think too much about the future,' he said evasively. 'It is too precarious. I try to live each day as it comes.'

'Yes,' she said. She had been striving to do that ever since she came to Hautvigne. 'It is the same for me.'

They walked on in silence, broken only by the crunching sound of the pine needles that carpeted the ground under their feet.

'Tell me about the man who brought you up,' he urged her, after several minutes had passed. If he could get her to relax and talk about her feelings, then that bleak look in her eyes would disappear and she might return to being the young innocent he had first met only a few short months ago.

But no, he told himself, she would never be that again. Already she had matured beyond her years, but that only increased his awareness of her as a desirable woman, the woman he loved above life itself.

'I led a very sheltered life as a child,' she said. 'Though I do not think I was spoiled.' She smiled ruefully. 'Well, perhaps a little. I wanted for nothing. And then. . .'

'You discovered you were the daughter of a French

nobleman and not of the man you had always thought
of as your father?'

Her cheeks flamed. She could not tell him the whole
truth, she really could not. Her bastardy was too shame-
ful to put into words. He watched her struggling with
her emotions and longed to help her, to tell her the real
truth. But that would mean revealing his identity, and
until they were safely out of France, he could not do
that. He had to make her trust him as he was.

'He was everything a father should be, generous and
caring. I remember how he sat with me when I had a
fever, telling me I would soon be well, and of course
I was. And when one of the horses was injured in a
hunting accident and had to be put down, he explained
that it had not suffered, and I believed him. I believed
everything he said, so you see the real blow when it
came, was doubly difficult to understand. . .'

'Perhaps he had his reasons for withholding the truth
from you,' he said, as if he could read her thoughts.
'Did you ask him?'

Already the resentment she had been harbouring
against her father was melting away. What had been a
furious rage at what he had done to her, now seemed
a fit of childish pique because he had kept the truth
from her. And it was this strange Frenchman who was
such a mixture of uncouthness and gentle understanding
who had wrought the change in her.

'No. I never spoke to him after. . .' She stopped and
the tears she had been valiantly holding in check,
tumbled down her cheeks.

He brought a surprisingly clean handkerchief from
his pocket and handed it to her. 'It does not always do
to keep things bottled up,' he said, longing to take her

in his arms and comfort her. 'The English do it all the time, but we French are more volatile, *n'est-ce pas?*'

She sniffed and mopped her face. 'I'm sorry.'

'Please don't apologise. There is no shame in having feelings.'

'No, but when the feelings are of guilt, it is a different matter. I wish I could tell Papa how sorry I am.'

'Perhaps one day, you will. When this dreadful war is over. Do not lose heart.'

She smiled wanly and handed back his handkerchief. 'It is the only thing that keeps me sane. I think I would go mad otherwise.'

'Oh, you will not go mad, *mam'selle,*' he said. 'You have too much courage for that.'

'Thank you.' For a moment she had forgotten she was speaking to a French soldier and should really have been more circumspect. He had managed to make her disregard that and talk to him as a friend. And how badly she needed a friend!

Could he do it? Could he obey his orders and deliver Juliette to safety at the same time? How far had the British advance come? How far behind him was Michel Clavier? He fingered the scar on his cheek. It was fading a little each day, but the major would recognise his own handiwork if they ever came face to face again and it was still too sore to be easily disguised.

'Juliette. . .' He turned and took her face in his hands and tilted it up so that he could look into her eyes. He wanted her to trust him, but he also needed to know that he could trust her. Had the time come to speak? 'Juliette, I. . .'

'So that's what the pair of you are up to, is it?'

Henri's voice startled them. 'Watch over her, we said, not ravish her.'

The captain had heard the voice, Juliette knew that by the involuntary tightening of his fingers, but he did not turn towards the sound, nor allow her to do so. She was forced to continue looking into his face while all the time wondering what Henri was doing behind them. Was there anyone else with him, creeping up, about to pounce?

Without warning, the captain laughed, enveloped her in a great bear hug of an embrace and kissed her. It was not a gentle kiss. His lips bruised hers and his hands roamed down her back and grasped her bottom. She struggled to free herself and he threw back his head and bellowed with coarse laughter.

'Henri, I *am* watching over her, can't you see? I was about to watch a little more of her when you so rudely interrupted. Go away, can't you?'

'No!' Juliette screamed, realising how foolish she had been to relax her guard. 'Get him off me!'

'Let her be,' growled Henri. 'You are abusing our hospitality. If you want a woman, go into Hautvigne, get yourself a whore.'

Philippe let her go and she dashed from him and along the path back to the house. He watched her go, cursing roundly in French. The moment for speaking had passed and she would not allow herself to be alone with him again.

'I beg pardon, *monsieur*,' he said. 'For a moment I forgot she was your kin, but you must admit she is a tempting morsel. She has fire in plenty and I like that.' They turned to go back, walking amiably side by side. 'Have you found anything?'

'No. I doubt there is anything to find, but Jean does not agree. For twenty years he has been hoping, ever since he married my daughter. . .' He shrugged. 'Me, I gave up long ago.'

'But the arrival of the Englishman and the woman set you all off again. Do you believe she is really Juliette Caronne?'

'If she isn't, she is remarkably like her. You knew the family, don't you think so?'

'Yes, I do. That delicate complexion and those huge expressive eyes and the shape of the brows, like little wings, are all Caronne features.'

Henri laughed suddenly. 'So that is what you were studying so intently when I came upon you.'

Philippe laughed. '*Touché, mon vieux.*' He paused. 'But what of the man? Do you think he is a spy?'

'Who knows? But he does have that letter with the royal crest at its head and the Emperor's signature at its foot. That cannot be easy to forge.'

They had just emerged from the trees and could see the digging party, still busy on the slopes. 'I should like a look at that letter,' Philippe said cautiously. 'Where does he keep it?'

'On his person, you can be sure.'

'Then I must think of a way to relieve him of it.'

'Shouldn't be difficult. He's more often drunk than sober. A little more wine than usual, a little added laudanum and he'll sleep like a babe.'

Juliette was disgusted with them. They were all drunk, even Anne-Marie, laughing and making lewd jests that sickened her. Dinner had been over for hours and yet they still sat round the table, passing the wine bottles round and then ordering her to fetch more.

She hated them all, she told herself, as she went down the cellar steps with a lantern in her hand, but most of all she hated Captain Philippe Devereux, simply because she had allowed herself to trust him, had melted under those probing eyes and confided in him. He was worse than the others because they did nothing to hide their animosity, but he had lulled her into thinking . . .

What had she thought? That he might rescue her, take her away? But where could he take her except to the battlefield? How foolish she was being!

The cellar was icy cold and she shivered as she reached the bottom stair and made her way slowly between the racks to where the last of the wine was stored. There was very little left now and she dreaded the day when James discovered it was all gone. James. Why had the captain been questioning her so closely about him? Was he suspicious? Ought she to warn James?

She reached the end of the cellar where the last of the wine bottles were kept and pulled two from the rack, only to discover they were not complete bottles, but the cut-off tops, complete with corks. At first she assumed that one of the workers, in that last year before The Terror, had been cheating the owners by stealing the wine and leaving these half bottles in their place, but then bottles filled with water would have done the same job.

However, when she put them back and wriggled them, they went no further in than the full bottles. She took them out again, reached into the back of the rack and her fingers closed round a small box about nine inches square. She pulled it out. Holding the candle above it, she brushed off the accumulation of years of dust and noticed it was intricately carved and inlaid with gold and mother-of-pearl.

She put the candle down so that she could open it, holding her breath in anticipation. If this was what everyone had been seeking, she held the future of the Caronne family in her hands.

The catch and hinges were stiff, but it was not locked. Lifting the candle again she peered inside, but all it contained was a scrap of parchment, a signet ring and a few tiny pieces of broken metal, which she thought might be silver, and a small blue stone. She knew, with sinking heart, that this was all that was left of the Caronne wealth, this and the ruby she carried in the pocket under her petticoat. It was a dangerous discovery.

Quickly she pushed it all back and replaced the half bottles before loading herself with full ones and returning upstairs. Later she would have to retrieve it because when she told Henri the cellars contained no more wine, he would come to down to see for himself and the hiding place would be found.

'Where've you been?' Jean grumbled.

'They were difficult to find in the dark.'

'Frightened of ghosts, are you? Afraid the spectres of the *comte* and *comtesse* might come to haunt you?'

'Why should they haunt the cellars?' she asked, her pulse quickening. She caught sight of the captain looking at her and it seemed to her that he was nothing like as drunk as the rest of them. James was the worst. He had already passed out with his head on the table among the dirty plates.

Jean seized the bottles from her and began opening

them. She went to shake James, but he did nothing but mumble incoherently.

'Let him be,' Henri said. 'I've no time for men who can't hold a bottle or two of wine.'

The captain got to his feet and ambled over to James. 'He's past caring. Shall we take him to bed, Countess?'

'You do what you like,' she snapped. 'I am going to my own room.'

She left them and, though aware that the captain had hauled James over his shoulder and was climbing the stairs behind her, she ignored him. Once in her room, she locked the door. The situation was getting worse and worse. James was useless and now she was sure there were no hidden jewels, their plight was precarious.

How much did Captain Devereux know? His questions about James had been very probing, as if he knew half the truth and needed to know it all. If only there was someone she could confide in, someone to advise her. Her idea that the captain might be a friend had turned out to be no more than fantasy.

She undressed and went to bed, discarding one plan after another until, from sheer exhaustion, she fell asleep. She did not hear the others rolling drunkenly to their beds, or the cock crow, nor the sound of a horse leaving at dawn. She did not know the captain had gone until she went down to breakfast at nine o'clock.

His departure left a void she would never have believed possible. In spite of his rough ways and watchful eyes, he had been someone she could talk to, someone who seemed to understand a little of what she felt, who had acted as a kind of buffer between her and the others.

And though he was a French soldier, he had been,

in some strange way, a link between her and all she held dear in England, perhaps because he encouraged her to talk about it, and James never did.

And now there was no one but James and he was incoherent because the captain had stolen that vital letter. Without it he was lost, an enemy of the country, a spy. At the mercy of the Caronnes, he dare not move from the château, not even as far as Hautvigne. 'We can't leave now,' he raged at Juliette.

They were alone in the kitchen; the others were sleeping off the excesses of the night before. 'We are stuck here for the rest of our lives. If I ever come face to face with that thieving bastard again, he'll wish he had never been born.'

'Why would he want it?'

'He's a deserter, isn't he? It would help him to go wherever he wanted to go. And it wasn't only the letter, he took other things. . .'

'What other things?' Whatever else he was, she did not want to believe the captain was a common thief.

'Papers, important documents. In the wrong hands they could be the end of us both.' He looked hard at her. 'You talked to him, did he tell you where he was going?'

'No. Why would he say anything to me?' She got up to fetch more bread from the crock in the bottom of the larder, bringing it back to the table to cut.

'I wonder. . .' He scratched the stubble which darkened his chin. 'Perhaps he found the jewels and made off with them. . .'

'That's nonsense and you know it. There is nothing to find.'

Something in her voice made him look up at her.

'You do know something!' He stood up and grabbed her arms. 'He has taken the spoils along with my belongings and you are going to meet him later and go off with him. That's it, isn't it?'

'Now, you are being fanciful. What interest could I possibly have in a French deserter?'

'You had your heads together often enough, even if he did pretend to treat you roughly. When you were alone with him, it was different, wasn't it? God, what fools we have all been!'

'You are gone mad!' she said, realising suddenly that he was right; the captain had only behaved badly when there were witnesses. He had been pretending, but not for the reasons James imagined. Then why? What had he been going to say when Henri interrupted them among the pine trees? 'I have no idea where Captain Devereux has gone,' she said. 'But I do know where the jewels were hidden.'

He stood and stared at her for a very long time, as if he dare not trust his ears. 'You do? Where are they?'

'I do not know. I said I knew where they were. They have gone.'

'Show me. Show me at once.'

She led him down to the cellar and pulled out the box. He grabbed it from her and opened it. His disappointment was so profound, she thought he was going to have a seizure. 'All for nothing,' he muttered, poking in the box with a finger that shook visibly. 'I gambled and lost. Lost everything. My country, Hartlea, my reputation, everything gone.'

She was puzzled. 'I cannot see that anything is different. Finding jewels here was always a long shot. You can still do whatever it was you came to France to do, can't you?'

'What are you talking about, woman?' he demanded.

'You work for British Intelligence, don't you?'

'British Intelligence?' he queried, then burst into raucous laughter.

'What is so funny?'

'Nothing.' He wiped the tears from his face. 'But how did you guess?'

She decided not to say anything of her conversation with Captain Devereux on the subject. 'There was always something strange about the way you arrived on that fishing boat, and meeting that man, Michel Clavier, in Richmond Park. I put two and two together. It was why you could not take me straight back to England when we landed, wasn't it? You had important work to do.

'That's why you brought me here, to be safe. Your search for jewels and your drunkenness were all part of your playacting to convince my cousins. As soon as you had completed your mission, we would return to England and a grateful government.'

'How clever of you!'

She did not detect the note of irony in his voice or, if she did, chose to ignore it. 'But I am tired of it all, James. When will it end? When can we go back?'

'When I have done what I have to do,' he said, shutting the box with a snap. 'But without the Emperor's letter, it will be nigh on impossible. Are you sure you have no idea where the captain was heading?'

'No.'

'He can't have gone far.' He thrust the box into her hands. 'Hide this in your room and say nothing to anyone else about finding it. I am going after him.'

He rushed along the lines of empty wine racks and disappeared up the cellar steps, leaving her to hide the box beneath her apron and make her way to her room and conceal it among her clothes. Now she really was alone and she dreaded to think of the outcome of a confrontation between James and the captain.

It reminded her of the duel that never took place, but this time there was no opportunity to intervene. That escapade had been less than three months before, but it seemed like a lifetime and a whole world away. Would James's opponent thwart him again? Deep inside her, so deep she was hardly aware of it herself, she hoped he would.

His tall figure, with its slight stoop, his rugged face, particularly his dark eyes, were engraved in her memory, just as Philip Devonshire's had once been. Sometimes one was overlaid with the other and made her more confused than ever. And again and again her thoughts turned to that last walk with him.

He had gone to great lengths to make sure the others were occupied in order to be alone with her. Was it simply that he wanted to kiss her or had he been going to tell her something, something for her ears alone? And it came to her in a flash which took her breath away that he had been going to speak in English. His last word was 'I', not the French '*Je*'.

And then everything fell into place, like the last piece of a puzzle; his sudden arrival, the way he spoke to her when they were alone, encouraging her to open her heart to him, the way he looked at her with those deep, dark eyes, conveying messages she could not read; the smell of his cigar, so evocative of home.

And even when he had kissed her for Henri's benefit, she had felt that same tremor of excitement and yearning she had felt when Philip had kissed her on the terrace on the night of her ball. It was because Philippe *was* Philip!

The similarities between them were not superficial, as she had thought, they went deep, to the character of the man beneath the skin. It was the differences that were on the surface, the reddish hair and untidy beard, the stoop and the scar, all easily contrived, though the scar was real enough.

She had had the man she loved here with her and had not even realised it. How could she have been so blind? Why had he not told her who he was? If only Henri had not interrupted them, he might have explained why he had come and what he meant to do. It could not have been to rescue her because he had gone and with him had gone all her hope.

The stoicism with which she had greeted each day in France, the determination to make the best of it, broke down under this new wave of grief, and she wept despairingly for a love that had been lost for a second time.

Philippe had not really doubted that the letter was genuine, but the rest of the papers certainly confirmed that James's treachery went far deeper than he had realised. In his hand was enough damning evidence to convict James many times over.

Here were state secrets that could be invaluable to Napoleon's beleaguered army; copies of despatches to Lord Wellington in Spain and letters to Prince Metternich of Austria, who had offered to act as mediator to a settlement in Europe, although Napoleon had rebuffed him and Austria had recently entered the war on the side of the allies.

How much more had been transmitted during the three years James had been working at the Horse Guards? Lord Martindale would never have suspected his own nephew and would have been more open than he might otherwise have been.

He had to get the information to the right quarter so that the breach in security could be repaired and nothing like it could happen again. But that meant leaving Juliette and going to Paris. He had toyed with the idea of taking her with him, but rejected it as impractical. While James was still obsessed by his search for treasure, she was in no immediate danger at Hautvigne and he would only be gone a week.

When he returned, he would be able to tell her the truth, but he had to admit to a little feeling of disappointment that she had not guessed who he was, which was illogical when he had taken such pains to conceal it. He would explain how Lord Martindale had rescued her as a baby and then he could take her home. The rest was up to her. He had slipped out of the château at dawn and ridden pell-mell, spurred on by hope.

It had taken him longer than he would have liked to reach the capital, even though his papers were impeccable. Every time he showed them, he had to give an account of how the war was progressing and answer questions about sons and husbands who had gone to fight.

Did he know so and so? Had he met this old woman's son, that man's brother? Were they safe? He fobbed them off with platitudes, but the delay made him fume. The longer he was gone, the longer Juliette was left alone with James Martindale. The man was mad enough to do anything.

'He will have to be stopped,' Martin Reynard said, when given the evidence. He was a portly little man apparently earning a precarious living as a baker in the shadow of the cathedral of Sacre Coeur. Philippe did not know his real name, any more than his was known to the baker. 'He could swing the whole tide of war round again just when we are beginning to smell victory.'

'Yes, I know.'

'Then you know what to do,' Martin said. 'Find him and silence him.'

It was an order Philippe had been dreading and he knew it would be useless to ask to be relieved of the task. The man deserved to die, but Juliette would never understand that. She might even think he had done it to rid himself of a rival and it would always be there between them, an obstacle to their love, even if he tried to keep it from her. He had been living in a fool's paradise if he thought they had any future together.

If he obeyed his orders, and he must do so, then he could not reveal himself to her as Philip Devonshire. The uncouth French captain had to live on.

Martin, unaware of the torment he was suffering, handed him a sealed package. 'Take this despatch to Wellington first. It is vitally important he receives it as soon as possible. There are moves afoot to offer peace, but we must be in an unassailable position before we do so. The further into France his lordship can advance the better.'

He smiled at the man opposite him. The last time he had seen him, he had been dressed as a naval officer and here he was now, a cavalry captain, and a very disreputable-looking one too. 'Whatever you do, do not allow yourself to be captured.'

Philippe took the package and left the shop. Looking carefully about him, he strode off to find his horse, hidden in a stable about half a mile away.

His route to the Spanish border would take him close to Hautvigne and, for once in his life, he intended to interpret his orders freely. Juliette must be taken out of harm's way before any confrontation with James Martindale. He dug his heels in and galloped through the night.

Chapter Nine

The family accepted the disappearance of the captain and James with indifference and tolerated her because they knew, jewels or no jewels, that she was truly Juliette Caronne. They even helped her in the vineyards and showed her how to prune the vines, talking to her of wine-making. The subject of the missing jewels was never raised. Neither did they mention James or the deserter

But Juliette, busy about her self-imposed tasks, could not helping thinking of them, particularly the captain, remembering the soft way he had sometimes looked at her even when he was taunting her, the things he had said. She recalled every word again and again, trying to make sense of it, to see some glimmer of light in the darkness of her despair.

Why had he come to Hautvigne and then gone away again without saying a word? Did he imagine she was happy with James? No, she decided, he was too astute for that. And there was that letter. He must have had good reason for taking it.

Surely he knew he could trust her? Would he come

back? How much danger was he in? Had he come to
France because of her? Then why leave without telling
her so? Her questions plagued her, night and day, but
she could find no answers.

She rose one morning, after a sleepless night, to find
the first frost of the year had touched the pines with
white. It was unusual to have frost so far south, Anne-
Marie told her when she went down to breakfast, though
later in the year it might snow on the mountains, but
there was no sign of snow today and she was glad to
go out and work on the slopes.

The year was drawing to a close and next year, with
luck, they might harvest some worthwhile grapes and
begin wine-making again. And the war might end.

The week before they had learned from a courier
who passed through Hautvigne on his way to Paris
that the British forces had established a toe-hold in the
south-west corner of France, and two weeks later, from
another going in the opposite direction, that Napoleon
had been decisively beaten at Leipzig. The tide of war
had, at last, turned against the dictator and she began
to wonder how long it would be before the allied armies
reached Toulouse, not so many miles to the south.

She remembered her father saying that when the war
ended, France and England would be friends again and
it would be possible to travel freely between the two
countries. When that happened, she might write to him;
he might even visit her, if Lady Martindale allowed it.
She had given up all idea of returning to Hartlea herself;
she had been gone too long.

Besides, how could she leave while Philip was in
France? He was Philip, wasn't he? She had not dreamed

it? The longer he was absent, the more questions she found to ask herself and the more her certainty changed to doubt. If and when he returned, she would be sure, but he had been gone ten days and so had James.

Had James caught up with him and killed him? He had been angry enough. That idea bothered her more than any other; she could not banish it from her mind. 'Lord, keep him safe,' she prayed, as she worked on the slopes, and it was for the enigmatic captain she prayed.

Hearing the sound of horses, she straightened her back and looked out towards the road which led down to the town, almost as if she expected to see him, and caught sight of a troop of cavalry, trotting up the narrow road towards the château. She put down her tools and went to meet them, arriving at the front door just as they came to a halt and Henri came out onto the step.

'We've nothing for you,' the old man said, assuming they were looking for food. 'Everything has already been taken. All we have left are a few scrawny chickens.'

'Rest easy, *mon vieux*, we are not after supplies,' their leader said. The sound of his voice made Juliette look at him more closely. It was Michel Clavier! He was wearing the insignia and red sash of a major of the Old Guard, and behind him, sitting easily in his saddle, was Pierre Veillard. He smiled and gave her a mock bow. 'Ah, *ma petite* Juliette, we meet again.'

Shocked to the core, all she could manage in reply was, 'What are you doing here?'

'What do you think, *mam'selle*?' Michel queried. 'We are looking for that double-crossing English husband of yours.'

Instinctively she moved to stand beside Henri, who had been joined by Jean and Anne-Marie. 'I have no husband.'

He grinned. 'Then we can save you the trouble of becoming a widow.' He pulled some documents from inside his jacket and handed them to Henri. 'I have orders to search the château and arrest James Martindale.'

'James Martindale?' repeated Henri. 'Who is he?'

Michel laughed. 'James Stewart, if you prefer. He has several names, that one. It depends where he is and whom he is trying to deceive. She will tell you.' He nodded at Juliette.

Henri, Jean and Anne-Marie turned in unison to look at her. 'What do you know of this?' Jean demanded.

'Nothing,' she said. Had someone discovered James was a British agent? 'I know nothing, I swear it.'

'Then you will not mind if we search the château,' the major said, making his way up the steps.

Henri, who had been standing in front of the door, moved aside. 'Do as you wish. You will find nothing.'

The men dismounted and crowded into the kitchen, demanding food. Juliette, helping Anne-Marie to serve them, wished they would go. James might come back and she did not relish the thought of what these men would do to him.

'The man left over two weeks ago,' Henri said, hovering over the major, anxious to rid himself of his unwelcome visitors. 'We don't know where. He had a letter. . .'

'Of course he had a letter. An Englishman in France would be courting an early death without one. How could he have done the Emperor's work without *carte blanche*?'

'The Emperor's work?' Juliette echoed, almost dropping the tureen she was carrying.

'*Naturellement*. Did you think he was loyal to King George?' He threw back his head and laughed, making his companions grin.

She did not answer. She was thinking of something the captain had said about James. *If he has been wasting his time here when he should have been elsewhere, then his masters will not be pleased. They will seek to punish him.* He had implied James was working for the French and she had chosen to believe differently. Had she been wrong?

James had agreed with her theory of why he was in France just a shade too readily and his strange laughter still echoed in her mind. And, on reflection, she realised he had not left the château at all until the letter had disappeared, which he would surely have done if he had had intelligence to gather.

His one obsession had been to find the jewels and he had wept with frustration when the box was found to be empty, not the reaction of a man who had been using the search as a cover. But still her mind refused to accept that he was a traitor.

'The devil of a job we have had to track him down,' the major broke in on her muddled thinking. 'If it were not for Lieutenant Veillard, we might never have traced him.'

She looked at Pierre who grinned sheepishly. 'I am sorry, *mam'selle*,' he said. 'I had to do my duty.'

'We are not the only ones looking for him,' Clavier went on. 'There is a certain cavalry captain. He'd have a scar, a new one. We have to get to him first.'

Juliette gasped. She looked across at Michel Clavier, whose lips were curled in a cruel grin.

'This captain,' she ventured, piling the major's plate with chicken, though her hands were shaking so much she thought they could not fail to notice. 'Who is he?'

Major Clavier, pulling the chicken apart with grubby hands, shrugged. 'We don't know his real name. We only know he is a thorn in our side, a snake in the grass, who creeps about in the dark and disappears when daylight comes. But if he is after our young English friend, then we must find him first. I have a fancy to end this war at home with a nice fat pension. This we have been promised.'

'There was a cavalry captain here,' Anne-Marie said, because Juliette had been struck dumb. She forced herself to pay attention as Anne-Marie continued. 'If we had known, we would have thought of a way of detaining both men, but we were glad to see them go.'

'No matter, we will find them,' he said, reaching out for a bottle of wine and tipping it up to his mouth.

As soon as they had disposed of everything that was eatable and drunk the very last bottle of wine, they began a systematic search of the château, not bothering to hide their frustration when they realised there was nothing to loot, not even a few bottles of wine, for the last of those stood on the kitchen table, or valuables in the form of jewellery.

The inlaid box they found among Juliette's possessions, but its contents were more than disappointing. And Henri, seeing it, laughed himself into hysterics. When they had satisfied themselves that neither James nor the captain were hiding in the house, they began on the outbuildings, but that search, too, proved fruitless.

'No matter,' Clavier said. 'We'll take the girl with us. She will be better than nothing and we will soon have her chattering like a magpie.'

'But why?' Juliette protested. 'I have done nothing wrong.'

They ignored her protests and ordered Anne-Marie to accompany her to her room and watch over her as she packed her few clothes in her old cloakbag. Half an hour later, she was put on Henri's old donkey and led away.

It was very uncomfortable riding the donkey with her hands tied and several times she thought she would fall off. By concentrating hard on keeping her balance, she stayed in the saddle, but it left her little time to dwell on her predicament, or her surroundings.

After a few miles they came to a river and followed its line through beautiful rugged scenery, with the sun at their backs, which meant, she concluded, that they were moving in a northerly direction, but it was not until they stopped for the night that she began to wonder where they were taking her and what they meant to do with her. They would not tell her when she asked.

They made camp in a clearing in a wooded area near the banks of the river, tethering the horses on a line strung between two trees and then building a fire to cook a meal. Juliette was glad of the fire because it was very cold and growing colder, and she sat on the ground as close to it as was safe. She ought to have been glad of the food, but it was an unappetising stew and tasted dreadful. She pushed the tin plate away. 'I'm not hungry.'

'Eat it,' Michel commanded. 'You'll get no more.

Food is scarce, had you not noticed? Everything is scarce.'

'It's the war,' Pierre added, almost apologetically. 'It has been going on too long. Nothing is left, no food, no weapons, no men.'

'No pay either,' someone else put in.

'Then why go on fighting?' she asked.

'What would you have us do?' another demanded. 'Give up? Or turn traitor like that slimy Englishman?'

'No.' She did not want to talk about James, traitor or patriot, for fear of doing irreparable damage to the allied cause. Her heart was English, as English as Lord Martindale's, whatever else she pretended.

'Where is he?' Pierre asked. 'If you told us that, we might let you go?'

'Who?'

'Martindale, of course. He promised information, reliable information, enough to turn the tide of war in our favour. He should have handed it over when he came on board the fishing boat at Lowestoft but when he found you he changed his mind. He said it was too important to trust to a courier and he was going to deliver it personally.' He grinned suddenly. 'He thought he could have the jewels and his pay.'

'Traitors, I spit on them all!' Michel said, suiting action to words and only just missing Juliette's skirt.

She hitched herself a little further away and spoke to Pierre. He seemed a little more civilised than the others. 'It was your idea for me to come to France. You arranged it.'

'So I did, but how was I to know our contact was your husband-to-be? I did not even know his name. I would never have brought you if I had. What is the

English expression, set the cat among the pigeons? That is what I did.'

'We need the information he brought to France with him,' the major said. 'And we need the man who followed him. I nearly had him once, but he's as slippery as an eel. Slid through my fingers, though I did mark him.'

She knew they were talking about Captain Devereux. Did they know who he really was? She thought it wiser not to ask. Instead, she said, 'But I am a loyal citizen of France, just as you are, though I was kept in ignorance of it until this year, just as I was ignorant of what James was doing.'

'Maybe,' Michel said. 'Maybe not. We shall soon see. Now get some sleep, all of you. We move on at dawn.' He went over to the line of horses and pulled a blanket roll from one of them, which he threw at Juliette's feet. 'Here, wrap yourself in this.'

She stood up and picked it up. It was smelly and dirty, but this was not the time to be fastidious. She dropped it, took up her own bag and set off for the river bank to perform her ablutions, but though they pretended not to look, she knew they were watchful and alert; running away was out of the question. Besides, the water was icy; she did not dally but washed quickly and put her riding breeches on under the old skirt she had been wearing when she left England.

When she returned they were all grinning, but she ignored them and, picking up the blanket, took it to a spot beneath the tree where the horses and donkey were tethered.

'Where do you think you are going?' Clavier demanded.

'Over there. To get a little privacy.'

He laughed. 'You prefer the company of horses to humans, do you?'

'Yes,' she snapped. 'They smell sweeter.'

He laughed again and ordered two of the men to stand watch, then made up the fire and rolled himself in his cloak beside it. Soon all but the sentries and Juliette were asleep.

Her mind was buzzing. Had James really betrayed his country? Was he a traitor or a British double agent? She could not understand how a man like James, heir to a great estate with everything to live for in England, could turn traitor. It was easier to believe he was a patriot. Easier, but was it true?

The more she thought about it, the more doubtful she became. But what did that make Philip? Was he a traitor too? Another escaped prisoner? A French spy? No, that was not possible, given all the years her father had known him. And she loved him. She had to escape before they forced her to talk.

She raised her head to look about her. The guards were talking together on the other side of the clearing. Then they turned and patrolled the perimeter, before retracing their steps.

She watched them make the circuit several times, wishing they would stop on the other side long enough for her to make a run for it, but there was never enough time. A twig snapped among the trees that encircled the clearing, and both guards dashed off towards it. Blessing whoever or whatever had made the noise, she seized her opportunity.

She rose, slung her bag over her shoulder, picked up a saddle from the heap nearby and hoisted it on to the horse Michel had been using, praying the animal would not whinny and alert the sleeping men. She did not notice the sentries return until she became aware of someone moving among the horses; he would reach her in a matter of moments. Having put the saddle on, she undid the rope that tethered all the horses and took hold of the reins. In her haste, she pulled too hard on the bit and the horse snorted and pawed the ground. Before she could calm it, someone grabbed her from behind and put a hand over her mouth. She struggled to free herself but he was far too strong for her.

'Don't make a sound.' The words were said in a whisper. 'Not this way, you will rouse them. Walk. Quietly.'

She recognised Philip's voice and suddenly she felt so happy she wanted to laugh and cry at the same time, but she did neither because he did not remove his hand from her mouth as he propelled her between the trees, leading the horse she had saddled.

The others were moving about restlessly as if, discovering they were free, they were uncertain whether to take advantage of it. Still holding her, he picked up a stick and hurled it at the horses. It hit one on the rump and, with a snort of annoyance, it trotted quietly away, followed by the rest. 'That should delay them. Now, if I let you go, will you keep quiet?'

She nodded.

He released her. 'I am sorry if I was rough,' he said, still whispering. 'But if you had simply ridden away, they would have heard you and caught you again immediately. Hurry now.'

He held her arm to help her along and five minutes later they came upon his horse tethered to a tree. He tossed her up in the saddle of Michel's horse, before untying his own and mounting. 'Come on, before they round up their horses and come after us.'

Almost giddy with relief and happiness, she rode out behind him on to a road that ran alongside the wood, sometimes in shadow, sometimes bathed in moonlight. There was no one else to be seen.

'How did you know I was with them?' she asked

'I was returning to the château when I saw them bring you out. I could not let them take you, could I?'

When he spotted the band of mounted soldiers, he had been riding along the rough unsurfaced road from Hautvigne up to the château, wondering how to persuade Juliette that her best hope of safety lay in going with him and whether to tell her he meant to take her to the Spanish border and the British lines or whether it would be safer, for her own sake, to keep her in ignorance.

He could say nothing about his Intelligence role because if they were ever captured, she would be interrogated, probably tortured, and he could not, would not, expect her to withstand that. The despatches he carried could shorten the war and save hundreds, perhaps thousands, of lives on both sides. But he had to protect her; if he allowed anything to happen to her, he would not want to live himself.

They had not seen him and he had lost no time in turning off the road and hiding himself and his horse in a ditch. Peering out, he had watched them ride towards him, six of them with Michel Clavier and Pierre Veillard at their head. And then he saw Juliette on the donkey. Her hands were tied and all her concentration was on trying to stay on its back.

He cursed under his breath, but managed to resist the

impulse to rush out and try to tackle them. He loved her with an intensity that burned in him like an unquenchable fire, but he had to guard against acting rashly for fear of endangering her. And he was only too aware of the despatches he carried and his orders not to allow himself to be taken. And where was James Martindale?

He had curbed his impatience and followed at a safe distance.

'Why not?' she asked.

'Why not?' he repeated and smiled. 'Because you are too young and beautiful to be left to their tender mercies. They have ways of making you say anything that suits their purpose.'

'About you or about James?' she asked, turning in the saddle to look at him. He did not seem half as uncouth as he had when she first set eyes on him, but that was because he was not the rough French captain he pretended to be, but her dearest Philip in disguise and a very clever one at that. Should she tell him she knew or wait until he chose to reveal himself?

'Where is Monsieur Stewart?' he asked.

She laughed suddenly. 'You know that is not his real name, don't you?'

'Do I?'

'Oh, yes. You followed us to France from England. It wasn't simply chance which brought you to Hautvigne.'

'Who told you that?'

'Pierre. He said James was a traitor, that he had used his position at the War Department to gather information. He was supposed to pass it on to someone in the French command, only he went to Hautvigne instead. You have been following him.'

'Do you believe that?'

'I do not know what to believe.' She was thoughtful for a moment. 'Do you remember telling me that if he was a double agent he was playing a very dangerous game?'

'Yes.'

'Perhaps that is the way of it.'

'Perhaps, but if that is so, should you be telling me?'

She smiled suddenly and the moonlight, falling on her face, gave it an ethereal beauty which made him catch his breath. 'Why not? I do not think you are the common soldier you pretend to be,' she said. 'Major Clavier was also very interested in you. He wanted to know where you were. He called you a thorn in his side.'

He laughed and it was Philip's laughter that fell on her ears. 'And what conclusion do you draw from that?'

'You are no Frenchman. I do not think you are Philippe Devereux at all. In fact, I know—'

She had guessed after all! His spirits soared, then plummeted again. If she had said that at Hautvigne, before that ride to Paris and he had been given his orders to dispose of James, he might have admitted the truth and sworn her to secrecy, but now it was too late. Much too late.

'Oh, but I assure you I am, *mam'selle*,' he put in before she could finish. 'I was born and raised in a little village close to Hautvigne, son of Antoine and Marie Devereux. I was not lying when I said my father knew Henri. He was our neighbour before he moved to the château.'

'I don't believe you,' she said. 'I understand you have your reasons for pretending to be someone else—

after all, we are in France—but you do not have to pretend with me.'

'There is no pretence, Countess. If we had time, I could prove it to you.'

'Oh.' She was bitterly disappointed and tears filled her eyes. She blinked hard to stop them falling, but one escaped and ran down her cheek. Ever since she had made the discovery, she had been buoyed up with hope, and now to find that he did not trust her enough to admit his identity, was the cruellest blow of all. But could she be wrong? Could there be two men so much alike? 'You really are French?'

'*Naturellement*, I am,' he said, watching the changing expressions flit across her face, the hope in her lovely eyes change to despair and fill with tears, and he hated himself for his continued deception. 'Did you think differently?'

'I thought. . .' She brushed a hand impatiently over her brimming eyes. How could she have been such a fool? 'Oh, it does not matter what I thought. 'Are you taking me back to Hautvigne?'

'Do you want to go back?'

'No, there is nothing for me there.'

'What about James? You are still betrothed to him, after all, and he will surely return for you and the jewels.'

'Oh, you are as obsessed by hidden treasure as he was,' she retorted angrily.

'No, I do not believe that fairy story,' he said. 'It is twenty years since the *comte* and *comtesse* went to the guillotine and the château has been looted more than once since then. It stood derelict for years until Henri Caronne was given permission to live there. Since then he has searched everywhere for the jewels. It is an open secret.'

'I found them after you left.'

'Did you? Well, I must own myself surprised. What did you find?'

'A box hidden in the cellar. It had nothing in it, except a piece of paper, a single blue stone and some bits of broken silver. Major Clavier has it now, so you see there is no point in returning to Hautvigne.'

'Then we shall have to think of something else,' he said. 'Now save your breath for riding.'

They rode on in tense silence, each immersed in thoughts they could not convey, feelings they dare not express, doubts and uncertainties and the knowledge that each had secrets that could not be told.

'I think we should rest,' he said, when dawn lightened the sky. 'It is dangerous to travel in daylight. Clavier is not a fool. He will guess you are not alone and will organise a search.'

'If you are a loyal Frenchman, then he is surely more interested in James than you.' Her voice was flat, every emotion seemed to have been drained from her.

'Where is James?'

'I told you, I do not know. He went after you to retrieve his letter. Why did you take it?'

'I thought it might be useful.' He would have liked to tell her the real reason, that without that piece of paper and the other documents James Martindale could not do his traitorous work, but to have done so would have revealed where his own loyalty lay. He spotted a shepherd's hut about half a mile away on the slope of a grass-clad hill. 'We will rest there,' he said, turning his horse towards it.

The hut was deserted; the sheep had been taken down to a lower level for the winter. They dismounted and tethered the horses between the hut and the rising ground behind it. He took a haversack and a rolled-up blanket from his saddle and ushered her inside. There was no furniture and it had a strong smell of sheep, but it was shelter from the cold wind. 'Not a palace, but it will do,' he said.

Juliette sat on the floor, leaning against the rough wall, her hands clasped round her knees, her skirt tucked around her feet. 'How long must we stay here?'

'Until dark.'

'Oh.' She could not stifle the little tremor of alarm she felt. To be riding beside him was one thing, but alone in the confines of this isolated hut, was another altogether. What would he do? What did she want him to do? Again she wondered if she was being rescued or whether he had some other reason for taking her. Did he imagine she would lead him to James?

'I am going out to feed and water the horses and make sure we have not been followed,' he said. 'I won't be long.'

He went out. She sat still, listening to him moving about outside, talking soothingly to the horses. If he was not Philip, then who was he? He was not the simple soldier he claimed to be, she was sure of it. The haversack lay just out of her reach. Could it hold the answers to her questions and his identity? She crawled over and pulled it towards her. She had just opened the flap when he returned.

'What are you doing?' he demanded, grabbing the bag and showing for the first time that he could be angry. She felt the colour flood her face and was glad of the gloom in the hut to hide it. 'I. . .I thought you might have some food. If it needs cooking. . .'

'It doesn't,' he said. 'We cannot risk a fire.' He sat beside her and delved into it, producing bread and cheese, cooked chicken legs and a flask of wine. 'You have nothing to fear from me,' he said, softly, laying out the food on a surprisingly clean cloth he had taken from the bag. 'But you must learn to curb your curiosity. It could be dangerous.'

'What would you do to me?'

'Not me, my love,' he said quietly. 'Others. I would not harm a hair of your head.' He smiled and reached out to push a tendril of hair from her face and tuck it behind her ear. His fingers were gentle, the look in his eyes belied his fierce appearance and she found herself trembling, though she was not particularly cold. 'Believe me I have only your safety and happiness at heart.'

'I know.' He was a inscrutable as ever but, in spite of her disappointment, she knew she could trust him.

'Have something to eat,' he said, handing her a chicken leg. 'And then you must rest. We have a long ride ahead of us.'

She gnawed at the bone. It had very little meat on it. 'Where are we going, then?'

'Did I not tell you I was returning to my regiment?'

'I did not believe it. I still don't.'

Maintaining his coolness and self-control was hellishly difficult, especially when she looked at him with those brilliant eyes and asked questions that required him to lie to her. He smiled. 'That is the second time you have doubted my word. If you were a man, I would not let you call me a liar.'

'You would call me out?' She giggled suddenly. 'Pistols at dawn, or would it be rapiers?'

'You would have the choice, being the one challenged.'

'Then I should choose feathers.'

He laughed. 'And tickle me to death. It is good to see you have not lost your sense of humour.'

'How do you know I ever had one?'

'Oh, I guessed,' he said quickly.

'You know, when you laugh, you remind me of Mr Devonshire,' she said, hoping to make him give himself away. 'He had a happy kind of laugh, as if he could always find something amusing in any situation, however serious.'

Must he also cease to laugh? 'And were you in love with him?'

'I am not sure,' she said slowly, unwilling to admit it. 'It seemed as though we had known each other for ever, though it was only a few weeks. We talked about being in love and agreed that it had to be a meeting of souls, a feeling that each could not live without the other. . .'

'And that did not happen?'

'I left before. . .' She smiled, giving her small face a piquancy that tore at his heart. 'You know, you are very like him, except Mr Devonshire was clean-shaven and did not have a scar. He was not a dandy by any means, but he was always impeccably dressed and his manners were exquisite.'

'Ah, I see now. In the depths of your despair, your imagination conjured him up. You transformed a rough and ready rogue of a French soldier into a London dandy.' He fingered his beard and smiled, sorely

tempted to tell her the truth. 'I must be a dreadful
disappointment to you.' He paused. 'War makes ruf-
fians of us all, *chérie*. If this were a London drawing
room instead of a shepherd's hut, I might be shaved
and dressed for the occasion.'

He smiled suddenly, making his eyes twinkle. 'Let
us imagine it, shall we? There is a sofa over there,' he
said, pointing. 'There is a table with chairs about it,
and more chairs against the wall. And above us there
is a crystal chandelier, blazing with light. And there is
an orchestra on a dais, playing a waltz. Can you not
hear it?'

'Oh, yes. And I am the belle of the ball. The eligibles
are all clamouring for me to stand up with them.' He
scrambled to his feet and executed an elegant bow.
'*Mam'selle,* may I have the honour of this dance?'

'Certainly, sir,' she said, offering her hand.

He raised her to her feet, put his hand about her waist
and whirled her round, humming the waltz tune they
had danced to at her come-out ball and for a little while
she was was back in London, wearing the white crêpe
gown of the Goddess of the Hunt. The tiny hut became
filled with glittering lights and the sound of music and
laughter.

'Juliette,' he murmured against her ear and now she
was sure it was Philip and not Philippe who spoke.

The imaginary music faded, the fantasy lights
dimmed, their steps slowed and they found themselves
standing in the middle of the earth floor of a crude
shepherd's hut, holding each other. She looked up into
his eyes, waiting for him to tell her the truth, and was
lost in the depths of them, sucked in and drowned. She
could not look away.

'Juliette,' he said again, savouring her name. Then slowly, so slowly she was not even sure of his intention, his face moved closer to hers, his lips hovered a few inches from her own. She waited, head tilted up to his. He touched her mouth with his, a butterfly touch, and drew back slightly, a question in his eyes.

She wanted him to kiss her, wanted it desperately. She opened her mouth slightly, passing the tip of her tongue across her lips. It was more than he could stand. He began kissing her in earnest, her forehead, her cheeks, the tip of her nose, her throat and finally her mouth.

She clung to him, savouring the shiver of excitement that ran through her from the top of her head down to her toes, now being lifted almost off the ground. And in the pit of her stomach, something stirred, a frisson of elation, of anticipation, of danger, of exquisite joy. She did not care what he called himself; it was enough that he was here with her. Her hands went up behind his head, holding him to her.

He stopped at last and drew back, watching her. Her eyes were almost fever bright, her cheeks were flushed and her hair had tumbled down about her shoulders in a silvery cascade. She ought to have been affronted, but she was not; her head was tilted back, the white arch of her neck inviting more. He could not let it go on, he had to defuse the situation somehow.

'How did I measure up to the impressive Mr Devonshire?' he asked, his smile pulling at the scar on his cheek.

She felt crushed and ashamed and angry too. 'There is no comparison,' she said flatly, resuming her sitting position back against the wall. 'He would not have kissed me like that.'

'Not even if you asked for it?'

'I did not!' she flared.

'No? Not in words, perhaps, but it was there in your eyes. Your eyes will always give you away, *má cherie*.'

She was silent, angrily pummelling her bag to make a pillow. Then she lay down and closed her eyes. If they were shut, then he could not read the longing in them, could he?

He had awakened her womanhood in a way that no one else had. That was why she had clothed him in the mantle of Philip, she decided, to make him more acceptable, more English. But Philip, the Englishman, or Philippe, the French Captain, she knew it was the same man. Had fate been making fun of her, and the reality was not in England but here, in France?

He sat down beside her and covered her with his blanket. 'I am sorry, that was unpardonable of me. Perhaps I am jealous.'

'Jealous?' Her eyes flew open again. 'Of whom?'

'Why, the gentleman in London.'

He was flirting with her, playing a game. She laughed to cover her confusion. 'That is absurd. Mr Devonshire has another love, he told me so.'

'He did?' he queried, puzzled. How had she come by that idea? 'How *ungallante* of him.'

'Oh, it was my fault, I was quizzing him. He said he was in love but could not marry, even though Papa encouraged him to offer for me.'

'Did he? Make an offer, I mean.'

'No, which proves he had another attachment. Unless, of course, he found me unattractive.'

'Never that,' he said. 'You are beautiful, he would have had to be blind not to see it.'

'Oh, what is the point of talking about it? It is all in the past. I must learn to live in the present and the present is here, with you.'

'And I am second best, is that what you mean?'

'No, no, I did not mean that. I meant. . .' She stopped. What had she meant? That she knew there was only one man? If she said that, he would only deny it again. 'Oh, when it comes to flirting, you are a master, aren't you?'

'It takes two to do that.'

'Oh, we are back to that are we? Now who is being *ungallante*?'

'I am sorry,' he said softly. 'That was unforgivable.'

'I am glad you realise it.'

It seemed there was no more to be said. He lay down a foot or so away with his back to her and pulled his cloak about him, pretending to sleep. She hitched herself up against the wall to look down at him. He was right; it did take two and she had wanted him to kiss her. 'Captain,' she said. 'I am sorry too.'

He turned to face her, propping himself on one elbow. 'Don't be. I should have known better than to take advantage of you. I ought to be the strong one.'

'Oh, you are! Immensely strong. And brave. Look how you rescued me.'

'You rescued yourself. It was very resourceful of you.'

'But it was you who thought to scatter the horses.'

'You untied them, so it was easy. Now, go to sleep.'

'Will you sleep?'

'Of course.'

'But you have given me your blanket. Won't you be cold?'

'No.'

'But you would be warmer under the blanket.' She lifted it to allow him to move closer and share it. He put his arm about her and she lay down with her head on his shoulder. It was disgraceful behaviour for a well-bred young lady, but she could not see that the rules of convention were valid in this situation. Besides, she was not a well-bred young lady, she was a love-child, which was a much pleasanter term than bastard.

She could hear his steady heartbeat against her ear, could feel his warm breath on her forehead and felt secure. It was a feeling she had not experienced since her childhood when she had always been protected and cossetted by her papa.

'Am I really such a wanton?' she murmured.

'No, of course not, but you certainly know how to tempt a man.'

'Must I apologise for that too?'

'No, I was trying to find an excuse for my bad behaviour.'

'I think it would be much better if we could always be honest with each other,' she said, remembering that she had not been entirely honest either. He did not know the true story of her birth. That was still an insurmountable obstacle. And so was James. But she did not want to think about him. It would spoil the moment and she wanted to savour it.

'Of course it would,' he said, wishing it could be so. 'Go to sleep, now. When it grows dusk we must move on again.'

'There is too much buzzing in my head, questions,

puzzles, uncertainties, keeping me awake. Tell me about the *comte* and *comtesse*.'

'The *comte* was a wise and good man,' he said slowly. 'He did not deserve to die in that dreadful fashion. He was prepared to adopt the new ways, to share his wealth, but simply because he had a title, he was one of the hated aristos. Someone denounced him. The whole family was arrested and taken to Paris for trial. It was a travesty, as most trials were in those days. They were sentenced to death, the *comte, comtesse*, their son Antoine and even the baby.'

'That was me?'

'Yes, you.'

'How did I escape?'

'I know only what I heard from others who were there. I was only ten years old myself at the time, you understand?'

'Yes, go on.'

He smiled to himself. The opportunity was heaven-sent. Now he could tell the true story without her knowing that it was his lordship himself who had told him. 'You were all being transported in a tumbril, which was how they took the convicts from the prison to the guillotine; it was meant to humiliate them.

'The *comte* and his son, who was the same age as me, stood together in the front of the cart, with the *comtesse* behind them, holding her baby daughter in her arms. There were huge crowds, all pressing in and shouting and being held at bay by the prison escort.

'An English gentleman pushed his way through so that he was walking alongside. He asked your mother to give the child to him and he would take care of her. She handed you over. Of course, it was only rumour and most people did not believe it could have happened that way, but the fact of the matter is that the records show only three executions that morning, not four.'

'Do you believe it?'

'The evidence is in front of my eyes, Juliette. I do not doubt who you are.'

'What was my mother like?'

'Beautiful. Everyone loved her.' The more he told her, the more she realised that he was who he said he was. But accepting that, opened up a whole new set of questions about Philip Devonshire. It was no good asking him because he would never answer them.

'Are you sure she did not know the Englishman? Could she have met him before that day? After all, it is a strange thing to do to give your child away to a stranger.'

'But they were all about to die. It gave you a chance of life, where there was none before.'

'I thought. . .' She stopped. How could she tell him what Lady Martindale had told her? He would be disgusted.

'What did you think?' he asked softly. 'Did you think you were the child of the Englishman?'

She turned startled eyes on him. 'What made you say that?'

'This is where all the questions are leading, isn't it?'

'Then do you know?'

'I have no proof, of course,' he said, picking his words with care. 'But you know you are the image of your grandmother, the *comte*'s own mother, the one whose portrait the lieutenant copied. It was a famous portrait, everyone was talking about it because it was such a good likeness. You, my dear Juliette, are a

Caronne and anyone who tries to tell you differently is either lying or mistaken.'

'Oh.' Why hadn't she thought of that herself? It meant Lord Martindale was not her natural father, but a very brave and benevolent man. As a child she had loved him with an unswerving devotion and believed in his goodness; she should have remembered that instead of condemning him. By running away, she had hurt him dreadfully and subjected him to unfair gossip. 'I wonder, will he ever forgive me?'

'The *comte*?'

'I was thinking of Lord Martindale. But yes, the *comte* too, if he can look down and see me now.'

'I am sure they both do.' He paused, then went on. 'Do you wish to return to England?'

'I thought I did. I longed for it. But now, I am not so sure. Except, of course, I should like to see Papa again.'

Lying in his arms, in the gloom of an animal shelter, with a keen December wind blowing in through the cracks, she realised that it did not matter who she was or what his name was. What mattered was that they loved one another.

'It is difficult to explain,' she said. 'But since I have been in France, I have learned that things are not always black and white, that people are not always what they seem. It is the same sort of thing as you were saying about honour and shame. Friend and foe cannot be decided by national boundaries. On this side of the road, everyone is my friend and on the other, there are only enemies and I must hate them. James, for instance, is no ordinary English aristocrat, might even be my enemy, I have no way of knowing. And you. . .'

'Me?' He affected surprise.

'I believe you are. . .' Whoever he was and whatever he was, made no difference. She would go along with his game of make believe until she discovered why he played it. 'You are my friend.'

'Good. Promise me, that whatever happens, you will always believe that.'

'Why? What is going to happen?'

'Nothing bad, I hope, but one can never tell. Now we have talked enough. Go to sleep.'

She slept, while he lay awake, wondering how much longer he could keep up the pretence. He had been a fool to suggest dancing and an even bigger fool to kiss her, but who could resist such temptation?

There were times when he was sure she had seen through him, when she hinted that she knew him, but others when she appeared to accept what he said. She would not have talked to him about Philip Devonshire if she had truly believed he was the same man. How angry she would be when she finally learned the truth!

But he would not be there when she did; he could not return to England. He had to obey his orders and that meant exile from the land he had thought of as home, ever since, as a confused ten-year-old, he and his mother had landed at Dover with Viscount Martindale. He had better try and keep his distance in future.

Chapter Ten

When Juliette woke, it was dark. He was already up and had fetched water and risked a fire to boil it, so that she could wash. It was another sign of his thoughtfulness, the way he anticipated her needs, but she had long-since ceased to think of him as a coarse soldier. The young men she had met and danced with in London paled into insignificance beside him.

Even her feelings for Philip Devonshire, she told herself, were no more than the immature longings of a schoolgirl. She had grown up.

She had ceased trying to compare the two men. It was as if, losing the first, a kindly Providence had produced a second, alike and yet very different. Philippe was his own man, stronger and yet gentler. Scar and bushy beard, beetle brows and quick temper were infinitely preferable to smooth cheeks and an even smoother tongue. 'I do believe that, under all that hair, you are a gentleman,' she told him.

'Why, thank you, my lady,' he said, executing a mock bow and making her laugh. The sound of her laughter lifted his own spirits and once again he found himself admiring her fortitude. He must not let anything happen to her and the only way of doing that was to part with her. And the prospect of that was breaking his heart.

'Why are you looking so sad?' she asked.

'I am not sad, *chérie*,' he said, forcing himself to smile. 'But we have a long ride ahead of us and cannot afford to dally.'

They ate and drank and left the hut to spend another night in the saddle. They stopped occasionally to rest the horses, but when dawn came, he did not suggest taking shelter as he had done the night before, but plodded on, along the river bank towards Hautvigne.

She wondered if he meant to leave her there after all and what her cousins would say about that. Even knowing she had every right to be there, she did not want to go back, but then they passed through Hautvigne, ignoring the track up to the château, and took the road to Toulouse.

It was strange, but now she was almost sure she was totally French, she felt more English than ever; however their slow, steady progress southwards seemed to preclude a return to England.

The strange thing was that she did not care. She was free of her bonds, free of the hostile atmosphere at the château, free of the constraints that had been forced on her by her place in London society, free to be herself, to love whom she chose. And that was the man who rode beside her.

It was easy to forget the wider implications of a war she hardly understood, when she was riding beside him through the quiet countryside that had not changed in hundreds of years. There were acres of vineyards, boulder-strewn hillsides dotted with sheep, small towns

and even smaller villages, people going about their daily
work, children playing, none of whom spared them
more than a cursory glance. It was like a waking dream,
this steady plod, without destination or meaning.

In late afternoon, when she felt she could go no further,
they reached Toulouse and he pulled up at an inn and
dismounted. 'We'll rest here,' he said as he came to
help her down. She was so stiff and saddle-sore, she
could hardly stand. 'Oh, *ma pauvre*,' he said, putting
his arm about her and helping her indoors, leaving the
ostler to see to the horses. 'I am a hard taskmaster,
am I not?'

She smiled weakly. 'Dreadful.'

He settled her on a sofa then went to arrange accom-
modation and food. He was gone less than two minutes,
but she was almost asleep when he returned. He picked
her up and carried her upstairs behind the innkeeper,
passed through a sitting room into a bedchamber and
put her on the bed. She was half aware of someone
pulling off her boots and covering her and then a blissful
slumber claimed her.

'Sleep, my little one,' he murmured softly. 'Sleep
while you can.'

He returned to the sitting room and the innkeeper
brought food and wine, but he did not wake Juliette.
Rest was more important for her than sustenance at the
moment because they still had a very long way to go
and he meant to be on the road again at dawn the next
morning.

They could make better progress during daylight
hours and, with luck, Clavier and his motley crew were
far enough behind not to be a threat. In any case, there

was something else he could do as an extra safeguard.

He rose and went into the next room. Juliette was sound asleep, her glossy hair cascading over the pillow, one hand flung out, her lips slightly parted. He bent and kissed her forehead. 'Sleep on, my love. I shall not be long.'

He left her and went downstairs, where he instructed the innkeeper to tell her he would be back for supper. On no account was he to allow her to leave. Then he strode off in search of the British agent he knew to be in the town. It was contrary to his orders to contact him except in an emergency, but as far as Philippe was concerned, this was an emergency.

It took him longer than he expected to find his contact. Emile—it was a false name and the only one by which he was known in France—was a very elusive man, which was why he was such a good agent, but he found him just as dusk fell, drinking with his cronies in one of the taverns in a back street.

Philippe was introduced as an old friend, a hero of Salamanca, and was soon made welcome and plied with wine and cognac. It was several hours before they could detach themselves and the moon was riding high by the time they left, staggering down the street, apparently the worse for drink. Once out of sight of their erstwhile companions, Philippe lost no time in telling Emile just what he wanted. If Michel Clavier put in an appearance in the area, he must be dealt with in any way Emile saw fit and if James Martindale showed his face, he must be securely held where he could do no more harm. 'I'll deal with him when I come back,' he said.

'When will that be?'

He shrugged. 'A week, maybe more. I have to deliver

something to the British lines. Do you know where they are?'

'Laying siege to Bayonne, the last I heard.'

'Will it hold out?'

'Not long once Wellington decides to move. You may tell him that the Boney has suffered a resounding defeat at Leipzig. The *Grande Armée* is so depleted he is faced with recruiting schoolboys and old men to carry on the fight.'

'There has been talk of peace terms.'

'The Emperor rejected them. Now there is nothing to stop our troops from carrying on into France. Bayonne will fall.' He smiled. 'After that, who knows? North or east? I hope they make for Toulouse, then I can go home.' He seized the other's hand. 'Good luck, my friend.'

'And to you.'

Philippe hurried back to the inn, where he found Juliette pacing the floor of their sitting room. Without stopping to think, she threw herself into his arms. 'Where have you been? I have been sick with worry. Don't ever do that again.'

He held her a minute, savouring the feel of her body against his, the faint scent of soap about her, then gently disengaged himself. 'I had business to attend to.'

'You could have told me. I thought you had been caught.'

'Caught? By whom? And why?'

'Major Clavier. You have been on edge all the time we have been travelling, looking about you all the time. And you said he would come after us.'

'But that was two days ago,' he said, sinking into a chair. He was weary beyond imagining but there was still a long way to go and he must rest. 'He will have given up by now. After all, he is a soldier, he cannot go chasing off wherever the fancy takes him. He has to obey his orders.'

'And you do not, I collect,' she said sharply.

He laughed. '*Touché, ma chèrie.*'

'Now it is dark, I suppose we must set off again.'

'No, we will go in the morning.'

He opened the door and shouted to the innkeeper to bring food and drink. It was brought promptly and they sat down to a meal such as they had not had in weeks: chicken soup, lamb chops and peaches, washed down with wine.

Afterwards, he escorted her to the door of the bedroom, but he did not follow her inside. Their earlier intimacy had gone; he was not disposed to tease her or flirt with her or even to talk. She was hurt by his apparent change of mood. Oh, how she hated this dreadful war, which made enemies of those you would rather love.

Where, oh, where was it all leading? The long day in the shepherd's hut had apparently been forgotten by him, but she could not forget it. Was that all she would ever have, a memory of such sweetness it hurt, deep inside her, whenever she thought of it. Better not to think at all.

He was already up and dressed, waiting for her in the little sitting room, when she rose next morning. They ate breakfast in silence, each determined to maintain a coolness that was the only way they could control their emotions, and afterwards he escorted her downstairs and out to where the horses had been saddled and were waiting. He helped her into the saddle, mounted himself and they set off again.

They travelled for two days, passing through vineyards, many as neglected as those at Hautvigne, and staying at little inns in the villages, pretending to be husband and wife, though he never took advantage of it, but slept in a chair. Their conversation was desultory; they seemed not to have the energy for the enthusiastic repartee and the sharp riposte which had characterised their exchanges before. They were like strangers, polite, but distant.

She supposed it might have something to do with the fact that they were nearing the fighting. They had been hearing the occasional boom of heavy guns for some hours and the roads were becoming clogged with the traffic of war, soldiers, mounted and on foot, guns on limbers, wagons, carts pulled by mules, women and even children. But they all seemed to be going in the opposite direction.

'Where are we going?' she asked.

'To Bayonne.'

'Why?'

He turned to look at her. 'That is where the lines are drawn.'

'Battle lines?'

'All the lines,' he said. Lines between friend and foe, between life and death, her life and his.

'Supposing I do not want to go?'

'There is no alternative.'

She did not answer, but plodded on beside him, not because she had no choice, but because that was where she wanted to be. Always.

They rode a little and walked a little, dodging patrols

and the remnants of the French army who were retreating to take up new positions. The ground around them was devastated, uprooted trees, broken-down guns, dead horses, deep holes filled with icy water, human bodies, men digging graves. She shuddered. So this was the aftermath of battle.

'It's inhuman.' She whispered, not because there was anyone taking any notice of them but because she felt it was respectful to do so.

'But of the animal kingdom, only humans wage war,' he said.

'It doesn't say much for the human race.'

'No.'

Suddenly they seemed to be alone on a hill overlooking a town. Beyond that was the sea. 'Come on,' he said, turning to look at her. She was exhausted, her hair had lost its sheen and her eyes had lost their sparkle; there was a smudge of dirt on her cheek and her skirt was torn, revealing the much-worn riding breeches.

But she was still smiling, this brave and beautiful love of his. He smiled too, though it was an effort. 'The last two or three miles are always the worst.'

'We are going down there?' She had noticed the flag fluttering from one of the tallest buildings and though it filled her with joy to see it, she was afraid for him, dressed as he was in a French uniform. 'Is that Bayonne?'

'No, it is the harbour of St Jean de Luz. The British command has its headquarters there.'

'We are going home, after all?' Her face lit with joy.

'Not me. You. I will see you safely through the British lines where you will be looked after and sent back to England. Viscount Martindale will welcome you back, I'll stake my all on that. . .'

'But why not you too? You are not the French soldier you pretend to be, I know that, even if you will not admit it, and even if you were, the prison camps are not so bad—there is one very near our home.' She paused, remembering how he had followed the escaped prisoners. 'But then you know that already, don't you? Philip Devonshire left England and Philippe Devereux arrived in France. And don't you dare deny it.'

He was very tempted to admit it, but when he thought of James and what he had to do, he knew nothing had changed. But he could not lie any more. Instead he said, 'We spoke of cowardice and dishonour, remember?'

She had not wanted to remember and she could not see that it had any bearing on the present situation. 'Oh, you make me so angry,' she cried. 'Fighting and killing, hate and revenge, it's all you live for, isn't it? I don't want you dead, I cannot love a corpse.'

'Love, Juliette?'

'Yes, love,' she shouted in English. 'Don't you understand, you buffle-head, I love you.'

He dismounted and ran round to lift her off her horse. He stood with his hands on her arms, looking down into her troubled face. 'Say that again.'

She repeated what she had said in French though she knew he had understood. 'Now, tell me I am shameless.'

He threw back his head and laughed, though his heart was breaking. 'Oh, you are very shameless, my love.' And he kissed her hungrily.

She clung to him, returning kiss for kiss, knowing now that he did love her and that what he was doing, the risks he was taking, were all borne of that love. But she didn't want his sacrifice; she wanted to stay with him. 'Take me with you.'

'No, it's impossible. I love you more than life itself and it is that love which is my greatest danger. Don't you see, my darling, only with you safe among your own people, can I go on and do what I have to do.'

'You love me?' It was the first time he had said the words and her heart sang to hear them.

'How could I not love you? You are everything to me. My life, my whole existence is bound to you. It was ordained from the beginning and will never change, no matter how long we are apart.' He touched her face with gentle fingers. 'But part we must. Please don't make it difficult for me.'

The tears were pouring down her face, though she made no sound. He had said he must be the strong one and he was, but he was asking her to be strong too. She wasn't. She was weak and she needed him. Why couldn't he see that?

He tethered the horses in a ruined barn. 'Horses are like gold,' he said, forcing himself to be practical. 'They will be confiscated if we take them with us and I need them both; riding them alternately will hasten my journey.' Then he took her cloakbag from her saddle and led her by the hand down the hill on to the road into the town.

Juliette found she was shaking, though she could not tell if it were caused by fear or the imminent parting from the man she loved. A figure loomed up in the darkness ahead of them and startled her. She clutched Philippe's hand as the soldier levelled a rifle and shouted, 'Who goes there?'

'Friend!' Philippe responded in English.

'Password?'

Juliette held her breath. 'Bucephalus,' Philippe said. 'And I have a package for old Hooknose.'

'Package, eh? And what might that be?'

He put up the hand which held Juliette's. 'This one.'

'What's so special about her?'

'Take her to Lord Wellington and you will see.'

'Do you think the Peer has nothin' better to do than entertain French whores?'

Juliette saw Philippe's jaw tense and the hand that held hers tightened so that she almost cried out in pain. 'I am English,' she called out. 'My name is Martindale. You have heard of Viscount Martindale? I am his daughter.'

Curiosity overcame him. 'Wait there.'

Juliette watched, with her heart in her mouth, as he disappeared into a building behind him.

'He has gone for the officer of the watch,' Philippe said. 'And I must go.'

'Philippe. . .'

He put two fingers on her lips to silence her. 'Listen, my darling. We must part. It breaks my heart to say it, but there is no alternative. One day, perhaps, when the world is at peace, we shall meet again. But, if we do not, know always that I loved you.'

'Don't say that. Oh, Philippe, don't talk as if this were the end. I cannot bear it.' She clung to him while the tears rolled silently down her cheeks unheeded.

He enfolded her in his arms, stroking the hair back from her forehead and tracing the outline of her face with a gentle finger. 'I need to know you are safe, my love. It is the only way I can go on. Go back to Hartlea, it is where you belong.'

'Do you remember once telling me to wait and you would be back?' she asked.

'Did I?' he said vaguely, though he remembered well enough.

'Yes. Only I didn't wait. I ran away and caused no end of trouble and danger for everyone. But this time I shall wait and pray for an end to all this enmity and carnage. I shall pray every day that you will come safe through and back to me.'

'I cannot ask that of you. You are young, one day you will fall in love and marry someone far more eligible than me. If you think of me at all, think of me with affection, as someone you met, a passing acquaintance with whom you once shared a short journey.'

'Philippe, how can you talk like that? You are not a passing acquaintance, you are my only love. You will be here, in my heart, always.' She pulled herself away from him and delved into her pocket for the ruby in its heart-shaped setting. It had been safely hidden there ever since Major Clavier had searched the chateau. 'Here, take this as a talisman.'

'No.'

'Please, Philippe.' She put it into his hand and closed his fingers over it, attempting to smile. 'Keep it safe, because one day I shall want it back and you with it.'

He took her face in his hands and kissed it, tasting the salt of her tears on his lips and tears sprang to his own eyes. 'Very well. I shall hold it in trust.' She was so absorbed in looking at him, trying to convince him that she meant what she said, she did not hear the sentry returning with the officer, but he did. He released her and turned her to face them. 'Go, my valiant one,' he said, putting her cloakbag into her hand. 'God keep you safe.'

She stood and watched the two men approaching as if in a dream. She knew she ought to walk forward to meet them, but her feet would not carry her. She turned back to the man she loved, but he had gone, melted away into the shadows.

The officer of the watch took her to his colonel, who had made his headquarters in one of the larger houses on the west side of the town, overlooking the little harbour. Here they interrogated her mercilessly, but she had nothing to tell them but the truth.

Unable to make her change her story and admit she was a spy, they took her bag from her to search it and it was then they found the package, clearly addressed to Field Marshal, the Duke of Wellington, Commander in Chief of the British forces.

'Where did you get this?' the officer demanded, holding it under her nose.

'I don't know anything about it. I don't know how it got there.'

'The Frenchie did say something about a package,' murmured the officer who had escorted her. 'We thought the fellow was referring to the girl.'

'Give it here. I'll take it to the Peer. Watch over her and give her something to eat and drink. She looks as though she could do with a good meal.'

He disappeared and by the time Juliette had made an attempt at eating the food they brought her, he had returned, smiling. 'Come with me.'

Five minutes later she was in the presence of the great man and acutely conscious of her unwashed face and torn clothes. But he didn't seem to mind that, as he asked her to be seated.

'Well, Miss Martindale, I have seen some very strange letter carriers in my time, but you are, indeed, the most extraordinary.'

She stared at him. He was not particularly tall, nor was he extravagantly dressed, but he had a commanding presence and a way of looking at those he was talking to as if he knew exactly what they were thinking. He reminded her of Philippe, but then her thoughts were so full of the Frenchman she saw him at every turn. 'Is that all I am, a letter carrier?'

'You think you have been used?'

'Wouldn't you?'

'Then let me reassure you, Miss Martindale, you are infinitely more than a letter carrier. That was my little joke and a very poor one, for which I beg pardon. You have brought me important information that will shorten this war by months. And you have brought me good tidings of one of our country's most trusted agents.'

'Philippe?' she whispered.

He smiled. 'Yes.'

'Why did he not tell me?'

'That would have been a very dangerous thing to do.'

'Yes, I suppose it would.' She paused and lifted her eyes to his. 'But why did he have to go back?'

'His work was not done. It won't be done until this war is at an end.'

'Then I pray it will end soon.'

'Amen to that,' he said. Then, suddenly becoming businesslike, he added, 'Now, there is a supply ship in the harbour which will be returning to England with some of the wounded. I shall send you on that, but in the meantime, I am sure you would like a wash and change of clothes. . .'

'Yes, thank you, but can I not stay in France until. . .' She paused. 'I want to be near at the end.'

'My dear Miss Martindale, we have no facilities for ladies. And we can never be sure the tide will not turn against us again.'

'I could work, help with the wounded, be a letter-carrier, if you like. I do not mind.'

'And what would Monsieur Devereux say to that idea, do you think?'

She was silent, knowing how much Philippe had risked to send her back.

'Viscount Martindale has been badly set back by your disappearance,' he went on. 'He will be overjoyed to see you safe.' Without giving her time to argue, he rang a bell on his desk and one of his aides appeared almost instantly. 'Find Miss Martindale a comfortable room and ask Sergeant Wetherby's wife to look after her and find her something to wear.'

Then to Juliette, with a disarming smile which took the sting from his words. 'I am not accustomed to being argued with, my dear. My orders are usually obeyed implicitly and at once. Now you must put yourself in our hands and before long you will be once again in the bosom of your family and able look back on the last few months as a bad dream.'

It was spring, a wonderful joyous spring after one of the longest and coldest winters anyone could remember. Flags and banners flew from every masthead, church bells pealed out from one parish to another, bonfires were lit and everyone was out, laughing and singing.

The war was at an end, the allies were in Paris and the tyrant had abdicated and been sent to the island of Elba. In England, everyone was preparing to welcome the heroes home, among those the Duke of Wellington.

When the news of the surrender came to Hartlea, Juliette was in the garden with Anne Golightly, in the same spot she had been occupying exactly a year before, to sit for her portrait, a portrait that had set in train a sequence of events which had changed her life forever.

Dressed once again in ladylike fashion, in a soft blue gown decorated with tiny embroidered rosebuds over a pale eau-de-nil petticoat and with her glorious hair brushed upwards and held so that its ringlets fell about her face in a silver cascade, she had become once again the fashionable debutante, far removed from the tearful ragged urchin who had faced Wellington in that bare room in St Jean de Luz.

While she had been away, Lord Martindale had convinced his wife that she had been mistaken in her belief that Juliette was his daughter and his brother had simply been making mischief in telling her that she was. Lady Martindale had asked and been granted forgiveness and their relationship had been strengthened because of it, but it had made Juliette's disappearance all the more distressing.

Just when they had almost given up hope of ever seeing her again, she had returned, escorted by an officer appointed by Wellington to see her safely home. Her French birth had been forgotten and she was, once again, the beloved daughter of Viscount and Lady Martindale, though now the adoption had been legalised.

The story everyone had been told was that she had

been abducted by a group of French prisoners of war to aid their escape and that James Martindale had set off in pursuit and disappeared. No hint was ever dropped that he was other than a patriotic Englishman who had risked his life to save the woman he loved and Juliette had never mentioned seeing him in France. She was afraid it would hurt her father too much to know the truth and so she had simply said a French officer had rescued her and helped her to reach the British lines.

In some ways, she supposed, Wellington had been right—it had been a nightmare—but in others, it had been the happiest and most glorious episode of her life. And though she could not have asked for a more fervent welcome home from her Mama and Papa, her thoughts were constantly with the man she had left behind in France, the man who held her heart.

While everyone rejoiced, Juliette began thinking of what had happened there, of Henri and Anne-Marie, of James and Michel Clavier, but most of all of Philippe Devereux, who was undoubtedly a Frenchman; it was Philip Devonshire who was not real.

How had a man so honourable and brave made the decision to help the other side? If his clandestine activities helping the allies were to become known to his compatriots in France, he would be branded a traitor. Would he be punished or would the British forces protect him?

Ever since she learned that he was a trusted British agent, she had realised that he and James could not be on the same side and it followed that James was a traitor. Thinking about his behaviour, his manner towards her and the escaped prisoners on the fishing boat, his anxiety about losing Napoleon's letter, and his extraordinary laughter when she told him she thought he was a double agent, had convinced her.

As far as the world was concerned, they were still betrothed, and if she was not out and about in Society, it was because she was waiting anxiously for his safe return. If he came back, pretending nothing had changed, could she remain silent? She could never marry him, not only because of his perfidy, but because she was forever pledged to Philippe Devereux.

Earlier in the year she had attended Lucinda's wedding to Arthur Boreton. Lucinda, gowned in heavy oyster satin and bedecked with jewellery, had fairly glowed with happiness. Juliette did not begrudge her friend her joy and had been one of the first to wish her well, but the occasion served to remind her of what she had lost and she had been glad to return to Hartlea to wait for the end of that terrible war, praying that Philippe survived.

Now the waiting was done, the guns were silent and the men coming home. In France, too, soldiers would be returning to their loved ones and her thoughts constantly drifted to the other side of the English Channel. She would not allow herself to dwell on the possibility that Philippe had been killed; she held on to the conviction that their talisman, the ruby pendant, would keep him alive. 'I shall want it back,' she had told him. 'And you with it.'

But he had made no promise to return to England, even though she had said she would wait for him. She remembered him saying that when the war was over, he would go home, and home was a village close to Hautvigne. She would ask Papa to take her to Hautvigne. She could visit Henri and Jean and Anne-

Marie and look for him from there. She hurried back
to the house to put the idea to her father, impatience
and hope lending wings to her feet.

His lordship had been spending more time at home
as the war drew to its conclusion and he was not wanted
so frequently in London. But he still received intelligence, was still visited by government officials and as
she approached the house, she became aware of a carriage clattering to a stop at the front door. A tall man
in a blue superfine coat, buckskin breeches and shining
leather boots jumped down almost before it had come
to a stop and hurried up the steps.

He was too far away to recognise, but she assumed
he had come to see her papa on business and now she
would not be able to ask about going to France until
he had left. Her footsteps slowed. By the time she
entered the house, the two men were already shut in
the library.

'Philip, how good it is to see you.' His lordship
embraced his visitor. 'It has been so long, I had almost
given up hope.'

The young man smiled. 'I am not easily disposed
of, my lord. And I had a very strong reason for
staying alive.'

'Sit down, my boy.'

Philip seated himself in an armchair by the hearth
and watched silently as his lordship poured two glasses
of brandy from a decanter on a side table and handed
one to him. 'Now, tell me everything.'

'First I must know if Miss Martindale arrived
safely home.'

'Yes, she did, thanks to a certain French cavalry captain.'

Philip smiled at the memory. 'I was an ugly brute, long red hair, bushy brows and a stoop which gave me excruciating backache. Did she say she recognised me?'

'No, but I guessed it might be you. I had asked you to find her and I have never known you fail.' He smiled, raising his glass to the young man. 'Here's to the unknown French soldier who undoubtedly captured her heart.'

'Did she tell you this?'

'No, but I know by the way she has been behaving, asking questions, demanding to know how the war was going, what would happen when it ended, whether the French army would be disbanded and what would happen to its soldiers, especially those who had helped France's enemies.

'I own it gave me a little heartache too. I tried to find out what had happened to you through other channels, but no one knew where you were. There were those in our Intelligence who said you could not have survived.'

Philip smiled ruefully. 'The situation became so confused I could not contact our people. Down in the south the news that the allies had entered Paris and Napoleon had surrendered did not reach us in time to prevent the battle for Toulouse. There were casualties. I am afraid Emile was one of them.'

'Bertie Wainwright,' his lordship mused. 'A very brave officer.'

'Yes, sir.' He paused. 'He was killed by a stray shell trying to cross the lines. It is ironic that if the news had reached the Peer sooner, there would have been no battle and Bertie would still be with us.' He paused. 'I am afraid James Martindale also died.'

'Oh.' He was thoughtful for a moment. 'Do not spare me the details if you know them.'

'When I left Miss Martindale I went back to Toulouse. I knew *Le Merle* was there and I suspected James would be there too.'

'He was the traitor,' his lordship said quietly. 'I suspected it.'

'Yes, my lord. I had hoped you might never know. I planned to offer him a way out, stay abroad, play dead and I would see that he was a hero in England. I didn't want to hurt you or Miss Martindale.'

'I think, like me, she has guessed the truth. She never mentions him, but do go on.'

Philip sipped his brandy before continuing. 'By the time I found out where he was, it was too late. *Le Merle* had executed him, believing he had double-crossed them. By then everyone was preparing for the battle and I found myself on the wrong side of the lines. I was obliged to take part, though I was careful not to inflict casualties.'

'I would like to think that perhaps James regretted what he had done,' his lordship said. 'Like his father, he was a weak man and a gambler. The more money he owed, the more he gambled.

'I tried to help him by finding him a post in the War Office, but that was a grave mistake. He was vulnerable to our enemies there and the suggestion of debts being cleared in exchange for a little information was too attractive a proposition to resist. Once in, there was no way out and the whole thing escalated until he was out of his depth.'

'Yes.' Philip was relieved to know that his lordship had not been so blind as he had thought. 'He wanted to get out of his obligation and when he found Miss Martindale on that fishing boat and heard about the ruby pendant, he thought it was a way out. A fortune in gold and jewels would see an end to his troubles.'

'But there was no fortune, so my daughter tells me.'

'No.' He paused. His duty had been done without having to carry out the order that would have barred him from ever returning to Hartlea. Now all he wanted was to be reunited with Juliette. 'How is Miss Martindale?'

'She is well, but as I said, a little despondent.' He smiled. 'But that will lift as soon as she sees you, I am sure.'

'You will allow me to speak to her?'

'Of course. Nothing will give me greater pleasure.'

'But I have nothing to offer.'

'I am sure a grateful country will reward you for the sterling work you have done. And with James dead and no heir, I intend to break that entail at the earliest opportunity. You are my ward; if you marry Juliette, Hartlea will be yours.' He smiled and, putting down his glass, left the room, leaving the young man to pace from the hearth to the window where he stood gazing out on the sunlit scene, wondering if Juliette had changed since returning home.

Could he bear it if she rejected Philip Devonshire simply because he was not the romantic Philippe Devereux? Time and place played havoc with the memory.

*   *   *

Papa and his visitor had been talking a very long time, Juliette decided, as she and her mother sat in the with-drawing room, each busy with a piece of needlepoint.

'I wonder if your papa is going to ask him to stay?' Lady Martindale mused. 'I think I should go and warn Cook and order a room to be prepared.'

'Perhaps he is in a hurry,' Juliette said. Now she had made up her mind, all she wanted was to talk to her father about going to Hautvigne and she could not bear the delay that entertaining a guest would cause. 'He might decline.'

'Possibly, but I would not want to be thought wanting in manners.' Her ladyship rose and left the room, leaving Juliette to put down her sewing and wish fervently that the man would go.

She was wondering how to broach the subject she most wanted to discuss with her father, when he came into the room with a broad smile lighting his features. 'Ah, Juliette, there you are. Come into the library, there is someone I would like you to meet. He has an interesting story to tell.'

Mystified, she rose obediently and followed her father to the library, where he stood on one side to allow her to enter first. She was surprised when he did not follow her, but shut the door softly, leaving her to confront the young man who was standing between her and the window, his face half in shadow.

He turned to look at her for a long, long moment, drinking in the sight of her. She was wearing a blue cambric morning dress with a high neck and two rows of ruched trimming around the hem and under the high waist. Her glorious hair was loose about her shoulders, framing a face that was even more beautiful than he remembered it. Her large eyes were surveying him with some puzzlement as if she was not sure how she ought to greet him.

'Miss Martindale.' The voice was soft with a well-modulated English accent, reviving memories of her come-out ball, the garden at Martindale House, the picnic at Richmond, but why did it suddenly stir memories of the pine-clad woods behind the chateau at Hautvigne?

'Sir. You wish to speak to me?'

He moved forward. 'Oh, my love, are you always so easily deceived?' His laugh jolted her into looking closely at him and, as he stepped towards her, she saw the scar, much fainter than it had been but plainly there, nevertheless. It was the same shape, the same length, and the brown eyes, looking down into hers, were as familiar as her own when she looked into a mirror.

'Philippe?' Her legs buckled beneath her and she would have fallen if he had not caught her in his arms.

'Steady, my love.'

'Is it really you?'

'Yes. Who else? Here, come and sit down beside me.' He led her to a sofa, put his arms about her shoulders and drew her to him to kiss her tenderly.

She did not doubt that it was Philippe but she was so confused, she kept shaking her head from side to side. 'I can't believe it is you.'

'Why not? You have seen through my disguises before, haven't you? There was that time when I came to the ball as a cardinal. . .'

'But it was different in France. That was not a game, it was deadly serious. And in spite of everything I said, you stuck to your story and convinced me you were Philippe Devereux.'

'That is because I am Philippe Devereux.' He smiled, touching her hair, her nose, her lips with gentle fingers, making her shiver with delight. 'Your father rescued me from The Terror, just as he did you, except that he brought my mother out too. She died in England soon afterwards and I became Philip Devonshire and grew up as his lordship's ward.'

'But why had we not met before last year?'

'I am afraid your mama wanted to keep us apart. She thought I knew what she believed was the truth about your birth and she was afraid I might tell you, or noise it abroad. His lordship never understood her animosity, but he always deferred to her and so we always met at Horse Guards or his club or my home.'

'Poor Mama. It has all been put to rights now. She and Papa are happier than they have ever been with each other.'

'I am glad. It was my indebtedness to your papa and because I could see the dreadful consequences of Napoleon's greed for power, that I agreed to return to France as an agent.

'I no longer thought of myself as French. I had been ten years a French boy and I have been twenty years an Englishman and hope to be so for many, many more years. So you see, we both have good reason to be grateful to your papa, me especially because it was through him, I met you.'

'Why couldn't you have told me?'

'It was a state secret. Only your father knew the truth. It would have jeopardised my work if others had known.'

'Even me?' She smiled. 'How you must have been laughing at me when we were in France.'

'No, my love. I hated myself for deceiving you, but I had to do it, there was too much at stake. One slip, a careless word. . .' He paused to kiss her again. 'Can you forgive me?'

She laughed, suddenly carefree. 'In France I often found myself making comparisons, the eyes and the laugh seemed so familiar. But you spoke in that difficult French dialect and you had long red hair and a beard and that scar.' She reached up to touch it. 'Philip Devonshire did not have that.'

'He has now. It was given to me by Michel Clavier when I landed in France and went after him to find out what had become of you.'

'Why did you?'

'Because your father asked me to and because I loved you. . .'

'Even then?'

'Yes, even then though, because of my work, I felt I could not declare myself. I tried to explain it to you once, but it all went wrong. And then you accepted James Martindale. You have no idea what that did to me. I could cheerfully have run him through.'

'But you didn't,' she said, thinking of that aborted duel. Was that the reason he had allowed himself to be branded a coward? 'What happened to James, do you know?'

'When I left you with Lord Wellington, I went back to find him, but I am afraid Clavier killed him before I reached them. I was unable to prevent it.'

'Was he really a traitor?'

He smiled; there was no need for her to know the truth. James was dead, killed by his own accomplices, and it was only because he had not had to put an end to the man's life himself, he had felt able to return. 'No one will ever know for sure, will they?'

'No, I suppose not.' She paused, glad that James's treachery need never become public. If everyone thought he had died a hero, then no shame would reflect on her father. And she had all she wanted, here in Hartlea, loving parents, her home and the man she loved. 'And now the war is over?' she asked. 'What will you do?'

'Become a model English gentleman, marry and have a family. That is, if you will have me.'

She laughed, looking up at him with eyes alight. 'Sir, is that a proposal?'

'Indeed, it is.' He felt in his pocket and drew out a package which he carefully unwrapped. 'I promised to return this to you, didn't I?'

Juliette gasped. The ruby pendant lay on his hand, but it was not the broken piece she had given him, but a whole necklace, not as ostentatious as the original with its crowded jewels, but, even so, a fine piece of work, with several smaller rubies on either side of the large one on a silver chain. 'Oh, Philippe, it is beautiful.'

'It is our talisman,' he said. 'It brought us together and it will keep us together, through all our lives.'

She flung her arms round his neck and kissed him. He laughed and kissed her back. 'Wanton.'

'She giggled. 'Am I? Well, it is your fault. You never would have told me you loved me if I hadn't said it first, would you?'

'I was afraid for you. Your safety was more important than my feelings.'

'I know, but now we are both safe and the war is over, you can tell me.'

'I love you. I love you.' He kissed her again and again. 'Will that do?'

'For a beginning, but I shall expect the same every day for the rest of our lives.'

'Is that an acceptance?' he asked, grinning.

'Of course, it is. How could you doubt it?'

His lips traced the contour of her face, roamed down her neck, sending delightful tremors tingling through her, banishing all sad thoughts from her mind. The privations she had endured faded into insignificance in the face of a love she knew would endure all their lives.

She had been uncommonly attracted to Philip Devonshire before she ever went to France and it would be Philip Devonshire she married but it was Philippe who had made a woman of her. They were indivisible, the man beneath the skin was the same, whatever he was called. Her love. Soon to be her husband.

She pulled herself from his arms at last. 'Don't you think we had better go and tell Mama and Papa our news?' She stood up, hauling on his hand. 'They will be imagining all manner of indiscretions.'

'Not without justification.' He rose, laughing, and allowed her to lead him to the withdrawing room, where Lord and Lady Martindale waited.

Historical Romance™

Coming next month

THE NEGLECTFUL GUARDIAN
Anne Ashley

Miss Sarah Pennington had taken matters into her own hands! If her guardian, Mr Marcus Ravenhurst, was not prepared to acknowledge her existence, then she would leave Bath and stay with her old governess. For propriety she became Mrs Armstrong, but her travels were cut short by snow and she found herself stranded in a wayside inn!

She didn't know that Marcus was hot on her trail. He might not have visited the chit, but he'd given her everything her companion had requested! Then the weather foundered him too, and he walked into that same inn, unaware that the delicious young widow called Mrs Armstrong was his missing ward—or that she had a marked propensity for getting into trouble...

THE BECKONING DREAM
Paula Marshall

When her brother Rob was held for seditious writing, the only way Mistress Catherine Wood could ensure his release was to accompany supposed merchant Tom Trenchard—pretending to be his wife!—to Holland on a spying mission. With roguish charm Tom made no bones about wanting Catherine in his bed—after all, Catherine was an actress!—but she was determined to hold him at bay. It surprised her to realise how hard that was, more so as they travelled into danger and depended upon one another, needing all their wits about them...

FOUR FREE
specially selected
Historical Romance™ novels
<u>PLUS</u> a FREE Mystery Gift
when you return this page...

Return this coupon and we'll send you 4 Historical Romance novels and a mystery gift absolutely FREE! We'll even pay the postage and packing for you.

We're making you this offer to introduce you to the benefits of the Reader Service™– FREE home delivery of brand-new Historical Romance novels, at least a month before they are available in the shops, FREE gifts and a monthly Newsletter packed with information, competitions, author profiles and lots more...

Accepting these FREE books and gift places you under no obligation to buy, you may cancel at any time, even after receiving just your free shipment. Simply complete the coupon below and send it to:

MILLS & BOON READER SERVICE, FREEPOST, CROYDON, SURREY, CR9 3WZ.

READERS IN EIRE PLEASE SEND COUPON TO PO BOX 4546, DUBLIN 24

NO STAMP NEEDED

Yes, please send me 4 free Historical Romance novels and a mystery gift. I understand that unless you hear from me, I will receive 4 superb new titles every month for just £2.99* each, postage and packing free. I am under no obligation to purchase any books and I may cancel or suspend my subscription at any time, but the free books and gift will be mine to keep in any case. (I am over 18 years of age)

H7YE

Ms/Mrs/Miss/Mr_____
BLOCK CAPS PLEASE
Address_____

_____

_____ Postcode _____

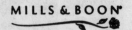

MILLS & BOON®

Christmas Treats

A sparkling new anthology
—the perfect Christmas gift!

Celebrate the season with a taste of love in this
delightful collection of brand-new short stories
combining the pleasures of food and love.

Figgy Pudding
by PENNY JORDAN
All the Trimmings
by LINDSAY ARMSTRONG
A Man For All Seasonings
by DAY LECLAIRE

And, as an extra treat, we've included the
authors' own recipe ideas in this
collection—because no yuletide would be
complete without...Christmas Dinner!